What are people saying about Susan Wells Bennett's work?

You find yourself falling in love with the main character and cheering at the end. *Grace Guerra, Amazon Reader*

Her plot is easy to follow, with characters that somehow grab my attention while there is always an element of mystery and surprise. *Alex Caton-Dutari, Amazon Reader*

She weaves in all the characters and the last part ties it all up in a profound way that may leave you needing a whole box of tissues. *Janet Brown, Amazon Reader*

This is a story about a writer. What he does affects everyone around him and he finds that he doesn't always see how it will affect them. Isn't that true for all of us? I quickly loved the other characters and found that many of the ideas expressed were unique, fascinating and thought provoking. It took me longer to love the main character, mostly because I was angry with his choice. It has some twists and turns as well as a few laughs. It made me look at life differently.
Earleen Smith, Amazon Reader

This one deserves your attention and five stars.
Arthur Levine, author of Johnny Oops

Just One Note

By

Susan Wells Bennett

Published by Inknbeans Press

Cover: Nikki McBroom, Trident Art

Just One Note © January 2013
Susan Wells Bennett
and Inknbeans Press

ISBN-13: 978-0615764429 (Inknbeans Press)

ISBN-10: 0615764428

This is a work of fiction. Names, characters, places, organizations, businesses or incidents portrayed in this novel are the product of the author's imagination, used fictitiously or with permission given to the author for use

For Dan. I wouldn't change a thing.

If you love her, marry her immediately -- and never tell her about 12/31/69.

First

I know a lot of women who would tell me -- hell, have told me -- they would happily trade their lives for mine.

Fuck them.

Just because a life looks good from the outside doesn't mean it is. I never planned to end up here -- an inmate in a nursing home at just eighty-one years old. I know, I know...I'm not a prisoner. I can leave anytime I want. Only I can't, can I? How the hell would I support myself, when all my money is tied up in the fucking apartment my children thought was such a perfect god-damned solution?

If you're blushing, get over it. I lived most of my life smiling graciously and holding my fucking tongue. What did that get me? Not a damned thing. I'm old, I'm alone, and I wasted my life.

I had a gift, once. When I was a child, I had a golden voice -- that's what my voice coach, Miss Louella Stroman, told me. Imagine -- a little girl like me with a voice Ethyl Merman or Barbra Streisand would have envied. Of course, when I was six, I had no idea who Ethyl Merman was. I only recognized Barbra Streisand's name because my father played her songs in the shop.

Let me tell you about my father, Nick Mogens. He was a wonderful man. He saw the beauty in abused things -- scratched-up dressers, chipped porcelain, ragged dolls. He owned an antique store in an old city-turned-suburb called Glendale, Arizona. It's a ghost town now, like all the rest of that forsaken valley. I haven't been there in decades. But once upon a time, I practically lived in his shop. Mogens's Memorabilia, it was called. Maybe you remember it -- no, I suppose not. It wasn't famous, and the sign came down over fifty years ago now. But Dad kept a nice place with an ever-changing collection of antiques and a merry-go-round of regular customers.

He met my mother around the time "Like a Virgin" was making its way up the charts. That's what he told me later anyway, when I would ask him to tell me how he met my mom as he tucked me into bed. "She was humming 'Like a Virgin' and looking at the jewelry collection," he would tell me. "She pointed to a flower made of copper and topaz and asked me how much. I fell in love with her right then and there." And I would drift to sleep, imagining this romantic first encounter between them.

My sister Demi told me the truth when I was eleven or twelve -- not that she was there to witness it. But she was Mom's confidante, so she heard the story from her instead. Mom -- born Charity Woodhouse -- was married before, to a professional basketball player. The part about her shopping at Mogens's was true. Heck, probably the whole story was true as far as Dad was concerned, but Mom's version wasn't nearly as romantic.

I got my looks from Mom -- there's no doubting that. The blonde hair, the heart-shaped face -- that's all her. When you put our high-school graduation pictures side by side, you would swear I was her clone; there's no evidence of my father in my face. Unlike me, though, Mom didn't have a talent for anything other than looking pretty. She was a catalog model before she met the tall, ebony athlete who was Demi's father. I never met him myself, but Demi showed me a picture she had torn out of a magazine once. He was long-limbed with high cheekbones and eyes that slanted up slightly, just like Demi's did. When I was a kid, I wanted to look like Demi; she wanted to look like me.

Nick Mogens and the basketball player were like photo negatives of each other, physically and mentally.

Dad was lanky and blond. He was mild mannered and patient. He would never have hit my mother, no matter how badly she treated him -- and she treated him like crap. The basketball player, on the other hand, had pulverized her left eye socket in a fit of jealous rage, leaving her eyes permanently out of alignment.

Miss Louella Stroman was the first music teacher to tell my father that I could sing. "Your daughter has a real gift, Mr. Mogens. With a little training--"

"Miss Stroman," Dad interrupted, "we don't have a lot of extra money for private lessons. If that's your angle here, you're barking up the wrong lamp post."

"Hardly. I'm more than happy to give Diana lessons *gratis*...for free."

My father's eyelids slid halfway closed. He hated the way the teachers at my school assumed all of the parents in the neighborhood were dull-witted. "Yes, I understand this 'gratis' you speak of."

The young teacher reddened. "I'm so sorry. I didn't mean--"

"No, I'm sure you didn't." My father shifted on the short chair beside me. I'd never considered how an adult would look sitting on the tiny chairs; my father was like a daddy long legs spider, with elbows and knees poking out in all directions as he attempted to look respectable. "Why would you want to put time into Diana's talent? There is no benefit for you."

"Not everything is about money. She's amazingly talented and incredibly sweet. I love spending time with such a wonderful little girl."

"I'll have to run it past her mother." Mom was on another one of her "vacations": random disappearances lasting anywhere from one week to two months.

"Of course. When could you let me know?"

Looking at me, Dad hemmed and hawed for a minute before answering. "You know what? You just go ahead and get started on 'em. If Charity has a problem with the lessons, we'll reevaluate."

I had my first lesson the next day.

Charity Woodhouse was a beautiful woman -- Demi and I used to flip through the scrapbook that proved it. She was a little shorter than I was -- at five-nine, she was an inch too short to find real success as a runway model. As a result, she never made the cover of *Vogue* or *Cosmo*. But she didn't rely on her looks alone -- she knew how to get invitations to the best events in L.A. That's how she met the basketball player.

But the pictures in the scrapbook weren't of her real life; they were staged shots of her modeling this dress and that pair of pants, that bracelet and this lace top. She wore her smile like an accessory.

I remember always thinking my mother's smile was calculated -- as if she never wasted a millimeter of it on anyone undeserving. I don't remember her ever smiling at Dad. She saved her sweetest looks for Demi. The grim, sad grin she used with me suggested she expected me to be her biggest disappointment.

I had been taking lessons from Miss Stroman for four weeks when Mom came home from her latest "vacation." She looked tan and relaxed, as if she had spent the last six weeks stretched out on a beach in the Caribbean. She hugged me distractedly before pulling Demi to the couch. "I missed you, baby girl!" she exclaimed, squeezing my sister against her. I knew better than to stay in the room -- Mom would only tell me to leave when she noticed me again. I slid out of sight, into the hallway, hugging my big pink stuffed rabbit to my chest and listening to the melody of Mom's conversation as she spoke softly to my sister.

I must have fallen asleep there, because the sound of the front door closing startled me. Dad's deep voice rolled through the house like a wide, warm river: "Girls? Are you home?"

Demi nearly tripped over me as she scurried to the hallway. She dropped to the floor behind me and wrapped her arms around my middle.

"Nicky, baby, I'm home," Mom cooed.

Demi and I held our breath, waiting for how Dad would respond.

"Sweetheart! Did you have a good trip?"

We relaxed -- this was going to be a happy homecoming.

"Lovely. Did you miss me?"

"Yes, of course. It's not the same around here without you. Have you seen the girls?"

"They're in their room. I spent the afternoon talking to Demi. It's amazing how much she's grown."

"She's going to be taller than me. Did you talk to Diana at all?"

"Not much. Why?"

I heard Dad take a few steps and drop into his old recliner. "I was called to the school a few weeks ago by one of her teachers."

"What did she do?"

"Turns out our girl can sing."

"Why would she be in trouble for that? Was she belting one out in the library?"

"She's not in trouble, Charity. The music teacher wanted our permission to start private lessons with her."

"And you said yes?" Mom's voice rose an octave. "You let your daughter be alone with some kind of musical freak?"

"Calm down, sweetheart."

"How can you even say that to me? Knowing what happened--"

"Charity! The teacher is a woman -- Miss Stroman."

"Diana!" my mother called suddenly. "Diana, come out here now!"

Demi gave me a quick squeeze before shoving me to my feet. Holding my stuffed rabbit in front of me like a shield, I advanced toward the living room.

"Diana! Do you hear me?"

"Yes, Mom?" I asked, emerging wide-eyed into my parents' battleground.

"I understand you're a singer now. Sing something."

I stood still, my brain searching for the words to a song -- any song.

"Go on, I want to hear this 'talent' of yours."

"Charity, you're putting her on the spot," Dad said. "Come here, honey." He opened his arms and I sidestepped toward him, never taking my eyes off my unpredictable mother. He gently pried my hands away from my rabbit and set it on the ground at his feet. "Why don't we sing together? Like at the shop, okay?"

I nodded. Mom crossed her arms and tipped her head to one side.

Dad started: "Memories light the corners of my mind..."

I joined him, softly at first: "Misty water-colored memories of the way we were..." Dad sang with me for another line or two, as my voice gained strength. I remembered Miss Stroman's words: *Sing from the diaphragm, Diana, not from the lungs. Don't move your shoulders, hold them still. Control your air flow -- don't waste all of your breath on one word!* I didn't know if I was a good singer or not -- all I knew for sure was that I was good enough for Miss Stroman to want to spend time with me.

When I finished the song, I stood in the silence of the room as my mother's eyes bored into me. After what must have been moments but felt like hours, she clapped. "Very nice, Diana. Now, tell me about Miss Stroman."

Miss Stroman never married. She had no family of her own. After the water system failed and the nuclear plant melted down in the valley, I wondered if she made it out. I even looked her up on the Internet and sent her a message, but I didn't get an answer. That's no guarantee that she didn't get out -- if her messages went to a server in Phoenix, they wouldn't have gotten to her.

I wished I'd stayed closer to her; we only talked every five or ten years after I stopped pursuing my singing. She never said she was disappointed in me, but I felt I let her down. After all, she spent eight years of her life molding me and my voice into a force to be reckoned with. By the time I hit high school, I was blowing my competition away. I sang most of the solos in my high-school choir; I played the lead female roles in all of the theater department's musicals. I even won roles in a few community-theater productions. The busier I was, the less time I had to spend at home.

Mom never liked Miss Stroman much, but she let me take the singing lessons. I didn't care why. It wasn't until I was an adult that I realized she preferred me to be out of the house. That gave her more time to spend with Demi. To my sister's credit, she never rubbed it in that Mom preferred her to me.

I should have visited Mom after Dad died. Even if she couldn't recognize me -- even if Demi was full of shit for telling me Mom wanted to see me -- I should have gone. Because the truth was that Demi wanted to see me. And when we were growing up, Demi did everything she could to protect me.

I know Demi and Mom didn't make it out. While the Internet didn't care about elementary-school music teachers, it did care about Olympic-gold-medalist basketball players. Demi and her wife were prominent among the casualties. One of the asshole television preachers even pointed them out as the reason Phoenix was destroyed -- as if they were the only gay people in that melted metropolis.

I was married to Joe and pregnant with my third son when the police called to tell me my father had been murdered. It was a random act of violence -- some meth head decided that Mogens's Memorabilia was a good place to rob. Dad gave him all the money in the register and the asshole still killed him. Demi told me that the guy said Dad moved too slowly.

Mom wasn't around when Dad died -- she was on another one of her vacations. When she came back and Dad was dead, she had some kind of mental breakdown. It left her catatonic for the rest of her life. Mom's breakdown came as a shock to me -- I didn't think she loved Dad that much.

I was so close to delivering Phillip that I couldn't go to Phoenix for the funeral. Later, when Phillip was weaned and life had moved on from that disastrous moment, I didn't want to go. Demi kept calling me...for a while. "Mom would like to see you," she would say. How could she know what Mom would like? From what she told me, Mom was barely capable of lifting a fork to feed herself.

I never should have married Joe. Don't get me wrong -- I loved him more than anyone else I ever met. But marrying him was a huge mistake. I should have known it the first time he told me about this crazy theory he had.

"Look at this," he said, holding his cell phone out to me. We were sitting in the commons at college, just hanging out together until our next classes started. On his phone's screen was an email with no sender and no content.

"So? You got a blank email. Must be a glitch."

"Look at the date."

It read 12/31/69. I laughed. "So you got an email from the past."

"I know this isn't your area of expertise," he said in that patronizing tone of his that just made me want to smack him, "but email didn't exist in 1969."

I rolled my eyes. "So you think it's from...what? 2169?"

"Don't be ridiculous. Why would someone be trying to reach me from a hundred-and-fifty years in the future?"

"You're a famous computer scientist and they want to pick your brain?"

"Um...probably not. But it might be from 2069."

"Okay, who would be emailing you from seventy years in the future?"

"Me, most likely."

"So you're saying that you...future you is sending you blank emails?"

"Well...no. But I think I could."

I blinked at him doubtfully.

"I'm serious here. All of the emails--"

"All? You've gotten more than one?"

"Yes. Haven't you?"

"No, I've never received a single one."

He stopped and frowned.

"Wait...have other people?"

"A few...other computer geeks, mostly."

"Where do they think they are coming from?"

"Most of them think it's a computer glitch some-where...a bad piece of code."

"I'm no genius, but that sounds plausible."

"Yes, but where is it? Because if the emails are all being generated by some bad source code, how are they being delivered to all of these different systems?"

"I don't understand. What 'different systems'?"

"It's complicated," he sighed. "But the upshot is that I think that if you send an email to yourself on December 31, 2069 -- the same date as this email -- you'll receive it here and now."

"You mean they'll all come to 2010?"

"No...yes, but only if you want it to. You know how you can set an email to deliver at a particular time?"

"You can do that?"

He nodded slowly. "Yes, Diana, you can. Where have you been?"

"Learning to sing like a trilling bird, remember?" My music and voice lessons were all-consuming. Coupled with my theater commitments, I rarely had free time to spend with Joe. These lunch-hour breaks three times a week and Sunday afternoons were all I had left. I had an email account, of course, but I only checked it once a week or so. A blank email would have been deleted without a second thought. And I never had a reason to delay a message; most of my messages were days late to begin with.

"You can set up an email to be delivered anytime in the future. As long as your email server is up and running at that time, the message will be delivered."

"But you can't deliver to the past."

"Not yet. But maybe, just maybe..."

I laughed and shook my head. "You're incredible, you know that?"

He grabbed my hand and squeezed. "I'll prove it to you."

"How?"

"Just you wait...on New Year's Eve in 2069, I'll have the last laugh."

He was full of speculative theories like that one -- always asking "what if..." when his bosses wanted to know "if...then." I spent fifty years with him -- that dreamer, that man with his impossible theories.

Marietta called me last night. She's such a good girl. Sometimes I find it near impossible to believe that Donny and his bitch of a wife produced such a wonderful daughter. Marietta has my voice, and she's going to do what I only dreamed of doing: she's going to be a star on Broadway. She's only won a few roles so far, but they've been good ones. She even got a solo in her last musical.

I was supposed to see that one -- I was flying to New York the day after I broke my hip. Had to cancel the trip, of course -- just about broke Marietta's heart. She wanted to fly back to California immediately, but I told her the show must go on! Nothing is more important than her career -- not me, not her parents, and definitely not a man.

She has a boyfriend, of course. She's sent me a few photos of him, and I saw him in the background during a recent call. I haven't been introduced to him officially yet. Marietta says it's not serious; he's talking about going to China, and she doesn't see a future for her there.

My sons called me last night too, of course. Not a single one of them thought they should visit their mother on Christmas -- a call is apparently all I'm warranted. I guess they don't call them "calls" anymore -- they're holochats. It's almost like my family is in the room with me, except my hand goes right through them. It's a cruel trick, I think: technology that almost -- but not quite --

allows you to touch. My sons, they think it's as good as being here. They're wrong.

Joe never stopped believing that on December 31st of this year, we would be able to email ourselves. He didn't talk about it all the time, just every once in a while -- and usually on New Year's Eve. I once asked him what he would tell himself and when.

"That's easy: I'd tell myself to marry you sooner."

I laughed. "That's it?"

"Yup," he said, pulling me tight against him. "You are everything I will ever need. And I figure the messages will need to be short and to the point."

"Why?" I asked, not raising my head. I didn't want him to see the guilt I feared was etched into my face.

"Either the recipient--"

"You, in other words."

"Not necessarily. Maybe, given the chance, I would send the email to someone else. Your dad, for instance," he said softly, waiting for the words to sink in.

Realizing that not only would Joe choose me all over again but also save my father with his one chance to change his life, I felt a tightness in my throat. I waited until I could talk without betraying my emotions. "Okay. So you wouldn't tell yourself anything. Shouldn't the message be long so that whomever receives it will know that it's for real?"

"There's no way for me to prove the veracity of my words to a past version of anyone."

"If you were writing to yourself, you could tell yourself something that only you would know."

"Maybe. But why would you trust someone who probably read your diary?"

I could hear the amusement in his voice; I tried

again. "You could tell yourself what was going to happen to you in the next few days."

"That wouldn't help. If you knew what was supposed to happen in the future, you might change it just by virtue of knowing."

"What about something in the news? Reference a news story totally unrelated to you or anyone you know as proof."

"And who's to say that someone else won't be using this same loophole to change that event?"

"Loophole? Is that how you think of it?" I felt his chin against my head a few times and knew he was nodding. "You think this is the only time in history that changing the past might be possible?"

"Let's just say it's the only time that you and I have a chance to change things. Who knows what might be possible in the future?"

I was frowning against his chest. "Why should the message be short?"

"Because a short piece of advice, delivered at the right time, might sway your decision-making process."

"What if you aren't making a decision? What if you are just going along with the flow of life?"

"Then game over. If you aren't able to find a yes-or-no, right-or-left moment of decision in the person's life, then you aren't going to change anything. He or she might ponder the email for a few minutes, but, ultimately, the advice will be disregarded."

I knew where that moment was in my life -- my "right-or-left" decision. And I knew, given a little nudge, I would go left instead of right.

I wrote the email yesterday. It's simple and to the point. Now, here I sit, on December 31, 2069, trying to work up the courage to change the past. It's hard to believe the day has finally come -- decades of "what-ifs," little games I played with myself whenever I thought about my wasted life.

I know you don't think it was wasted. You think a happy marriage and three handsome sons would be more than a satisfying life to lead. But it just isn't -- not when you know there was so much more out there, so many missed opportunities to shine. I hid my light under a bushel until it went out and left me a withered husk of a woman, full of bitterness and regret.

I've spent the whole day arguing with myself. Joe will be fine without me -- he'll find another woman to love. He'll have other sons, a different -- maybe better -- marriage. I don't know how this works, really. Does this life cease to exist? I think it must. I never asked Joe about that. As I sit here, my finger hovering over the send key on my tablet, I realize I could be erasing not just my life, but the lives of my children and grandchildren. Don't they deserve their chance to live? Doesn't Marietta deserve her chance to shine?

Eleven-fifty-eight. Less than sixty seconds left to decide. What should I do? Accept my past decisions or reclaim my life? It won't work, anyway. This is just another one of Joe's failed theories. Send the email or don't -- the world won't change.

I press the button.

Second

If it hadn't been for the timing, I might have deleted it: an email with no sender dated 12/31/69? And the message: "Don't move to California. Go to New York and pursue your dreams." It was weird -- like someone was inside my head. If I had told anyone...but I hadn't. Not yet.

The day before, I auditioned for a special performing arts program in New York.

"Diana Mogens?" The assistant was pretty enough to be a star herself, if only she would shed the serious, black-framed glasses that made her look like a nerd.

"Here!" I answered with my hand raised, like some kind of ridiculous high-school student.

"Mr. Carlyle will see you now." I followed her down the short hallway to the empty conference room where the auditions were being held. I would have preferred to be on a stage, with bright lights in my eyes to keep me from having to look right at him as he gave me a cynical once-over.

"Ms...Mogens, is it? Scandinavian?"

"Yes, sir. M-my father's side." I bit my stumbling tongue in irritation.

"That a stutter, or just nerves?"

"Nerves, sir."

"Then let's get right to it, shall we? Will you be singing or acting first?"

I sucked in a deep breath and let it out slowly. "Singing."

"And what will you be singing?" He tapped his pen against the small table in front of him a few times before uncapping it and writing something in the file in front of him.

"Um..." I swallowed hard, searching my brain for the name of the song I had spent the last several weeks preparing. "It's from *Les Miserables*."

He closed his eyes for longer than a blink and I knew I had already blown the audition. He recapped the pen and leaned back in his chair. "Go ahead."

I didn't want to sing anymore. I wanted to run out of the room and back to my dorm, where I would hide my head under my pillow and scream in anguish. My voice cracked on the first note.

Mr. Carlyle smiled with all the warmth of a velociraptor and said, "Perhaps you'd like to do your reading first."

"I...can I reschedule?"

"I recommend you pursue a less-demanding career, Ms. Mogens. I don't believe you are cut out for the theater."

"But I've been studying for this my entire life!"

"Look, I'm sorry you're suffering from PMS or whatever other malady may be affecting both your memory and your voice, but the show must go on -- especially on Broadway. You, my dear, simply aren't made of the right stuff to find success there. This program is only for those who can handle the pressure -- even then, half my students won't graduate from the program. I'm afraid you don't have a chance."

"No...but...I'm really good. I swear..."

"Sweetheart, if everyone who wanted to be a star were as 'good' as their mother, father, teacher, or lover told them they were, Broadway would stretch down the East Coast and Hollywood would make four times as many movies. But you know the old saying -- those who can't do, teach. Finish your degree and encourage a new crop of hopefuls to trip the light fantastic. Have Sylvia send in the next one on your way out." He looked down at the file in front of him, drew a big "X" through the page, and closed it.

I slunk from the room in shame. Sylvia shot one disinterested glance at me and called the next name on her list. I went back to my dorm room and lay down, so drained I couldn't even muster tears. When my roommate -- an ugly girl named Tessa who was forever flattering me -- came in, she asked how the audition went.

"Not bad," I answered. "I don't know if the program is right for me, though."

"Of course it isn't, Diana! You don't need any more training -- you just need to show those New York producers and directors what you can do!"

"That's kind of you to say, but--"

"Don't forget, I've seen you on stage more than once. You are terrific -- better than anyone I've ever seen!"

"Better than Bernadette Peters?" I asked, sitting up. Sometimes her flattery was worth listening to, especially when my ego had taken a beating.

"Definitely."

"What about that blonde chick from *Wicked*?"

"You're ten times the singer she is, and you're a better actress to boot."

"Thanks, Tess."

"You're welcome." She tossed a massive book from an English Lit class onto her bed and flipped it open.

"What are you studying now?"

"Victorian poetry," she said, rolling her eyes. "I wish I had a gift like yours -- no one will ever pay me the big bucks for explicating the poetry of dead white men."

A laugh bubbled out of me.

"What are you doing tonight?"

"I have a date with Joe."

"I can't believe you found the only computer nerd on the planet who also looks like a movie star. Why can't I get that lucky?"

"There aren't a lot of guys like Joe around." I would never tell her why I thought she didn't have a boyfriend: her standards were too high. She was less than average looking, with a big nose and eyes too close together. The extra thirty pounds she had gained in the last three years didn't help. Yet she thought she should be able to find a guy who could be the model of the next Disney prince. Still, she was smart, friendly, and easy to live with. She took her studies seriously, as did I. Even though we didn't have much in common beyond that, we had been roommates since our freshman year.

I pulled out a textbook about music theory and tried to study. My mind wouldn't let go of the horrible audition, though. I had really wanted to participate in the program; I was nervous about moving to New York after college, and I thought a summer there between my junior and senior years would calm my nerves. After reading the same paragraph three times -- something about the effective use of disharmonic chords -- I pushed the textbook away and laid my head on my arms.

"Are you okay?" Tessa asked, glancing up from her studies.

"Yeah. I just need a nap."

"Go ahead and take one. What time do you need to be up for your date?"

"Five-thirty."

"I'll wake you before I leave for dinner."

When Joe arrived at six-thirty, I had showered, fixed my hair, and applied a fresh coat of lipstick, the only makeup I wore regularly. He kissed me on the cheek to avoid smudging it.

"May I have a real kiss?"

"Later. I prefer my lips their natural color. You ready to go?"

"If you are."

We walked down the stairs and out to the sidewalk in the direction of the town square. "Let's go to the Chinese restaurant, okay?"

"I thought we were on a burger-and-fries budget until payday." My hand felt warm in his larger one. I loved that he was so much taller than me. At five-ten, I was as tall or taller than most of the guys I went to high school with. When I met Joe my freshman year, he had me the moment he stood up -- all seventy-five inches of him. I didn't care what he was studying...he was my dream date.

"I'm feeling celebratory. Besides, we need to have a talk."

My stomach flipped. Crap. I didn't want to have any "talks." Talks were bad -- serious shit. I wasn't ready for anything serious yet -- positive or negative.

He squeezed my fingers. "Relax. It's all good, I promise."

"Okay," I mumbled. The spring air smelled strongly of lilacs, and their sickeningly sweet scent did nothing to calm my nerves. The red-and-black faux-pagoda was within sight; I tried to concentrate on it.

"After you," Joe said, holding the heavy door open for me.

The lilac scent was instantly overpowered by the aromatic Asian spices used in the dishes served there. A young woman wearing a traditional Chinese dress -- yellow with red bursts -- led us to a booth near the back of the small dining room. She bowed slightly as she handed us our menus. Growing up in Phoenix, Asians weren't an unusual sight: several Japanese families grew flowers and ran florist shops, Chinese restaurants were common, and most pedicure places were run by the Vietnamese. Here, though, the Lotus Blossom Inn was the only place, outside of college, that I ever saw an Asian face. I wondered where they lived and shopped.

"What are you thinking about?"

I cleared my throat and focused on Joe. "Nothing important. Do you want to talk now or later?"

"Let me order for us and then we'll talk."

I frowned, but closed the menu and slid it away from me. "Is this an exercise in trust? You're not going to order octopus and eel, are you?"

He laughed. "No, of course not. I figured I'd get us the 'Yum Yum's Feast for Two or More.'"

"That's the most expensive meal on the menu! What did you do today -- rob a bank?"

He smiled as he beckoned the waitress over to order our dinner. When she was gone, he reached across the table and clutched my hand. "Let's talk about you first. How did your audition go?" I frowned and his face fell. "I'm so sorry, babe."

I shrugged like it didn't matter. "It probably wasn't the right fit for me anyway. It's more of a singing boot camp for actors than an acting boot camp for singers."

"I don't know why you would need it either way. You're a great singer and actress."

"Now you sound like Tessa."

"Your number-one fan can't be wrong." He shot me a cheesy smile.

"Who's that? You or her?"

He ignored my question. "Anyway, I'm glad. I didn't want to lose you to New York anyway."

"You wouldn't have--"

"Of course I would have. But I'm hoping you'll consider something different."

The waitress brought out the pu-pu platter and set it between us. Joe released my hand and picked up a skewer of beef.

"What? I'm on pins and needles here, Joey! Tell me your news already!"

"I got a call today from Silicon Valley."

"In California? Wait...I didn't think geographical areas had phones."

He rolled his eyes at my joke. "It's a startup company with a new idea -- something that hasn't been tried before."

"What is it?"

He grimaced. "They won't tell me until I sign on -- and even then, there's a confidentiality agreement that will keep me from telling you about it."

"So, someone from Silicon Valley called to tell you they're working on something they can't tell you about? And they want to hire you? Why?"

"You remember Dakota?"

"Nerdy guy, horn-rimmed glasses and limp brown hair that was always hanging in his eyes?"

"That's the one. He's in on the new company. He's practically begging me to come to California."

"I don't know...he doesn't seem like the most reliable--"

"He's a legacy -- his dad started one of the first big tech companies out there."

"But what about finishing college? You've still got another semester to go."

"I don't need a degree to be successful, Diana. And neither do you."

"What are you saying?" I pushed myself back in the booth and frowned.

"Why do you need a degree to be a star?"

"I...I don't. The degree is my backup plan. You know that."

"Why do you need a backup plan? You are beautiful and talented."

"So you think I should just, what? Take off for New York right now?"

"No. I think you should come to California with me."

I was speechless.

"Just think about it before you say no," he went on quickly. "New York isn't the only place where you can become a star. Silicon Valley isn't that far from Hollywood -- we could get a place somewhere in the middle."

"I want to be on Broadway, though."

"Diana, you are bigger than any stage. You need to be something more -- a movie star."

"I still have a full year of college."

"Why bother? You're wasting time here."

"How will I support myself?"

"You won't have to."

The waitress brought our soup. Joe pushed the still-full pu-pu platter to one side. I barely glanced at the yellow liquid in front of me.

"What do you mean?" I asked. "If I'm not in college, I'll have to start paying my own bills -- that's the deal I have with my dad."

"I'll take care of you."

"And what happens when you run off with some geekette you meet in the company cafeteria?"

He smirked. "I don't want a geekette. I want you." He picked up his porcelain spoon and noisily slurped a spoonful of soup.

"You say that now..."

"I will always say that. You're special."

"I can't let you support me."

"One-hundred-thousand dollars a year."

I felt my jaw drop -- it took some effort to bring it back to its normal position. "For an entry-level position?"

He bobbed his head from side to side. "It's a little more than entry level."

I knew Joe was smart, but I hadn't understood until that moment how smart.

"Listen, babe, I know this is a lot to drop on you right now. I already told Dakota I was finishing this semester, since it's too late to get a refund on classes anyway. He's not expecting me until June first. Take your time deciding. Just know that I love you."

"What are you going to do?" Tessa asked as soon as I'd finished telling her about Joe's proposal.

"I don't know. On the one hand, I love Joe and I don't want to be without him -- even for a little while."

"On the other hand," Tessa answered, "he didn't propose. What if you get to California and he dumps you? You know your mom won't let your dad bail you out."

"Joe says that won't happen. Besides, I could always call Demi -- she'd help me if I needed her." I threw myself onto my bed face first, screaming into my pillow in frustration. I heard Tessa jump.

"Are you all right?" she asked, alarmed.

Rolling over, I said, "No, I'm not. I'm clueless."

Ever the organizer, my roommate sat down on the edge of her bed and pulled out a blank sheet of paper and a pen. "Let's make a pros and cons list."

"Seriously? This seems like too big of a decision--"

"Not to make a list," she interrupted pointedly. "This is not a decision you can make lightly." She drew a line down the middle of the page and said, "Pro: Joe loves you."

"Shouldn't this list be about my feelings?" I sat up, hugging my pillow to my middle.

"Okay. Do you love Joe?"

I searched my heart and answered, "Yes."

"Took you long enough."

"I just wanted to be certain."

"Okay, so that goes in the 'pro' column."

"Maybe we should call them the 'California' and 'New York' columns."

Tessa blew out an irritated breath, crossing through the "pro" and "con" and replacing the labels with "CA" and "NY." "What else?"

"I always wanted to be on Broadway."

"You can't do that in L.A." She added Broadway under the "NY" column.

I hesitated. "Should there be a third column?"

"For what?"

"Staying in school?"

She frowned and put her pen down. "I just assumed you'd be staying in school if you took the New York option."

"I'm not certain about that. Joe may be right -- why do I need a college degree to be a successful actress? Aren't I just wasting my youth here?"

"Your father will lose his mind if you don't finish this degree. He's already paid for three years--"

"I can always finish later."

"Don't be ridiculous, Di. If you don't go to California, you've got to stay and finish college."

"Why?"

"For your backup plan, remember? What if you don't make it big? What if it takes you longer than you think it will? How will you support yourself?"

"High-class call girl?"

"That's not funny, you know. Plenty of women have ended up on that road."

"I think that's an urban legend."

"Even urban legends are based on some bit of truth."

"How is a music degree going to save me in New York? Every other aspiring actress probably has the same sort of background. Not to mention all the other already-employed music and drama teachers."

"Okay. If you go to California, though, Joe will support you. I'm putting that in the 'CA' column."

"My degree would probably be worth more in L.A."

"But you won't have a degree, because you will have quit college. I'm adding a BA to the NYC column." The boiler kicked on and Tessa fanned herself. "I wish they would stop heating these rooms after spring break."

I leaned back and opened my window to let in some fresh air. "This isn't going to help."

"Of course it will. Making a list always helps."

"Not this time. I can already see that the lists will be equal."

"But they won't. Given enough thought..."

"No. I'll always have another reason to add to the column that's fallen behind."

Tessa set the paper aside and asked, "Then what are you going to do?"

"I don't know. Maybe I'll go see that fortune teller in town. Or call Demi and ask for her opinion. Or just flip a coin."

Tessa pressed her lips together and stared at me as if I were a particularly obscure poem. Finally, she threw her hands up. "Sometimes, I just don't get you."

The mysterious email came the next day. If it hadn't seemed to address my situation so clearly, I would have shown it to Joe. Only a few weeks had passed since he had shared his theory about the blank emails from the "future." I still didn't know if I believed him, but the message I received that morning went a long way toward convincing me. "Don't move to California. Go to New York and pursue your dreams." Who, besides Joe, Tessa, and me, even knew I was trying to make that decision? Joe might have the technical expertise to pull off a stunt like this one: set me up with his theory and then zing me with the email punchline. But if that were true, wouldn't the email tell me to go with him to Silicon Valley? Tessa, my Luddite roommate, only used her computer for writing papers -- she definitely didn't send me the message.

Was I actually sending myself advice from the future? If I was, what did that mean? The thought over-whelmed me, numbed my fingers, toes, and brain to the point where I could only drop onto my bed and try to maintain an even flow of air. Inhaling, exhaling, wondering what sort of life would lead me to email myself sixty years in the past. How old would I be in 2069? I did a quick calculation: eighty-one. I lived to be eighty-one and regretted a decision I made as a junior in college so much that I was willing to change everything.

I knew what I had to do.

I finished college and headed for New York. As it turned out, Tessa came with me -- she was accepted by Columbia University's graduate program. With her parents still supporting her, she was able to secure a small but safe apartment for the two of us. The place had just enough room for two twin beds, which we disguised as sofas during the day. She wouldn't take my half-heartedly offered rent money.

Tessa immersed herself in her classes while I spent my days going from audition to audition. My meager savings dwindled. A much-needed infusion of funds showed up on my birthday, thanks to my generous sister, but a thousand dollars didn't go too far in the city that never sleeps.

By the time Tessa's first semester was over, I was down to two-hundred dollars. Mom sent me a plane ticket home -- one-way. I shredded it, piece by tiny piece, even though I knew the action was more symbolic than real; the ticket would still be available if I changed my mind. I doubted myself every day. What kind of idiot takes advice from an anonymous email? This kind.

But then, shock of shocks, I got a callback for a musical revival. The director liked my blonde-bombshell looks -- said I was perfect for the part! Rehearsals would start on the first Monday in January.

I wanted to celebrate -- I called Tessa and offered to treat her to a fancy dinner on the last of my "scraping-by" money. She said she was thrilled for me, but she was leaving town that night for the holidays. I hadn't even realized that Christmas was upon us. I ended up eating tuna fish out of a can while leaning over the kitchen sink. I pulled out my laptop and posted my good news on all of the social media sites, receiving sterile, typed words of congratulations from friends scattered across the country. Only Miss Stroman called me.

"I'm so proud of you!" my childhood music teacher sang into the phone.

"Thank you for calling me."

"I always knew you would be a star, Diana. You just have that ethereal quality about you. And your voice...I have never taught anyone as naturally gifted as you are," she enthused.

"Thank you," I repeated. I felt the corners of my mouth tip upward.

"You be sure to let me know when the show opens. I'm going to come to New York to see my star pupil perform -- how exciting!"

By the time we hung up, I had decided to go out to a club and find someone to celebrate with.

#

Between my rehearsal schedule and Tessa's studies, we drifted further and further apart. It didn't help that she disapproved of my boyfriends. She accused me of being too quick to open my legs; in retaliation, I posted online my suspicions that she harbored romantic intentions toward me, and I was definitely not interested. We didn't talk much after that.

As soon as I had enough money saved, I got my own place -- one that was closer to the theater. I had a new circle of friends, a few boys following me around with their tongues hanging out, and a budding career. Why did I need a hanger-on like Tessa, anyway?

Miss Stroman -- I mean, Louella -- came to New York to see my performance. She was more supportive than my own family. My father called to congratulate me, of course, but my mom alternately pretended that I was starving to death or working as a prostitute.

Demi promised to come see me when her team came to New York, but she didn't. She told me she had a bad case of the flu and didn't want to get me sick. When I saw a picture of her out on the town with one of her teammates on the front cover of a tabloid, I left her a nasty message and told her not to bother with an excuse the next time she was in town. When she called me back, I let her go to voicemail. She told me her girlfriend had never been to New York and just wanted to go clubbing. She apologized, but, as far as I was concerned, it was too late to fix our relationship -- the damage was done.

I spent a year in that musical -- I even won a Tony. After that first role, I was a hot commodity. I went from someone who had to audition to someone directors offered parts to before casting had even begun. I even did some television -- though only shows filmed in New York. By the time I was twenty-five, I needed a full-time assistant. I offered the position to Louella, and she accepted immediately. Her first assignment was to find us a bigger apartment.

Someone was tapping at my bedroom door, interrupting my sleep. That never happened. I reached over and clicked on my lamp. The clock read three in the morning -- I'd only been home from the theater for three hours. Frowning, I called out, "What's wrong, Louella?"

My former teacher pushed open the door hesitantly. "I'm sorry to wake you, dear, but the police are on the phone."

"Why would they be calling? Wouldn't they just come to the door? It must be a prank." I pulled my sleeping mask back over my eyes and fell against my pillows with a huff.

"It's not the NYPD, Diana. They're calling from Glendale."

My internal organs felt as though they had suddenly turned to stone and I was too weak to haul them out of bed. "Did they say..."

She shook her head. "She won't tell me. She says she needs to speak with you directly."

I held out my hand and beckoned. "Bring me the phone."

She crossed to the bed and handed me the small cell phone that served as my connection to the world.

"Hello?"

"Is this Diana Mogens?"

"Yes."

"Ms. Mogens, I'm afraid I have some bad news."

I don't remember much of what happened after that phone call. Louella made the travel arrangements, packed my bags, called my director. I barely noticed. I kept thinking about all those afternoons working in the shop with him, singing along with Barbra Streisand records. I hadn't been home in years -- too busy. He came to see me once, without Mom. When he got home, she was gone on one of her "vacations" for the first time in years. He didn't dare leave her again.

Demi met me at the airport. I was thirty, so she was, what? Thirty-four? Thirty-five? Her left shoulder had gone out a year or two earlier. She was the color commentator for her former team now. Her wife was still playing, though. She'd put on a few pounds since her retirement; her hips were wider and her face was fuller, but she was still beautiful. She hugged me to her and I cried for the first time since I found out he was gone.

We didn't talk on the way to her house. She and her wife -- Ranice -- lived near the center of Phoenix in a renovated cottage-style home on a large piece of land. Ranice was the same woman who didn't care to see me on stage several years earlier; I didn't want to like her, but she was surprisingly warm and charming. Mom was sitting on the striped couch in their lavender and yellow living room. I went directly to her, hugging her. She didn't hug me back or acknowledge my presence.

"She's been like that since we found her." Demi had a hand on my shoulder.

"What do you mean?" I straightened and looked at my sister.

"She was on one of her vacations when he died."

"I thought she stopped doing that."

Demi shrugged. "For a few years, yeah. After Dad visited you in New York, though, she started up again."

"How did you find her?"

"I knew where to look." The warning in her eyes was implicit -- I shouldn't ask anything else.

Demi and I planned my dad's funeral while Ranice looked after our mother. Demi was inclined to get the best casket we could afford -- and, let's face it, between the two of us we could afford the top-of-the-line model. But Dad had told me years before that a pine box was all he wanted -- "All you're burying is a shell, Di." When the funeral director implied that I must not have loved my dad as much as my sister did, I almost slapped the guy. Demi beat me to it.

"You knew Dad best. I'll follow your lead," she said to me as we left that funeral home. We went to the one down the street from Mogen's Memorabilia instead, even though Dad never liked the guy who ran it very well. He was an unusually cheery man, given his line of work, but the funeral was perfect -- a plain casket, a message about the power of love to transform lives, and a quick graveside service. The mourners came back to Demi and Ranice's house, where a buffet was served on the expansive green lawn behind the cottage. It was February when Dad died, just a few days before Valentine's Day. The sky was a powdery blue, so different from the gray New York horizon I was used to. Whenever I was left alone, I found myself gazing up at it, wondering if Dad was looking back at me. It was harder to picture heaven without clouds.

I never heard my mother speak another word, though Demi said she did still talk sometimes. She and Ranice were afraid to leave her alone in the home she had once shared with Dad. Instead, they moved her into their cottage, and Ranice, who still had a few good years left in basketball, retired to care for her. Demi told me Ranice wanted babies before Mom got sick, but that dream went out the window when Mom became a permanent fixture in their cottage.

The guy who killed my dad was just some random druggie in need of a fix. A crime of opportunity, the detective said -- he saw Dad alone in the shop. The street was empty; no one saw him go inside. If Dad hadn't fought back -- if he hadn't gotten some of his skin under his nails as he tried to grab the guy's knife away from him -- the cops might not have caught him.

It was my second trip to Phoenix in as many years. This time, I brought Louella along. She booked us a suite at the Princess Resort in Scottsdale; she got to enjoy it pretty much by herself, since I was at the courthouse with Demi almost every day. There was no point in staying with Demi and Ranice -- their cottage only had two bedrooms, and any change to Mom's surroundings tended to upset her.

For the first three days of the trial, I stared at the back of the guy's head, willing him to turn around. Even though I hadn't recognized his picture, I still thought he

31

must know us. He must have known my dad was an easy target. Maybe Mom even put him up to it; I wondered if she wasn't talking because she was overwhelmed by guilt. On the fourth day, I was in the courtroom when they brought him in. He looked old -- at least fifty. I could see that most of his teeth were gone. His skin was scarred from years of meth acne. His eyes scanned disinterestedly over the assembled audience, not pausing when he saw Demi or me. It really was a random crime.

With the mound of evidence against him -- DNA, an ATM camera's footage, an eyewitness who saw him flee the shop on foot -- he took a plea deal that morning. Life, without parole. In a capital-punishment state, that was a good deal.

A sharp rap on my dressing-room door roused me from meditation. "Go away!" Everyone backstage knew better than to bother me before showtime. I inhaled deeply and exhaled slowly, attempting to erase the interruption.

Another knock.

"I said, go away!"

"Miss Mogens? There's someone here--"

"The curtain goes up in twenty minutes. Tell them they'll see me then."

"Miss Mogens, he has the password."

I frowned. No one except Louella and my agent knew the password, and they both knew not to use it unless absolutely necessary. "Just a minute." I wrapped a peach-colored silk robe around me, covering my flesh-colored leotard. I wore the leotard under all of my costumes by then -- loose skin gave away my age in a way that my voice and face did not. I was seriously considering a full-body lift. My cosmetic surgeon assured me I would look twenty-five again -- even in bed. Since my boyfriends tended to be a decade or two younger than I was, I could certainly see the appeal.

Someone tapped hesitantly on my door. With one more glance in the mirror to be sure everything was in place, I sang out, "Come in!"

The man in the doorway was tall and gray-headed. I estimated him to be about my age, but he didn't look familiar. "Hello, Diana."

"I'm afraid you have me at a disadvantage. You are?"

"It's me -- Joe. Joe Stones, remember?"

Of course I remembered him. Who forgets their first love? "Joe! My goodness, it's been years!"

"More than forty," he affirmed. "How are you?"

I spread my arms wide. "Living the dream. You?"

"Happy enough. Tessa and I are in New York for our anniversary and we wanted to see you."

"Tessa? My Tessa?" I felt a stab of pain. I hadn't known they ended up together.

"Yes. She was there for me after you...well...made your choice."

"But she was here with me!"

"For a while. She kept me up to date on what was happening in your life. And when I got over you, there she was."

"No wonder I never heard from her again," I mused.

"She had a feeling you wouldn't take it well. She's waiting outside, if you'd like to see her."

"Come in, come in. I still have a few minutes before they need me on stage."

He stepped to one side and ushered Tessa in. She was prettier than I remembered...or maybe she just aged well. Her hair was silvery white and her skin was still pale as moonlight, despite forty years of living in California. "You do still live in Silicon Valley, right?" I asked, voicing the thought that had already slid through my memories.

"Yes. Tessa's been teaching at a community college there and I, of course, own Stonesthrow."

I should have known, but my brain -- constantly focused on the task of learning new songs and new lines -- hadn't made the connection. "The fake teachers thing? That's you?"

He chuckled. "They aren't fake. They're amalgamated personifications of educational objectives."

I raised an eyebrow. "They're robotic replacements for humans. Isn't that what the teachers' unions are calling them?"

"Stonesthrow teachers are cheaper than actual instructors. Plus, they are preprogrammed with all of the information necessary to answer any and all questions their students might throw at them. And they're safer. Student-on-teacher violence is completely non-existent in schools using Stonesthrow."

"That's because you can't kill an android!"

"You know a lot about it, considering you don't have children."

"Most of my fellow actors are parents. When New York replaced teachers with robots, it was a big deal. Tessa, what do you think about this?" I asked, remembering her distaste for technology.

"It frees up a large percentage of the population to do more interesting things than teaching," she said with a shrug.

"But what about all the people who are already teachers?"

"It will be decades before Joe's droids replace everyone. And I honestly don't think they'll ever be up to the task of teaching more than the basics. Colleges will always require humans to lead lectures."

Joe took out his wallet and unfolded a digital picture album roughly the size of two dollar bills taped together. He kept it in the slot where men used to carry paper money. Handing it to me, he said, "These are our children and grandchildren."

Six adults and ten children -- none older than ten or so -- were shown gathered at an amusement park, a roller coaster in the background. I smiled politely and complimented them on their family, as if raising children were a true accomplishment.

Tessa smiled proudly. "The boys both work with Joe at Stonesthrow."

"And your daughter?" I asked.

"She's a nurse, but her husband's a doctor."

"I always admired the nurses more," I commented. "They have to know more and work harder." Remembering that long-ago email, I asked Joe, "Do you remember your theory about the emails from the future?"

He smiled indulgently. "Of course...the foolish preoccupation of a science-fiction aficionado."

"So, you don't think it's possible?"

"Highly unlikely." He frowned in curiosity. "What made you remember that?"

"I don't know...I guess it's one of the last things I remember discussing with you. You were so enthusiastic about it."

Tessa rolled her eyes and said, "Oh, yes. I remember now! The emails from 12/31/69 -- you were obsessed with that idea for a while...especially right after..." She dropped her eyes to her lap and stopped talking.

"Right after what?" he asked Tessa. When she didn't answer, he sat back and seemed to search his memory. Suddenly, his eyebrows shot up. "Oh, yes! Right after...you broke up with me, Diana. I was obsessed with changing our future -- emailing myself and advising me to marry you right away." He chuckled at the memory even as Tessa stiffened. When he glanced toward her and saw her distress, he took her hand reassuringly. "But everything happens for a reason, you know. As it turns out, Tessa was the right woman for me all along. I wouldn't trade our life together for anything...not even you, Diana."

A stagehand knocked and called through the door: "Two minutes, Miss Mogens."

"We'll get out of your way," Joe said, still holding tightly to Tessa's hand as he stood.

"It was wonderful to see you both. We should get together sometime," I lied as I gave them both quick hugs.

"Yes. Maybe you'll come to California someday," Tessa answered, but I could see in her eyes she sincerely hoped I would never do that.

When you know something like what I know -- that I can send an email to myself and change my past -- the question is not "Did I live a good life?" but "Did I live the best life possible?" I've had decades to think about this; sixty, in point of fact. Here it is, December 2069, and I still don't know that answer for certain.

I spent my life on Broadway, and I passed up opportunities for a bigger career in Hollywood. I can only assume that taking that long-ago email's advice was the right decision -- this life has to have been better than what awaited me with Joe.

I spend my days amid the awards and accolades collected in a lifetime of entertaining. Friends stop by from time to time, and I have a lovely assistant who doesn't get upset with me when I call her Louella. She understands that I am old and my memory isn't nearly as reliable as it once was.

I miss the real Louella. She was a mother, sister, and friend to me. She celebrated my triumphs as if they were hers as well; she wept with me when tragedy stalked me. And it did.

My sister, her wife, and my mother were all lost in

the Great Nuclear Disaster of 2047. A few years ago, when the government finally decided it was safe for people to return to Arizona, Louella and I made a pilgrimage to our home state. Not much was left. All of the wood and stucco homes had long-since disintegrated. I found my dad's old shop -- a brick building, of course. The last business there had been something called Twentieth Century Ties. I imagine it was an antique store, probably a lot like the one my dad ran there.

I found the cottage where Demi lived, too...what was left of it, anyway. Time and the desert weather had taken it down to half-walls. The steeply sloped roof and the charming half-circle windows were gone. I don't know for sure if they died in the nuclear blast or before, to be honest. The environmental terrorists -- extremists, the president called them at the time -- slipped something toxic and contagious into the water supply a week or two before they sabotaged the nuclear plant and caused the meltdown. Their stated reason for the attack was to return the desert to its natural state. At least, that's what their website said -- none of them survived the attack either.

My apartment overlooks Central Park West. Some days, I just sit in front of the window and stare out at the city. I haven't played a role in five years now. I tell the reporters...I used to tell the reporters that I just wanted to spend the rest of my life thinking my own thoughts instead of memorizing the thoughts of others. It didn't take long to fall out of New York's consciousness. I imagine that when I die, thousands of people will read my obituary and be shocked that I wasn't already dead.

Why didn't I save my dad's life with that one email? I could change anything in my life, and I chose to live on the East Coast instead of on the West. I can think of two good reasons for not saving Dad. The first one is that he didn't need saving. If I had moved to California with Joe, maybe Dad wouldn't have been at the shop that day. Maybe he was in California visiting me. Or even living there. Who knows? Maybe some other poor shopkeeper was killed by that meth head. The second reason? Maybe I thought that one email would change everything. Maybe I thought by me not being in California, Dad's life would change too. Scientists believe there is a pattern to everything. Changing one thing within that pattern alters history, or so they think. Maybe that's what I thought. Or should I say "she thought"? Am I the same person as she was? Am I the same person as I will be after I send my email?

Because, make no mistake about it, I am sending an email. I've had a good life, but it hasn't been perfect by any stretch of the imagination. A dead father, a catatonic mother, my sister's family destroyed in the Arizona disaster...no, there are things that must be changed. But how much should I tell myself? If I try to fix everything with one email, will I (she) spend my (her) whole life waiting for disasters that may never come?

No. I must make a choice: a single course correction that will send my life flowing in a different -- hopefully better -- direction.

Third

"This is odd," Louella said, looking up from the tablet where she was checking my messages.

"What?" I was having my nails done by a Long Island girl named Michelle. We had a standing appointment -- Monday mornings at eleven.

She laughed. "You have an email here that says, 'Take the film role.' Have you been offered a film role?"

I pulled my hand away from Michelle and turned to face Louella. "Who's it from?"

"Let's see..." She slid her finger along the tablet until she could see the sender's line. "Okay, this has got to be a joke. No sender."

I reached out and took the tablet from Louella. My hands trembled as I read the date sent: 12/31/69.

"What is it? Do you know who it's from?" Suddenly suspicious, she asked, "Do you have a stalker, Diana? You need to tell me these things--"

"It's not a stalker," I answered quickly. "You're right -- that's odd!" Handing the tablet back to Louella, I return to face Michelle, who is waiting patiently, nail file in hand. "Anything else interesting in my email today?"

"Not that I can see. Just the usual fan mail. Send the standard replies?"

"Yes, please." I took a few deep breaths and willed myself to relax. Another email. It had been five years since I received the first one. Another email from the same date and no sender -- what could that mean? I briefly wished that I could call Joe and ask, but that was out of the question. And besides, no film roles were even on my horizon, as far as I knew. I stuck the message to a mental note board in my brain and put it aside.

When my agent called a few days later, I wasn't as surprised as I should have been. "Diana, I just took a call from California."

"Really, Paul? How is she? Still sunny?"

"Ha, ha. You're a crack-up, doll."

"You know I hate it when you call me that," I sighed.

"Stop with the corny jokes, and I'll stop with the patronizing nicknames." Paul Foster was already in his fifties when he took me on as a client. He was short and balding and liked to chomp on cigars in a way that reminded me of Danny DeVito. Not that he was heavy -- not at all. In fact, he was concentration-camp thin. "Listen, Diana, I got a call from Ronnie. He's making a film of that little drama you were in last winter. What was it? *The Profits*?"

"*The Prophet's Wives*," I supplied.

"That's the one. He wants you to reprise your role out in Hollywood."

"He wants me to play Zoe on screen? Gee, I don't know, Paul..."

"What's to know? You were terrific in it."

"But it's not really film material, is it? I mean, it's mostly just three women complaining about an asshole of a husband."

"The script is being completely overhauled by the best script doctors in the business."

"Then how do they know I'll be right for the part?" I asked coyly.

"Don't be stupid, Diana...they're writing the part for you specifically. Your contract with the musical is up in two weeks. Take a chance! Maybe you're Hollywood gold. Katherine Hepburn was!"

"Come on, Paul. You know the star track travels West to East these days. The only New York performer to get anywhere in the last decade has been Kristin Chenoweth, and it has taken most of ten years for Hollywood to find her a suitable vehicle."

"You're a lot taller than Kristin, Diana. You have that willowy look they like out there. Plus, you look gorgeous even when you're just standing around."

I was about to tell Paul there was no way I was leaving my Broadway star power to become a Tinseltown ingenue when I remembered the email. "Have Ronnie's people send me the script."

"You'll do it?" Paul sounded overjoyed -- he probably dropped his cigar.

"I'll read the script and decide."

"You're lucky Ronnie's set on you, little girl. That kind of attitude doesn't usually go over well with the California types."

"Who are you kidding? That's exactly what the stars are like!"

"Yes," he agreed, "but you aren't a star yet."

I sent Louella to California a couple of weeks ahead of me, so that she could find us a suitable home for the duration of the movie shoot. Since the whole film was set in various parts of California, location shoots would require minimal traveling. All of the indoor scenes would be shot on the studio lot.

Even though the schedule said filming would take six weeks, Ronnie, the primary producer, specifically asked me to plan on being in California for a year.

"Why?" I asked. "I prefer New York."

"Because you're such an unknown factor out here," answered the Hollywood veteran. His boyish grin belied his age -- he had to be over sixty. "We're going to spend the next year building your reputation. You're going to have interviews, attend movie premieres, date actors -- the whole show."

"What if I don't want that?"

He shrugged. "Read your contract. It's not really your choice anymore."

Louella found us a home that resembled a stack of boxes from the outside, with a pool and hot tub in the back. The interior was stark -- lots of white and gray -- but spacious. At four thousand square feet, we could have fit three New York apartments like mine inside and still had enough space for a pool table. Louella spent a chunk of my signing bonus on brightly colored Danish-modern furniture that cheered the place considerably. By the time I arrived, the house looked like I had been living there for years.

The script was terrific. Even better, the casting was top notch. I was the least-known of everyone on the set, but the others were gracious -- none of the normal "New York" stigma seemed to have been attached to me. To be honest, I thought I was a little too old for the role of Zoe -- the teenaged third wife of the prophet. But when I saw the completed film a few years later, I was amazed at what post-production could accomplish. Of course, by then, I had my first Oscar on my display case -- right next to the Tony I'd won a few years earlier back in New York.

I didn't go back, of course. Not then...not with a stack of scripts on my coffee table, one handsome film-star date after another, and producers and directors constantly courting me. Even Louella was happier in the California air. She sat by the pool and skimmed scripts for me, tossing the ones she liked into a small pile and the ones she didn't into the "thanks, but no" pile.

Louella could afford to get a tan. I, on the other hand, stayed out of the sun -- I couldn't afford to age. Plastic surgery can only hide so much damage; it's much better to avoid the fine lines and folds if you can. There are only two ages in Hollywood scripts: young and old. Looking like anything other than that means you won't be getting a lot of work. I had an advantage: At just past thirty, I had spent only a minimal amount of time in the sun and didn't like to tan. I never left home without sunglasses and a wide, floppy-brimmed hat, though not for the reasons most stars chose to wear such items; I was protecting my youth. Directors were still thinking of me for roles as young as twenty -- which was just fine with me.

I had also practiced a form of serial dating that guaranteed, at the very least, a good opening weekend for my films: I dated my co-stars. The relationships usually lasted until the films were out of the theaters; after that, it was time to start over. Most of the guys were on board with that -- relationships bonded by celluloid.

Louella didn't approve of my boyfriends, but she didn't criticize me. Instead, she would say that she preferred the men I dated when we lived in New York, because they hung around longer. I was just as happy to change men out every six months. None of them were that interesting, and none of them were much different from the ones who came before or after them. The men in New York had been slightly better; though, on the whole, they considered me beneath them and therefore not worthy of a ring. Marriage was something other women did -- the ones who worked "normal" jobs and kept "regular" hours.

Sometimes I thought about Joe -- the man who wanted me to follow him to this golden dreamland. He wasn't far away now, yet he was lost to me. Silicon Valley might as well have been Istanbul. I mean, how does a movie star leave her sphere of orbit?

I was on my way home from one of the spring awards ceremonies -- I forget which one -- when Louella called me. "I'm almost there, sweetie," I said as my latest boyfriend, who was nominated but didn't win for some historical role, grumpily steered the car onto my street. He had wanted me to come to his place and console him, but I wasn't in the mood.

"Don't freak out, but the police are in the driveway, Diana."

"What?! What happened? Are you okay? Was it that stalker?"

"I'm fine. They won't tell me why they're here. They say they have to talk to you directly."

The house came into view and the sore loser hit his brakes. "What the hell?"

"It's okay. They're here to talk to me."

"Listen, Diana...I can't afford this kind of publicity."

"What are you talking about?"

"You and I both know that this thing--" he waggled his finger back and forth between us "--has almost run its course. I don't want to get caught up in your..."

"Drama?" I supplied, arching my eyebrows.

"Yeah," he sighed, relieved. "So can I just...?"

"It's a damn good thing you usually have writers to supply your dialogue," I spat. Stepping out of his car and slamming the door behind me, I regretted my shoe choice of gold satin stiletto heels. I was certain I'd break my ankle if I tried to walk home in them. Resigned to the fact that my hosiery would be shredded by the asphalt leading to my house, I slipped the shoes off and headed toward my door.

Thanks to the moonlight glinting off my sequined gown, one of the officers, a woman, spotted me. She drove down the hill and picked me up in one of the squad cars. She didn't ask why I was walking; I didn't want to talk about it. Of course, the next day, pictures of me stepping out of a squad car in front of my house were all over the internet. Right next to those photos were the ones of me leaving a party in my erstwhile boyfriend's car, with said man at the wheel. I took great pleasure in instructing my publicist to say, "no comment" when questioned about the nasty rumors as to why I was escorted home by the police.

#

My father was dead -- the victim of "random violence," according to the Los Angeles police officer who had been assigned to deliver the news. When the officers left, Louella made me comfortable on the couch and turned off all the lights in the house. We waited two hours for the paparazzi to disperse. Louella figured leaving in the middle of the night would give us the best chance of not being followed.

A little after three, we slipped into the garage under cover of darkness. Louella drove me to Arizona that night while I sat in the passenger seat and sobbed. As it turned out, we might as well have left the moment the cops drove away; another tribe of photographers was set up in my sister's front yard. Louella had to honk to get the bastards out of the long driveway.

When the horn sounded, I saw the blinds in the living room louver open and closed quickly. "Pull around to the back," I said to Louella.

"Off the driveway?"

"Yes. We can replace the grass later. Just get me in the house quickly."

She swung the car up to the back door, where my sister-in-law stood with the door cracked. We jumped out of the car and ran toward her quickly, pulling the door shut behind us. I hugged Ranice tightly.

"I'm so glad you're here. Demi is beside herself," Ranice said, hugging me back. "Your mama's in shock -- hasn't said a word since Demi found her."

"Was she in the shop?"

Ranice shook her head and bit her lip.

"Where did Demi find her?"

She wouldn't meet my eyes. "She was on one of her...vacations."

"I thought she didn't do that anymore."

45

"She hadn't -- not for a long time. Then about a year ago, she started up again. A few days here, a few days there -- not too much. We only knew about them because your mama told Demi. Your dad never said a word against her, you know."

The old anger and resentment welled up in me. I reached out and gripped Louella's hand -- she was the only one in whom I had fully confided. She smiled encouragingly at me. "Where are they?"

"We convinced your mama to take a sleeping pill. Demi's sitting with her in our bedroom."

I released Louella and rounded the corner of the kitchen that led to the hallway. At the end, I could see Demi, her eyes closed, sitting in a straight-backed chair next to the bed. Her normally frizzy hair was pulled back into a tight bun. Her caramel skin looked as if a layer of dust had settled on it. In the bed, our scarred, blonde mother was sleeping, her face more relaxed than it ever was in her waking state.

My foot landed on a loose floorboard, which creaked and caused Demi to open her eyes. She frowned, looking at our mother first. When she looked down the hallway and saw me, she smiled even as tears began to flow silently. She held up a hand to tell me to stay where I was. Standing, she stretched her tall body and rolled her shoulders and neck. She was a little wider in the hips than she had been in her prime, but she was still athletic. She negotiated the hallway, clearly stepping over boards she knew would creak. Wrapping a long arm around my shoulder, she pulled me close and squeezed. "Thank you for coming so quickly," she whispered.

"How could I not? My father..." I couldn't finish the thought, let alone the sentence.

"I know, I know. I'm so sorry, Didi," she said, using a childhood nickname I hadn't heard in fifteen years.

She moved us away from the bedroom and toward

the living room, where Ranice and Louella were already sitting. Louella stood and hugged my sister. "I'm so sorry for your loss."

"How long have the reporters been here?" I asked.

"Since they caught wind that the father of a major Hollywood star was killed."

"When was that?"

"About three hours ago. The first one knocked on the door at five-thirty."

"Fucking vultures."

"That's their job," Demi shrugged. "You can't blame them -- blame the public that demands such detail about their favorite celebrities."

Demi was able to fill in some of the details the LAPD hadn't been able to provide. My dad's killer had walked in off the street and demanded money. When Dad handed him everything that was in the register, the punk got angry and said he knew there had to be more. He knew I was his daughter -- that was why he chose to rob Mogens's Memorabilia. He hadn't gotten far; a Glendale cop who was friendly with Dad and heard the gunshot saw the creep leaving the store, the gun still in his hand. He dropped it right away and the officer apprehended him. The guy was so high he'd practically screamed his confession. Unfortunately, that didn't mean there wouldn't be a trial.

In the meantime, we buried my dad while the tabloids whispered from every grocery-store checkout lane that Mr. Sore Loser had left me high and dry at the first sign of trouble. He had a hard time shaking that rep -- they were still asking him about it in interviews ten years later, even as his career circled the toilet. After what he supposedly did to me, the female audience found him "disingenuous" and "creepy."

Back in Hollywood a few weeks later, I came home one night to find a bouquet of white roses waiting for me. That wasn't so surprising -- my very public breakup with my ex had brought a surprising number of suitors out of the woodwork. One of my former leading men -- a man with whom I had conducted my longest affair -- even showed up on my doorstep and professed his undying love for me. I politely told him I appreciated his devotion, but I wasn't interested in anything long-term at the moment.

These roses were different, though, and not just because they were white. The card attached showed they were from a chain florist, a sure sign that they weren't from anyone in the Hollywood solar system. "Who are these from?" I asked Louella, who, as usual, was waiting for me in the living room. Three stacks of scripts were piled around her.

"Someone named Joe," she said casually. "I've been looking all night for a script with that name on it -- it's got to be from a writer, right? I mean, who else uses the internet to order bouquets?"

I walked straight for the flowers and pulled the card. *So sorry about your father. All my love, Joe.* "I don't think it's a writer, Louella."

"Who, then?"

"You remember me telling you about my college boyfriend, don't you?"

"The computer guy?"

"Yeah, that's the one."

Louella abandoned the scripts and walked over to inspect the card. "Is it his writing?"

"No, of course not. He definitely ordered them off the computer. But it just feels like him."

"How can you know for sure?"

"I suppose I could search for him online."

She took the card from me. "I'll do it tomorrow. It'll

make a nice change from reading scripts. What's his last name?"

"Stones."

#

The next night, I returned home to find a dossier on Joe Stones waiting for me next to the roses. "No trouble then?" I asked Louella.

"Nope. He's quite the guy if you happen to be into technology. He's been a front runner in educational tech for the last few years." She stood up and stretched. "I'm going to bed. Happy reading."

"Thanks." I took the folder to my bedroom and stretched out across the huge, blue-covered bed. A picture of Joe, who was even more handsome in a suit than he had been in t-shirts and jeans, was on top of the pile. The next picture was the shocker, though: a family portrait featuring Joe, two sons, and his pregnant wife...Tessa!

I flipped through the Stonesthrow media package and the half-dozen interviews he had done over the last five years. There were more pictures: Joe playing catch with the older boy, Joe in front of a computer, Joe striding through some kind of nerd paradise that passed for an office. All the articles described him as charming, intelligent, and remarkable. The one article that commented on Tessa at all called her reclusive and unfriendly.

On the last page in the folder, Louella had scrawled a note above his address: "In case you want to send a thank-you note."

I did. I most certainly did.

I met Joe for drinks at a small bar known for its discretion when it came to celebrity clientele. It was so well disguised that even the paparazzi hadn't figured out that it wasn't just a therapeutic spa. Like a speakeasy from the 1920s, it was hidden behind smoke -- or steam, in this case -- and mirrors. With the right password, you gained access to a comfortably dim lounge where the most secret of deals were made.

When I arrived, Joe was already there, looking bemused and even a little starstruck. He smiled and stood when he saw me, wrapping tentative arms around my shoulders. "This is...amazing," he said, allowing his eyes to sweep the room.

I shrugged. "It's necessary. The photographers are so aggressive these days -- the owners of this place saw a niche and filled it."

We sat down and Joe took my hand. "It's so good to see you. You look beautiful."

"Thank you. And you look fantastic, as well. How are you?"

"Great. Well, good enough. I suppose you know about Stonesthrow." His chest puffed up just a bit.

"I read about it."

A waiter slid two drinks in front of us -- a gin and tonic for him and a lemon-drop martini for me.

"How did you know?" I asked, smiling.

"The waiter asked me who I was meeting. When I told him, he said that was your favorite drink."

"He's right." I picked it up and sipped it. "How's Tessa?"

"She's good."

"Good enough?" I queried, repeating his own words back to him.

His lips curled into a sardonic smile. "Yes, I suppose so."

I could feel the electricity between us -- chemistry had never been the problem. Under the table, I brushed my hand over his thigh. He breathed in sharply. "I've missed you," I whispered.

"Not as much as I've missed you." He threw back

50

most of his drink before continuing. "I have almost contacted you a dozen times since you made *The Prophet's Wives.* Seeing you up there, on that screen -- I knew I'd made a terrible mistake. But I was married! Tessa and I already had our first son. And Stonesthrow was just starting to get noticed. You'd be surprised how important fidelity is to the educational community. No matter how much better my software is than my competitor's, I would have lost half my business."

"What's changed?"

"Nothing," he admitted, "but I had to reach out to you after I heard about your father. What happened was so horrible..."

"Let's not talk about that," I said. So we didn't. We talked instead about the strange turns our lives had taken. I told him about my next project, which was a historical piece about Catherine the Great. He talked about his company and the coldness of his marriage (though I knew better than to trust his interpretation of their relationship).

We shared a kiss that afternoon -- a lingering memory of the love we once had mixed with the promise of illicit and passionate sex. For the first time in years, I didn't find myself plotting just where to put my hands or how to make sure the camera caught me at my best angle; I just relaxed into him, our flesh melting together as the temperature between us increased.

"When can I see you again?" he whispered against my ear.

"You can't. It's too dangerous for you."

"But I must. I can't go back to Tessa without knowing we'll be together again."

I laughed. "Don't be melodramatic."

He pulled back as if I'd slapped him. "I'm not. I love you. I never stopped loving you."

"What is the matter with you? If you want a mistress, pick someone with a low profile, Joe. I'm not the girl for you. I have a platoon of photographers following me around day in and day out."

He pushed out an irritated breath and set his jaw. "I don't care. I'd walk away from everything for a chance to be with you. Wouldn't you?"

How could I say no? Yet hadn't I walked away from him on the advice of an email? Who knows? Maybe Tessa did send that message to me all those years ago. "I made my choice, Joe, and you made yours." I hugged him goodbye and slipped back out of the club alone.

And that should have been the end.

I'm not sure how we kept it a secret for as long as we did. Louella helped, of course. No one seemed to realize how much older she was than me; and, of course, they weren't interested in whom she dated. Even though he was recognizable within the tech community, the Hollywood paparazzi seemed oblivious to his identity. If they had known who he was, our affair would have been exposed years earlier.

I did try to resist him, you know. I told him to go back to his wife repeatedly -- often as I was pushing him out of bed. I warned him that I would have other lovers -- and that they would usually be my latest co-stars. He told me he understood; after all, he was staying in a loveless marriage for business reasons.

To Joe's credit, he was never jealous, despite the gauntlet of magazines he had to walk through year in and year out: pictures of me dancing in the arms of one handsome man after another, dining in the most exclusive restaurants, strolling the streets of Paris or London or...well, anywhere in the world. When I came home, he would be there waiting for me.

"What about Tessa? Doesn't she find your absences

suspicious?" I would ask as I lay in his arms.

"She has her own life. She knows I have to travel for Stonesthrow."

"What if she has you followed? She'll know that you aren't here for Louella."

"Are you concerned about my reputation...or yours?"

That's where the conversation always ended.

The journalist who finally put two and two together and came up with four made a mint on the story. Viola Weisler was a serious-minded young woman who wanted to be a true journalist, not just a celebrity interviewer. The fact that it was she who figured it out and not one of the crazed photographers who stalked me actually makes me smile.

I still remember meeting her. It was less than a year after Arizona was ceded back to Mexico as part of the agreement worked out between the governments of our two countries. Demi and Ranice refused to leave their home, despite the dangers of being Americans living under Mexican rule. Mexico had re-embraced their Catholic heritage and it was no longer safe to be homosexual in that country, no matter where you claimed citizenship. After Demi and Ranice disappeared, Ms. Weisler arranged to meet me to discuss my sister's plight.

Viola Weisler was petite, and I towered over her in my stilettos. Even though I was nearing forty, I still looked and acted like a younger woman when possible. When I shook her hand, I noticed that her nails were unpainted but neatly kept. Her hair was very short, but she still appeared feminine. "It's a pleasure to meet you."

"Thank you for the interview," she said with a sincere smile. "I know this isn't the sort of thing you usually talk about."

"My sister is very dear to me. If there's any chance I can help her, this is the least I can do." I led her into my living room, where she set up her cameras -- three facing me and one on her. In the last few years, this had become the standard in interview journalism; interviewers had discovered that they received more authentic answers when the subject was only faced with a single questioning gaze instead of the stares of a camera crew. I knew the trick well...and I also knew how to hold my tongue. I settled into the sofa and waited.

The interview started with the normal preliminaries: a brief introduction of me and my oeuvre to the "audience," followed by a warm greeting from Viola. I answered her back in kind, and we chatted briefly about my latest role as an uptight corporate executive in a film about the evils of big business.

"But, of course, the new film isn't the reason you agreed to this interview, is it?"

"No," I answered, taking a deep breath to steel myself for the conversation to come.

"Demi Mogens, the WNBA mega-star -- the woman who, arguably, made the WNBA an institution in its own right, bringing it out from under the shadow of the NBA -- is your sister."

I smiled and nodded proudly. "The best sister in the world."

"And her wife, Ranice Jackson, was no slouch herself. She was inducted into the Basketball Hall of Fame just last year."

Again, I nodded and smiled.

"But they are on the wrong side of the recent land treaty the US made with Mexico. Demi and Ranice still live in what used to be Arizona, is that correct?"

"To the best of my knowledge."

Viola creased her brow. "I don't understand."

"Demi and Ranice chose not to leave Arizona because

of our mother, who has been mentally unstable since my father's murder ten years ago. Any change in her environment leaves her in a near-catatonic state for months afterward. I practically begged them to move here, but Demi believed doing so would set our mother back years in her slow recovery. She trusted that the government of Mexico would be too busy actually running the country to concern themselves with the private lives of two citizens. However, I haven't been able to reach Demi or Ranice in nearly two months now. I suspect that our mother has been left on her own, and she is unable to care for herself. The government will not grant me a visa to check on her welfare or my sister and her wife."

"Why not?"

"They say they cannot guarantee my safety."

"Because you are a US citizen?"

"No. Because I am a public figure who does not profess the same faith as they do."

Viola pulled back just a bit and smiled. "Here's where I'll add some information about the rejuvenation of Catholicism in Mexico and how it has become almost synonymous with national pride. I'll talk about the recent string of violence against women and homosexuals and how the church seemingly condones it."

"That sounds good. Thank you."

"I just hope we can get some publicity out about what's happening there. I mean, these are US citizens--"

"In name only. Demi and Ranice had to get visas to stay there for five more years. Of course, the treaty did smooth the way for them somewhat, but it still wasn't a 'rubber stamp' process. And if they decide to take permanent residency, they will have to give up their US citizenship."

"Do you think they'll do that?"

"Only if our mother is still alive. I think if Mom dies, she and Ranice will move back stateside."

"You're from Arizona, though, aren't you?"

"Yes." I smiled wistfully, remembering my years there. "I suppose I feel 'homeless' these days."

She swiveled her head, searching the house for something. When her eyes fell on Louella, she asked, "Isn't your companion from Arizona as well?"

I knew she was trying to catch me out -- the conservative rumor mill had recently switched from calling me a serial monogamist to suggesting I was a closeted lesbian. Of course, the LGBT community latched onto that one; after all, I had always been vocal about my support for gay rights. If I had, in fact, waited this long to come out, it would have been detrimental to my career. Everyone knew that the gay community was ridiculously faithful to known gay actors. In fact, I knew actors who were closeted heterosexuals -- a situation I'm sure the American moral majority of my childhood didn't see coming. I rolled my eyes. "Please. Louella is my personal assistant. Even if I were attracted to her -- which I'm not -- that would just be too weird. She was my first voice coach."

"Really?" Viola laughed. "I had no idea!"

"Yes. I have her to thank for my career...and really, she's been the guiding light for me since I came to Hollywood. She reads all of my scripts first. And, in a lot of ways, she's like a mother to me."

"You're right. That would be weird." She paused and looked at her notes. "Who are you dating these days?"

The standard answer would be my co-star, but, as it happened, I had no leading man in my latest film. "I'm happily single, thanks."

"No one at all?" she prodded.

"I'm afraid not. I think a little celibacy is a good thing, though."

We finished the interview and she shook my hand firmly. "Thank you again. I do hope Demi and Ranice are all right."

"Thank you. I'm trying to stay optimistic."

She was in the process of packing her cameras away. "That must be difficult, given your history," she said offhandedly.

"Excuse me?"

"I mean with your dad's death and your mother's illness, it must be hard to look on the bright side."

I looked at her for a long moment, trying to discern if this was part of the interview or friendly conversation. Finally, I smiled and answered, "It's not all dead roses and wrinkle creams. I've still got a few good years left."

"I'm sure you do! I didn't mean to imply...I didn't even realize you were forty until I did the research for the article!"

"Thirty-nine," I corrected, under my breath.

"Oh, that's right...your birthday is still a few months off. Anything big planned for the occasion?"

Joe and I were planning to slip away to Europe for a few days -- one of our few trips together. "Not really. I might take a short vacation."

"Where to?"

"I'm not sure yet...maybe Paris. I do love France."

"Parlez-vous français?" she asked playfully.

"I do speak a bit, but the Parisians always reply in English. The language only comes in handy in the countryside."

Viola swung her camera gear onto her shoulder. "I know what you mean. I spent a semester at the Sorbonne during my senior year of college. Outside of the other students, it was nearly impossible to get anyone to speak French to me."

I led her toward the door. "When will the interview be posted?" Almost all interviews appeared on the Internet first by then, and I knew she had a contract with a major online news provider.

"I'd say by next week at the latest."

When the doorbell rang, I did something I will regret for the rest of my life: I answered it. "Come on in, Joe."

"Mr. Stones!" Viola exclaimed, surprised. "What a coincidence meeting you here!"

Joe's eyes widened and stayed that way a second too long. "M-ms. Weisler!" he finally said, pasting on a smile. "A pleasure to see you again."

I knew our normal cover story was impossible now -- this woman would know that Joe was married with children. Unsure of what to do, I stalled for time. "You've interviewed Joe too?"

"Yes. He was kind enough to give me half an hour of his precious time last week." She turned to him again. "Have you had time to watch the finished piece yet?"

"Not personally, but my assistant briefed me on it. He said it was accurate and relatively flattering. I appreciate that."

"I didn't say anything that wasn't true. Your company has made amazing advances in the science of education. It's obvious that you are passionate about your work." She paused and looked back at me. "I have to say, it's a little odd to run into a computer genius at a Hollywood star's home. I would have been less surprised to find Brad Pitt on the other side of your door."

"We're old friends. We went to college together." I heard the patio door slide open. "I suppose you need to be on your way," I said, then cursed myself for sounding so abrupt.

She didn't seem to notice. "You're right. I've got a lot to do before this interview is in the can, so to speak."

Louella, in her navy-blue one-piece swimsuit and loose white crocheted pullover, appeared at Joe's side. "Hello, sweetheart," she said, reaching up and pulling Joe into a more-than-friendly hug. Joe's eyes bulged in horror.

Viola's eyes widened a little. "I wouldn't let Tessa

see you hanging on him like that," she said. "She seems like the territorial type."

Louella, who wasn't much of an actress, instantly jumped away from Joe as if he were an electrified fence.

The smile that lit up Viola's features was predatory. "Have a great day," she said as she retreated to her car.

It's easy to second-guess yourself -- to think of what you should have done -- after the moment is nothing but a memory stored in the recesses of your mind.

We should have canceled our Paris rendezvous; if we had, Viola wouldn't have had photos to back up her assertions that Joe and I were a couple. Tessa wouldn't have divorced him and taken half the business. Stonesthrow wouldn't have been destroyed from the inside out, like a cancer growing at warp speed. I wouldn't have felt obligated to marry him. I wouldn't have suddenly found myself in the actor's version of no-man's-land: too old to be a romantic lead, but too young to be the latest ingenue's mother. Married actresses -- especially those who marry below their "station" -- simply aren't romantic-lead material.

I suppose I was lucky, to tell the truth. I had made so many films in fifteen years and had been so well paid for those roles that even Tessa's vengeful lawsuit against me for stealing her husband didn't really cause us to suffer. Parting with twenty million dollars was a small price to pay to have her out of our lives.

Unfortunately, Joe also lost his children because of us. Out of loyalty to their mother, none of them would even agree to meet me. Joe's heart was broken. Though he claimed to love me, I don't think he could feel much of anything after that happened. We stayed together, but the relationship was hollow.

On second thought, it's short-sighted of me to think

that simply canceling the Paris trip would have changed the way things turned out. Viola was like a lioness hunting a pair of giraffes: our heads stuck out way above everyone else's. All she had to do was stay low and wait. And if it hadn't been Viola who caught us, it would have been someone else. You can't be who Joe and I were and not end up devoured.

I should never have met him at all. I should have sent him a thank-you note and been done with it. Who knows what my career would have brought me? Perhaps I never would have married -- but singing and acting were my true loves anyway. Maybe I would have been able to segue from actress to singer during those turbulent years between ingenue and matron. No one is worried about your crow's feet (or lack of them) when they are listening to you sing.

But Joe would never have sent me flowers in the first place if my father hadn't been murdered.

Fourth

The message popped up on my cell phone this time. This was a new email address...one I had created for only close friends and family members to use. It was anonymous enough that no one outside of my circle could possibly have known it -- just a few numbers and letters in a random pattern. And yet, here was another email from an unknown sender.

I took a deep breath and opened it. "You need a vacation. Take your father. Stay gone until the end of the month." It had to be from a future me; no one else, besides Louella, knew that I actually could take a vacation right now. I was between movies, and the relationship with my current co-star was all but over. Shooting for my next film wasn't scheduled to begin until the summer. But why would I take my dad? As much as I adored him, we weren't as close as we once had been. Besides, if I took Dad, I would have to take Mom as well. My film career had done nothing to increase her affection for me; if anything, she was more bitter than ever before. Still, the emails had been right up to now -- at least as far as I could see. I dialed my phone.

"Diana! What a surprise!" My father sounded jovial and healthy enough.

"Hi, Dad. How's things?"

He rambled on about the shop. He had recently acquired a jukebox replica that played CDs and was expecting to double his money on the thing. One of his friends, a guy who ran a gun shop not far from his store, recently had a heart attack, but he was already back at work.

"How's Mom?" I asked dutifully. He hemmed and hawed for a few minutes before I realized the truth. "She's on one of her vacations, isn't she?"

"Yes," he sighed, "I'm afraid so."

"I thought she'd stopped that."

"Me, too. Then, about a year ago, she started disappearing again. She always comes back, of course," he hastened to add.

Maybe he needed to get away for a while, after all. "I'm planning a little trip, Dad, and I'd like you to come with me."

"Oh, you know I can't do that. I've got to stay with the shop! It's snowbird season here. Now if you call me in a few months--"

"I'll be on set then," I interrupted. "Come on, Dad! When was the last time you had a proper vacation? And you've always wanted to see London, right?"

"London?" His voice rose slightly, and I knew I had him on the hook.

"Yes. I'm thinking we'll do the whole Western Europe tour."

"Paris and Berlin as well?"

"And anywhere else you would like."

"Hmm," he sounded, but I knew it was a token reservation. "I can't really afford it..."

"My treat."

"How long will we be gone?"

"At least three weeks," I answered, glancing at the date on my phone. "I'm going to book us flights for three days from now. Is that enough time for you to get ready?"

"Three days! I don't know if I'll be able to get your mother home that quickly."

"Don't bother. Just close up the shop and come with me. She takes her little vacations without you all the time!" Silence fell on the other end of the line and I waited, holding my breath, for his final decision.

"Let's do it."

"Great! I'll have Louella send you the itinerary later, okay?"

"Okay, sweetheart. Will she be coming along?"

Louella had been by my side for years now, but I sensed my dad wanted me to leave her out of this trip. "No, just you and me. I love you, Dad."

"I love you, too."

I canceled all of my commitments for the rest of the month and ended my relationship with my co-star. He didn't seem particularly bothered, but then, we were both well aware that our relationship had more to do with the cameras than any real feeling on either of our parts.

Louella planned and booked the trip for me, securing suites in London, Paris, and Berlin hotels. When I told her she wouldn't be coming with me this time, she was actually relieved. "I think I'll visit some friends, if that's all right."

"You can take a vacation whenever you want, you know. You aren't my slave."

"Of course I'm not," she said, squeezing my hand, "but I hate to leave you on your own. I think you need someone like me in your life."

I smiled and hugged her. "Thanks for taking care of me. You have no idea how much I appreciate it."

"Happy to do it. If I'd had children, I'd want them to be just like you."

I called my agent and let him know I was going to be out of the loop for a few weeks. He promised to let me know if anything critical came up. I rather hoped he would take care of any little emergencies.

Three days later, I stepped off the plane at Heathrow. Dad's plane would arrive about an hour later. The paparazzi hadn't realized I was leaving the country -- a rarity. I pulled my floppy hat down over my ears and slid my big sunglasses over my eyes, hoping to continue my lucky streak. Since I was traveling without an entourage -- I was even carrying my own bag -- I managed to slip past the spotters with nary a flash. I found a bench and sat down to wait.

When I saw my dad walking toward me, I was shocked -- his hair had grayed completely in the last two years, aging him considerably. I silently reprimanded myself for not visiting more often, as if my presence could have kept him from graying. "Daddy!" I said, standing to hug him.

"Oh, Diana...am I glad to see you, my darling girl!" his arms encircled me and squeezed tightly for just a moment. "I'm so glad you had this idea. I've always wanted to see Europe, and your mother was never that interested, you know."

I slid one warm hand into his cool one and picked up my well-packed travel bag with the other, looping it over my head and across my shoulder. I noticed he didn't have a bag with him. "We need to go to baggage claim?"

"Yes, of course." He frowned at me. "Is that all you brought? I thought we were staying for several weeks."

"We are. But the hotels have laundry service."

"I wish I'd known that," he grumbled. "I had to pack two suitcases to get enough clothes."

The trip was a fantastic success. In less than a day, Dad and I had settled back into our easy relationship, joking and playing with each other. Mom seemed a distant memory as my father ogled the displays in the British Museum, took in the view from the top of the Eiffel Tower, and had a beer in Berlin.

The paparazzi didn't catch up with me until midway through our week in Paris, when the news hit that I had broken yet another leading man's heart. The European press are a little more forgiving though, particularly in

France. Ever since they were blamed for Princess Diana's death decades ago, they have maintained a policy of not chasing celebrities -- even American ones, who presumably can handle the pressure.

One did finally get close enough to ask me a few salient questions. First, was it true that my co-star and I had split? Yes, I said. Was I to blame? The decision to part was mutual, I said. Is this my new love interest? No, this is my father, I said. The reporter thanked me and left us alone. Apparently, my traveling across Europe with my father wasn't likely to sell a lot of magazines. Once the news spread, the paparazzi backed off.

All too soon, it was time to leave. I caught a flight to LA and Dad headed home to Phoenix. Louella had arranged for a car to pick me up when I got in to LAX that afternoon. After talking with Louella briefly about the trip, I collapsed in my bedroom for the next twelve hours. When I woke up the next morning at a little before five, I wasn't surprised to find Louella was still sleeping. Stretching as I walked through the house, I headed for the kitchen to make myself a cup of espresso and get my day started. Flipping on the radio, I caught the tail-end of a report: "We send our sympathies to the lovely Diana Mogens."

My heart thudded so hard I thought it would flip out of my chest and onto the floor. I clicked off the radio and headed for the living room, forgetting my espresso. Before I had the television turned on, someone buzzed from the gate, causing my phone to vibrate in my robe pocket. Agitated, I pulled the device out and answered, "Yes?"

"LAPD. We need to speak with Ms. Mogens."

"You are."

There was a longer-than-normal pause. "Ms. Mogens, may we come up to the house?"

Now I hesitated. Minding Louella's advice, I turned on the television and switched to the camera feed. A police car sat at the gate. "Yes," I said into the phone, "just a moment." I pressed the "open gate" button. Dropping the phone back into my robe, I rushed toward my bedroom to dress. "Louella!" I shouted. "Get up...I need you!"

I dressed quickly and ran a brush through my hair. I looked like hell -- I hadn't showered since leaving Germany more than two days before.

"What's wrong?" Louella was standing in my doorway, wearing a bright-blue embroidered Mexican dress. With her naturally curly hair already brushed into something resembling normal, she looked more prepared to greet our visitors than I did.

"Could you get the door?"

"Who's here at this hour?"

"The police. I'd really like to take a shower first--"

"The police?! What's happened?"

"I don't know...exactly. I turned on the radio and heard the announcer say something about me, but I can't be sure what."

Louella looked genuinely worried. "You can't get in the shower," she said, walking over and putting her arms around me. "If the police are here, you need to talk to them now."

"But I haven't done anything..."

"I'm sure you haven't." She took the brush out of my hand and turned me so that she could work with my hair. I let myself relax under her gentle touch. Louella was so much more like a mother to me than the woman who bore me into this world. "There now," she said, reaching for a hair tie lying on my dresser, "that's better."

I glanced in the mirror and saw that she had tamed my greasy, straggly mess of hair into a sleek and smooth French braid. "Thank you," I said, smiling at her reflection in the mirror.

"It's what I do," she said, smiling back. "Let's go meet the officers. We've kept them waiting long enough."

She put her hands on my shoulders and guided me to the front door.

"I'm sorry to keep you waiting," I said as I opened it.

The two officers, both women, were standing on the other side. "That's all right, Ms. Mogens. We know it's early," said the woman who had been speaking into the intercom at the gate. Her voice was slightly raspy, as if she were a cigarette smoker; I knew she couldn't be, of course. Cigarettes were illegal in California.

I stepped to one side and gestured for them to come into the house. "May I get you something to drink, officers?" Louella asked. "Espresso? Tea?"

"We're fine," the lead officer answered for both of them.

I led them to the dining table. "Louella, I could really use an espresso."

"Of course."

"Are you sure we can't offer you something?" I asked, again addressing the officers.

The second officer finally spoke. "Since you're already making some, I would appreciate an espresso."

Louella nodded and stepped into the kitchen to prepare both drinks.

I sat down at the table and invited them to do the same.

As soon as the lead officer was across from me in the morning light, I could see the fine lines at the corners of her eyes -- she was either fifty or she had aged badly in the California weather. "Miss Mogens, we're here about your parents."

"My father? He was fine two days ago...we just flew home from Germany!"

"Should we wait for your friend?" the other officer asked. She was younger -- probably twenty-five or so -- and wore her hair in a mannish style.

Suddenly anxious for support, I nodded. "If you

don't mind."

"Of course not."

We sat in awkward silence. The younger officer, wanting to fill the gaping and growing canyon between us, said, "I saw your latest film this weekend. It was great."

"Thank you."

"Your co-star -- what was his name again? -- he's talented."

"Not as talented as he thinks he is."

The older woman gave the younger a look that conveyed a command of silence.

The younger woman cleared her throat and sat back in her chair.

Louella came back into the dining area and set two steaming cups of espresso in front of the younger officer and me. She sat down at my side, facing the two officers.

"As I was saying," the older officer began again, "we're here about your parents."

"But her parents are in Arizona," Louella pointed out.

"Yes. Normally, the Glendale police would have contacted you via telephone. Unfortunately, the media got hold of the story before the sun even came up. We were hoping to reach you before you turned on a television or radio this morning."

"You were a minute late," I replied, smiling ruefully. "I caught my name at the tail-end of a report just before you rang the call-button on the gate." I could feel numbness settling into my fingers and toes, as if my heart were sucking all the blood in my body toward itself in preparation for whatever horrible news I was about to hear. I kept my cordial-star smile firmly in place.

"Ms. Mogens, I'm sorry to have to tell you that your mother is dead."

All the blood in my body stopped for a second before it began heading back toward my extremities.

"How terrible!" I exclaimed. The officers looked at me strangely; even I was unconvinced by my acting. "How did it happen?" I asked, pushing onward.

"Your father allegedly stabbed her thirteen times."

I felt myself freeze solid in that moment -- flash-frozen like a fish stick or some equally bland food product.

Louella's arm went around my shoulders. "That's not possible."

"I'm afraid it is," the officer said softly. "He called 9-1-1 to report her death. The first officer on scene disarmed him."

Louella was talking again, but I couldn't hear her. Was this why I had sent myself the latest message? Did this happen in another time line, too? If so, I'd done a lousy job of stopping it from happening. Why would I allow him to go home to her at all?

I downed the espresso and wandered away from the table, certain that I was dreaming. I don't remember saying goodbye to the policewomen. I fell back onto my bed and closed my eyes; my ears were ringing so loudly I couldn't hear the clock ticking in the hallway. I tried to sleep, but every time I drifted off I would see my father stabbing my mother to death and come awake with a start.

I don't know how long I was in my room. Hours, I suppose. I remember Louella stepping in and talking to me, but I couldn't make out her words. Finally, she just pulled the door of my room shut and left me alone.

Louella told me later that Demi was relieved when the cops did what she couldn't bring herself to do: tell me what had happened. Their conversation was brief, but Demi was able to fill in some of the details the cops hadn't known. Apparently, Dad came home just in time to find Mom packing up her stuff to leave him. After more than three decades, she was going back to her first love -- the abusive basketball player who had stolen her beauty and refused to acknowledge Demi as his daughter.

Dad was incensed. He had taken Mom -- pregnant with Demi at the time -- into his home and vowed to protect her from her violent ex. He had spent more than thirty years by Mom's side, accepting her absences and reappearances as if they were perfectly normal. He had loved and raised Demi as if she were his own child. He stabbed Mom to death, then called Demi and confessed, begging her forgiveness the whole time. Stunned and in shock, she told him to call the police and report the murder. She didn't fully believe our mother was dead until the cops knocked on her door a few hours later.

The media picked up the story immediately, thanks to the recent paparazzi shots of Dad and me in Europe. If it hadn't been for that, the story wouldn't have been splashed across the internet and on every news program from coast to coast before I was even out of bed that morning. Louella contacted a director friend of mine, and he arranged for his production company's private plane to fly us to Phoenix that evening. A car was waiting for us at the airport, and it took us directly to the jail where they were holding Dad.

I don't know if visits like this were normally allowed or if I received preferential treatment due to my celebrity status, but I was hugging my father in a private consultation/visiting room that night.

"What happened?" I asked as we sat down at the rectangular table in the middle of the room.

He shook his head, keeping his eyes on the scarred surface of the table. "She was leaving me, Diana. After all these years of taking care of her...protecting her. She was going back to that asshole who tried to kill her." He was tapping his finger against the table now, stabbing repeatedly at a carved heart with the initials "ML" in the center.

I reached across the table and laid my hand over his. His fingers were cold compared to mine; I worried that the jailers would put him somewhere drafty. Then I remembered we were in Arizona -- even a drafty place would be warm this time of year. "Dad. Why did you kill her?"

He shrugged. "She needed killing. Might as well be me."

Any other questions I had seemed to fly away on the breeze of his words. I squeezed his hand. "I love you, Dad."

His troubled expression cleared and I saw the father I'd known my whole life. "I love you too, Diana."

An officer escorted me back to my car, just in case any reporters were hanging around waiting for me to show. Everything was quiet, though. I stepped back into my car unaccosted.

"How is he?" Louella asked.

"I think he's lost his mind," I answered, staring straight ahead.

"What do you mean?"

"He's not himself. He said she needed killing. All the things she's done over the years -- he's never said that before. He always claimed to understand her need to escape."

"Should we find a lawyer for him?"

"I think it would be best. Find someone with experience in temporary insanity defenses." I closed my eyes and tried not to think about the manic man I'd seen inhabiting my father's body as the car drove us to the luxury hotel near the NFL football stadium.

Demi was at my suite's door at ten o'clock the next morning. Ranice, her new wife, was at her side, almost holding her in an upright position. Demi's eyes were bloodshot and rimmed with red. She didn't look like she had slept at all in the last two days.

I opened my arms to hug her but she skirted me as if I were a volcano threatening to erupt. Ranice shot me an apologetic smile as she helped Demi to the couch.

"You've seen him." It wasn't a question -- Louella must have told her that I was going straight to the jail last night.

"Yes." I sat down on the plush green chair across from her.

"You forgive him?" she asked, looking directly at me, her eyes squinting as if I were too bright to watch so intensely.

I didn't know if "forgive" was the right word. I avoided answering instead. "He's our father."

"No!" she spat. "He's your father!"

I leaned away from her, eyes wide. I had never seen my sister like this -- infuriated, vengeful, dangerous. "Mom is gone," I said softly. "I'm going to do whatever I can to take care of Dad."

"You never loved her. You're glad she's gone, aren't you?"

"She was my mother too. Of course I loved her."

"But if you had to choose a parent to lose?"

"If I have to choose between losing Mom or losing Dad, you're right: I'd pick Mom."

"Traitor," she whispered.

"Why are you mad at me? I didn't kill her!"

"Maybe not, but you're going to defend her murderer. You're a gender traitor. Nothing but a Hollywood whore."

"I'm a whore? What the hell was our mother then?" I stood up and pointed at the door. "Leave. You aren't welcome here anymore."

"Now, Diana, you don't mean that," Ranice said

soothingly. "Demi, tell her you're sorry."

"I'm not. She's as guilty as he is. She always made Mom feel like a bad mother."

I felt the hair at the back of my neck stand on end. "That's because she was," I said slowly. "In fact, I'm absolutely thrilled she's gone."

Demi lunged toward me from the sofa with the speed of a cobra. Her basketball reflexes hadn't completely deserted her after all. She pinned me against the wall, her huge hand around my neck. I could feel her fingers quiver against my throat. Her eyes stared into mine with intense hatred, but she didn't say anything.

Ranice appeared over Demi's left shoulder. She placed a calming hand on her shoulder and whispered, "Demi, darling, let her go. Let her go. You can't do this -- let her go."

Demi's grip loosened and her eyes softened. At last, her hand fell away from my throat and she collapsed into her wife's arms. As Ranice led my sister out of my suite, she met my eyes once more and mouthed the words 'I'm sorry.'

I shouldn't have bothered to find my father a good defense lawyer. He disregarded their advice and pled guilty at his arraignment. He was sentenced to life imprisonment -- which turned out to be a ridiculously short sentence. He died of a heart attack less than a year later. Suddenly, my whole family was gone -- and I felt as if I'd never really appreciated them.

More surprisingly, my film career seemed to have evaporated in the months following my mother's death and my father's incarceration. No one in Hollywood wanted to work with me; I might as well have had a tattoo on my forehead that proclaimed me "untouchable."

My agent had an idea. "Come back to New York, baby doll," he cooed over the line soothingly. "Come back to your roots. You always wanted to be a Broadway star, anyway."

Louella, on the other hand, was lobbying for me to record an album. "No one cares what you look like when you're a singer," she reasoned.

I studied my appearance in the huge white-framed mirror that hung on the far side of my bedroom. From a few feet away, I didn't look any different -- all my curves were still in the right places. Closer inspection, though, revealed the truth: the stressful year had left behind signs that the camera would pick up easily: three lines between my eyebrows, deep channels from my nose to my lips, and crow's feet. I was no longer an ingenue.

For the first time in my life, I prayed that one of those damned emails would arrive and tell me what to do next -- even though the last one had clearly gone awry. What horrible event had I been attempting to avert by taking my father to Europe? Was it worse than what had happened? I would never know. If I never received another email, all I could hope for in the future was the chance to do some damage control -- maybe I'd be able to salvage my relationship with Demi.

I was back in New York by the fall of my thirty-first year. I hadn't seen my agent Paul in person since moving to Hollywood, because he claimed there was no valid reason to leave New York in the digital age. Walking into his office was like stepping back in time. Even Paul seemed unchanged -- a little smaller, maybe, but only in stature, not in attitude.

"Diana, sweetheart! You look like a million bucks!"

"Only because I made you that much last year," I

answered, slipping onto the beat-up black leather chair next to his desk. "Why don't you spend some of that dough on fixing this place up?"

He ignored me. "You're still gorgeous, baby doll. Just a little more...mature. So you come back home, you do some theater, in a few years, you go back as a 'serious' actress."

"I thought I was a serious actress!" I laughed incredulously.

He shrugged in that way only New Yorkers can. "You were Meg Ryan. In a few years, you can be Meryl Streep."

"You're aging yourself, Paul. Meg and Meryl's heyday has long-since passed."

"Sweetheart...you're killing me. Do you want to end up like Meg Ryan? Fine. Go back to Hollywood. Have a few surgeries. See who will hire you then."

He was right -- I didn't want to become a parody of myself. I slumped into the seat. "Fine. What's next?"

He rubbed his hands together in glee. "A revival of *Cat on a Hot Tin Roof.*"

"What? You're kidding me, Paul. I'm a song-and-dance girl. And from a distance I still look young, right? Can't you get me *Sweet Charity*? That did wonders for Christina Applegate's career a few decades ago."

He shook his head. "Sorry, kid. Musicals are out for now. No one's heard you sing since the Teens. Besides, a serious role is what you need -- that's the sort of thing that will get you back on screen."

"If you're sure..."

"Have I ever steered you wrong?"

Up to that point, he hadn't. I took his advice and began rehearsals for my turn as Maggie.

The reviews were lukewarm at best. Most of the critics said I didn't have the bite that an actress needed to do the role justice. I was too tame, too pretty, too nice. When I tried to be wilder, uglier, and meaner, the critics were even less impressed. Now I was overacting, in their humble opinions. Still, the audiences came, if only to see the Hollywood star with the murderous father and dead mother. On the strength of my notoriety, we kept the curtain rising for six months.

About half way through the run, one of the ushers brought me a note from an insistent audience member. "I'm sorry to bother you, Miss Mogens, but there's a man here who insists you are old friends and that you would want to see him."

"That's fine," I told him. "Let me read the note."

He handed me a program, on the back of which was scribbled: "Diana, it's Joe from college. Remember me?" Of course I did. Even if I didn't want to, the internet was prompting me to remember him almost daily. His educational technology firm was a rising star -- some were predicting that he was the next Steve Jobs because his innovations seemed so far ahead of the curve. I had even read an article or two about him -- enough to know that he had married my ugly college roommate, Tessa. I smiled at the usher. "Send him back during the break."

"Yes, Miss Mogens."

I was back on stage a moment later and trying to keep my smile more on the inside than on the out.

At intermission, he knocked on the door.

"Come in!"

As soon as he opened the door, I felt a rush of warmth steam my blood. I hadn't had sex since I broke up with that forgettable co-star back in Hollywood -- in fact, I hadn't even thought about the caress of a man since my father killed my mother. Seeing Joe, though, I knew what I wanted -- and he was it. His eyes told me everything I needed to know at that moment. I walked across the room and wrapped my hand around his neck, pulling his lips to mine. His tongue slid against mine and I felt a rush of moisture flood my loins.

"Wait," he said, "we can't--"

"Intermission is only fifteen minutes, Joe," I said, unbuckling his belt. "We have ten minutes left. Do you want to talk--" his pants slid to the ground "--or do you want me?"

He responded by turning me so that I was against the door and pressing his mouth against mine hungrily. All the times I had faked my way through bad lovemaking as if it were just another scene for a film melted away under the intense heat of our passion. When he entered me, I remembered what it felt like to be desired as more than just a rising Hollywood star. Our fever reached its peak as the lights dimmed and I momentarily wondered if we were draining the electricity from the building. He leaned against me and the door heavily, trying to catch his breath. Feeling as much as hearing his breath against me, I soaked up the warmth of his body for a moment more.

When I pushed him away, it was with regret -- I knew I would never touch him again. He was a married man, and I didn't need one of those following me around, threatening to tarnish my image. I went to the mirror and carefully reapplied lipstick and smoothed my hair. On my way toward the stage -- I pressed my lips against his cheek and whispered, "It was lovely to see you again, Joe. Give my best to Tessa."

It's amazing how interested the reporters were in me when the baby bump became unmistakable. Louella, my ever-faithful friend and assistant, spread the news that I had opted for in-vitro fertilization because I wanted children even though I wasn't in a permanent relationship. It wasn't long before the usher who had brought me Joe's note floated his own story to the tabloid sites: I had a visitor named Joe one night around the time I got knocked up. You've got to give the press their due -- it only took them a few days to compile a list of Joes and Josephs I had been connected with over the years. The internet is the one invention I wish I had preceded by a few decades; I envy movie stars like Marilyn Monroe and Marlena Dietrich, who were able to conduct their love affairs in relative secrecy.

The list the tabloids came up with wasn't too long: a film director who worked with me on two films back when my career was just taking off; an actor who never lived up to his potential; a star who recently married for the fourth time; and my Joe, the computer genius with the billion-dollar company and devoted wife.

In one of the only decent breaks I have ever gotten in my personal life, the usher turned out to have prosopagnosia -- more commonly known as face blindness. He had no idea which of the "Joes" had been to see me that night. Popular opinion seemed to finger the failed actor, who actually got a bump to his career when he smiled slyly at the cameras and refused to answer the paternity question.

Meanwhile, Louella continued to stick by the in-vitro story. When the play's run ended, I told Paul I was going to take some time off and raise my child.

"I think that's a mistake, baby doll," he said, tapping his pen against his desk uneasily. "You should capitalize on your new-found popularity in the media."

"Don't call me that, Paul. I'm no one's baby doll," I answered irritably. "My Hollywood career is on hold for the next decade, my Broadway career will be too demanding when the baby comes--"

"Isn't that what Louella is for?" he interrupted. "I

mean, she can take care of it, right? After all, you're the breadwinner."

"What are you trying to say?"

He shrugged and frowned. "In-vitro fertilization? Long-term female roommate? No boyfriend in the last year? You know being a lesbian isn't the detriment it used to be, right? Ellen broke that barrier decades ago..."

My jaw was hanging open. Why did everyone think I was gay? "I'm just single, Paul. Just another one of those crazy unmarried mothers."

He snorted like he doubted my word. "I don't remember you ever mentioning a passionate desire for motherhood."

My heartbeat sped up, but I managed to keep a neutral expression. "It just seemed like the right time."

He agreed to abide by my decision to take the next two years off. After that time period had passed, he would begin fielding my name for movie roles only, though he frankly told me that my career would be dead in two years' time. I didn't really care. Even though I had been unprepared to become a mother, the thought of a child -- particularly one with Joe's and my genes -- suddenly seemed wonderful.

Joe, for his part, sent a card -- a thank-you note, to be exact. In it, he wished me happiness and told me to contact him if I ever needed anything. I understood what he meant -- if our child ever needed anything, he would be there. That was more than I ever would have asked of him, but I appreciated the gesture.

My daughter, Demi Ella, was the best child I could have hoped for. She was beautiful and talented and sweet-tempered. She had blonde ringlets and green eyes -- just like her father's. Her porcelain skin, bow-shaped lips, and plump cheeks made strangers stop and stare as we went about our lives in New York. The attention we received was so great, in fact, that Louella insisted we move to

Connecticut. She found us a farmhouse -- the very one I'm in now -- and we made a good life for Demi Ella. Louella taught her to sing and play the piano and guitar. She never asked about her father -- she believed me when I told her she was planned and wanted. By the time she was twenty, she was well on her way to musical super-stardom -- and I was just a footnote in her biography.

My career -- such as it had been -- slipped into the past almost without me noticing it. Sure, I got a few small roles -- mostly mothers, occasionally older "friend" roles. When I was nearly sixty and Paul had been dead a good ten years, a television producer approached me about playing a boozy, ex-"B-movie" actress in a comedic mystery series they were calling *The Brass Monkey Gang*. I told him it was a terrible name for a television show and I wasn't interested.

He sent me the first script anyway. Louella, now well into her seventies, nearly fell off the porch swing laughing as she read it one afternoon.

I glanced over at her from my favorite rocking chair. The stack of scripts was less than a tenth of what it had been in my heyday, but it was still enough to keep her in reading material. "What are you reading?"

"It's called *Brass Monkeys*. The female lead is hilarious!"

"Sounds familiar...I think I already turned it down."

Louella clucked disapprovingly. "Seems like a mistake to me."

"What seems like a mistake?" Demi Ella asked, emerging from the house with a towel wrapped around her head. She was home for the first time in months after a spectacular multi-continental tour.

"Your mother has turned down one of the best roles I've ever read for a woman of her age."

"It's a sitcom, Louella," I said. "How can it possibly be a good role?"

"Actually, it's more like a witty *Murder, She Wrote*."
Demi Ella wrinkled her nose. "What's that?"

"Never mind, dear," Louella said. "It was on television decades before you were born."

"So, I'd be a detective?" I laughed. "Now I'm sure that I'd look like a fool. And I'd have to be away from here for months at a time."

"I don't think so." Louella frowned and, flipping to the front of the script, read some handwritten notes. "That's what I thought! This show is being shot in twelve-episode seasons. The shooting schedule will be twelve weeks long."

"So three months in California?"

"Actually, they're shooting on location in Arizona."

I hadn't been to Arizona since my father died. Even after I named my daughter for her, Demi refused to acknowledge me. I lost my whole family in one fell swoop. Maybe that's why Demi Ella is so precious to me. "I don't think it's a great idea. What about all the political unrest?"

"Mom, I was just there a few months ago. It's actually very safe now. And with the wall...." She hesitated, no doubt remembering my repeated rants when Arizona succeeded in seceding from the U.S. and erecting a wall around the former state -- now independent nation -- to keep the "undesirables" out. A couple of other states attempted to follow their lead, but found themselves unable to become truly self-supporting. Having grown up in the state, I have no idea how the Arizonans are able to do it now -- though they do make a fair amount of money on tourism. The Grand Canyon is a major part of their economic plan.

I ground my teeth together in irritation. "I doubt they would let me in the state."

"You have dual citizenship, you know. Automatically, because you were born there," Louella answered.

"Maybe so, but since so many people assume I'm

gay, I'm sure I wouldn't be welcome."

Now Demi Ella chimed in: "Actually, they don't actively discriminate against native homosexuals. They just won't let them emigrate."

"How forward-thinking of them," I said dryly.

Demi Ella shrugged. "It seems to work for them. Even Aunt Demi--" She stopped talking and clapped a hand over her mouth, her eyes wide.

"You've seen Demi?"

She looked everywhere but at me. "Only once or twice."

"How many times?"

"Three times," she answered with a sigh. "She and Aunt Ranice came to my concert a few years ago. This time, I invited them to join me for dinner after the concert. Since the next day was Sunday, I was stuck in Arizona. They invited me to spend the day with them."

My heart ached, unsure of whether it was happy or angry. I had always wanted Demi Ella to meet her aunts -- but I had hoped to be part of the family reunion. "Is she still mad at me?"

Demi Ella knelt next to my chair. "No, Mom, she's not. She hasn't been angry for years now -- but she didn't know how to apologize."

Of course, you know I took the role. How could I not? Sondra Lane was practically written for me -- except for the red hair, of course. I dyed mine for three months out of the year for the next decade. *Brass Monkeys* was a cultural phenomenon -- partly because of its "exotic" location. Arizona was a mystery to most people. The other major part in the show -- Sax Ridley, the grizzled, gay bartender-turned-private eye -- was played by a straight actor who had also fallen off the radar for a few decades.

He wasn't a very convincing gay man as far as the American public was concerned, but then, that was what the role required. The gay population loved Sax for exactly that reason -- he wasn't portrayed as a stereotype.

Unfortunately, my sister was already failing when I arrived to tape the first season of the show. She was diagnosed with multiple sclerosis and quickly lost her motor skills.

"Is there anything I can do?" I asked Ranice and Demi as soon as I arrived in Arizona. I was sitting in their beautifully furnished central-Phoenix bungalow. "There are treatment options in the United States. I could arrange for you--"

Demi held up her hand to silence me. "They aren't guarantees. I'd rather stay here, with Ranice, and live out my life."

"But you're not that old! Wouldn't you rather have a longer life?"

"The best treatments available involve genetic manipulation. If I have that done, I won't be allowed to return to Arizona."

"How will they know?" I looked around the living room, taking in the oil painting of the two of them together and the other artwork they had accumulated over the years. "And besides, even if they did find out, you could always join Louella and me in Connecticut. The house is too big for just the two of us anyway. Demi Ella is hardly ever home...and she's nearly thirty! She'd probably love the excuse to move out."

"We appreciate the offer," Ranice answered, "but Arizona is our home." She squeezed Demi's hand lovingly and they looked at each other with a devotion I'd never experienced in my life. The pang of envy that shot through my heart was unexpected, but real.

"I'm sorry about how I behaved when Mom...died," Demi said. "Dad was a good man. I know he just couldn't take it anymore."

"He would never have done what he did if he had been in his right mind," I offered. "I know he loved her more than anyone else in the world."

"And I know you were just doing what you thought was right for him."

Ranice stood up. "Would you like something to drink?"

"Tea would be nice," I said, smiling.

"Of course." She disappeared into the kitchen.

Demi caught my eyes and held them. "My real father contacted me after she died."

"Oh?"

"Yes. He asked me if I knew who he was -- as if I somehow thought that Mom and Nick had miraculously birthed a mixed-race child," she snorted.

"What did he want?"

"My silence. He wanted me to agree never to name him as my father."

I slid to the edge of the sofa and took one of her soft hands in mine. "I'm sorry, Demi."

A tear slipped and fell down her cheek. "He tried to tell me that Mom would want me to keep the secret -- after all, she had kept it for more than thirty years."

I shook my head. "Why did she keep going back to him?"

Demi, her eyes full of understanding for our long-dead mother, answered, "Because she loved him."

"I guess I've never loved anyone that much."

"I doubt that. Don't forget -- I've met your daughter." She looked at me sideways, a small smile on her lips. "She looks familiar."

"I don't think she looks too much like me." I smiled, hiding the truth behind my teeth.

"I didn't say she reminded me of you."

Ranice reappeared, balancing three glasses of iced

tea. She handed me mine first before setting one in front of Demi and sitting down next to me on the sofa. "What are you two talking about so intently?"

"Family resemblance," Demi answered. "It's hard to believe Diana and I are sisters, isn't it?"

"Not really," Ranice shrugged. "You both have your mother's eyes, I think. And her--"

Demi's glass of tea slipped out of her hands and toward Ranice and me, splattering us with cold, brown liquid. Thankfully, the "glass" was actually plastic -- it clattered against the wooden floors but didn't shatter. The shock of the wetness soaking into my clothes was more surprising. As soon as the moment passed, I began to laugh. Demi, for her part, looked horrified. Ranice responded by immediately hurrying to the linen closet to get a few towels. She tossed one at me and took the other one to Demi, drying her legs even as Demi's eyes rained down more liquid than had actually fallen on her.

As soon as my mind registered how upset my sister was, I was able to stop laughing. "It's okay," I soothed, "accidents happen."

"My whole life is an accident these days -- one right after the other."

As I lay in bed that night, my memory sent flash after flash of my sister, the professional basketball player. I'd seen her glide through the air with the speed and grace of Michael Jordan. She had been the heroine of an entire generation of female athletes; she made the WNBA a real league. Her love of athletics led directly to the establishment of professional female leagues in all the major sports -- even football. No wonder dumping a glass of tea brought her to tears -- it reminded her of the life she once had.

I spent every spare moment I could with her and Ranice -- making up for lost time, I hoped. We never talked about Demi Ella again, though I'm sure Demi knew who her niece's father was. After all, Joe and I had been together throughout college, and I had brought him home for winter and spring breaks more than once. Demi had even taken me aside -- back before I received the first email -- and told me that she would be proud to have Joe as a brother-in-law.

After three months in Arizona, the first season of *Brass Monkeys* was in the can. Before I came back for the second season -- nine months later -- Demi was dead. I like to think that we were better -- that our relationship was healed -- but I know we could have used more time to sort things out. I didn't come back to Arizona when she died because Ranice didn't want to give Arizona the benefit of a state funeral for her. All that pomp and circumstance over a dead lesbian just because she revolutionized women's sports? That seemed like the height of hypocrisy to my sister's widow. If I had shown up, though, she would have had a hard time convincing the officials to back off.

Ranice, bereft of her wife after forty years, seemed unsettled when I saw her...almost as if she didn't know what to do now that she was free to do whatever she wanted. I offered to send her anywhere in the world, but she wasn't interested. "Besides," she said, "I have plenty of money, Diana. If I want to take a trip, I can afford to go anywhere -- even on one of those Mars flyovers!"

She was visiting me on the set. I had a pre-fab home set on a cement slab, right next door to the actor who played Sax. It wasn't very large, but it was fine for lounging between shots. The production team even sent a chef in to prepare my lunches every day. I had invited Ranice to join me for lunch, and I wasn't due on the set again for at least another hour. "I'm sorry. I didn't mean to--"

She waved my apology away. "No, no. I should apologize to you. I'm afraid I've turned into a crusty old woman since Demi's death."

"You miss her."

She nodded. "Terribly. I suppose you'll understand

better when sweet Louella passes on."

"We're not--"

She laughed, cutting me off. "Maybe not physically, Diana, but you and she have passed a lifetime by each other's side. That's a level of devotion most married couples don't experience these days."

By the time I came back to film the third season of *Brass Monkeys*, Ranice was gone. She left the bungalow she had shared with my sister to Demi Ella.

I was lucky enough to play the role of Sondra Lane -- thereby securing my stardom with a new generation of fans -- for a decade. I spent my nine months between each season back in Connecticut with Louella and occasionally Demi Ella. When Demi Ella was in her mid-thirties, she married her guitar player. He was a nice boy, though a little younger than my daughter. They got off the road and bought a house not far from us. Before long, I had a couple of beautiful granddaughters to dandle on my knee. When filming resumed each fall, Louella would come with me to Arizona, where we would share the home formerly occupied by my sister and her wife.

If youth is dedicated to meeting new people and discovering new things about the world, old age is about losing each of those people and things gracefully. Louella went first, about ten years ago now. *Brass Monkeys* had finished its run just a few months before. We'd had a lovely Christmas dinner with Demi Ella's family and come home full of food and happiness. The last thing I said to my dearest friend in the world was, "Sleep tight. See you in the morning." I didn't get the chance to tell her once more how much I had appreciated her devotion over the years. She had been a part of my life longer than anyone -- from the time I was a child until I was seventy. When I woke up the next morning, I knew something was wrong before I pushed her door open and confirmed it. The house felt empty in a way that it never had in the many years we had lived there together.

Louella was still in bed and could have been sleeping. She had passed peacefully in the night -- the best death either of us could imagine. I called the police and Demi Ella, unlocked the doors, and sat down next to her body. I didn't cry until my daughter was next to me, and then the tears were more for her than for Louella or me -- I hated the look of despair I saw on my daughter's face.

Demi Ella wanted me to come live with her, but I wasn't ready to give up my independence -- as if I'd ever had any real independence. In my long life, I had never lived alone for more than a few weeks at a time. At least I had the scripts to keep me busy -- Louella's position as script reader was irreversibly vacant.

I took a few roles in the next few years -- roles that reminded me of Betty White, for the most part. Bawdy grandmothers, crusty and sarcastic old women, the occasional female letch. Betty's been dead for decades now, but it seems like these roles were written with her in mind. They're still being written that way now. It's almost a form of reverse-typecasting: all little old women of a certain age are expected to be like Betty White.

I tripped on set a few years ago and broke my arm. After that, Demi Ella insisted I retire. "What if you hurt yourself on location somewhere and I can't get to you in time?"

"In time for what?" I asked, passing her a glass of lemonade. My left arm was still in a sling, but I was managing fine with just my right arm.

She pressed her lips together worriedly in a manner that reminded me of her father, though I didn't dare say that aloud.

"What?"

"Hmm?" I sat down opposite her at the small white-wicker table I kept on the porch in the summer months.

"You said something about my father."

"Did I? How odd." I attempted to channel the doddering fool persona that some old people found so easy to play.

"Mother," she said slowly, "what aren't you telling me?"

I looked at my daughter, so beautiful even in her mid-forties. My sister had been correct -- Demi Ella favored her father's features. Who was I keeping the secret for now? Only myself. Joe had died around the same time I lost Louella -- I saw the notice on the internet. I smiled and reached for her hands; trustingly, she gripped my fingers. "Darling girl...you weren't a laboratory baby at all. You were -- are -- the product of a remarkable passion."

Her eyes widened and I felt her try to pull away from me.

"I promise you," I said, tightening my own grip, "that you have been treasured your whole life -- from the moment I discovered you right up to today."

"How could you not tell me? I have a father?" She pulled harder and her hands slipped from my grasp.

"You did. He was my college sweetheart. A wonderful man named Joe."

Her face contorted through anger, shock, and distress, finally settling on puzzlement. "Why tell me now?"

"I thought...well, there's no one left to keep the secret for. He's gone."

"But if you loved him, why didn't you marry him?"

I thought about that first email from so long ago. "Someone I trusted advised me not to."

"So when I was conceived...?"

"He was married. He had a family."

"I was an accident," she said flatly.

"A happy accident, yes! I didn't know what true, soul-stirring happiness was until the day I found out about you."

She wasn't looking at me, but at her hands in her lap. "Joe who?"

"Joe Stones."

Her eyes snapped up. "The education-tech guy?"

I nodded.

She shook her head in disbelief. "I always thought that the reverse-DNA test was ridiculous."

My spine tingled with terror; I never considered that she would submit to one of those tests. Of course, they had been readily available for years -- decades -- now. But I thought she believed me when I told her she was the product of a sperm-bank father. "Why would you have that done?"

"The obstetrician recommended it when Jake and I decided to have Mia. The test came back with not only the requisite genetic information but also the probable identity of my father."

"Why didn't you tell me?"

She shrugged. "I thought they'd made a mistake...or that maybe he had been a sperm donor. Of course, I knew who he was; everyone knew who he was. But I didn't see any connection to you. I mean, if he knew you had me, he would have--"

I shook my head, stopping her mid-sentence. "He knew I had you, but we thought it would be best if he didn't have any contact with you. He wasn't going to leave his wife and children -- and I didn't want him to. What happened between us was a one-time thing -- a moment of mad nostalgia, so to speak."

She seemed to accept that explanation, but our relationship has never been the same. I regret telling her, even though she had a right to know. I believe it made her think much less of me.

The date is approaching -- New Year's Eve is just around the corner now. First, Christmas, then Boxing Day and the anniversary of Louella's death, then...December thirty-first, 2069. I've had such a good life, despite the bad things that have happened. The last email I received gave me a lifetime of good memories of my father...and who knows what horrible thing it attempted to protect me from? Maybe my father was simply destined to murder my mother, and no amount of time away would have prevented it.

With so little to gain and so much to lose, do I really want to change my life? Yes, I have decided, I do. I don't want to lose my sister for decades the way I did this time. If I make that small change, my life will be perfect.

Fifth

Deflated despite the adrenaline coursing through my veins, I collapsed into the sofa, which was surprisingly soft for hotel furniture. Demi and I had never fought like that -- not even as children. We'd always known that she was Mom's favorite and I was Dad's -- it was obvious, even logical. After all, I was definitely Dad's daughter. And Demi was the result of Mom's relationship with the basketball player -- the man she loved more than all of us combined, even though she hadn't been able to live with his rage. Demi had to know that I would defend Dad to the ends of the earth, no matter what he had done to Mom.

I heard my phone vibrate against the glass-topped end table next to me. Picking it up, I immediately saw another of the emails from the future that had guided my life to this point. The last one had been only a few months before -- the one that had prompted me to get my father out of the country for a while. With a certain amount of trepidation, I opened it. *Apologize to Demi now -- don't let this wound fester. If you do, you will lose your whole family.*

Apologizing wouldn't be enough. I would have to agree to not defend my father, and I didn't think I could do that. But the future me must have known something I didn't. I called Louella and told her to hold off on hiring an attorney.

"What's wrong?" she asked.

"Demi was just here. She's furious."

"Of course, she is," Louella soothed. "Your mother just died. But she'll get over it...she's not just a daughter, she's a sister, too."

"Maybe so, but she was much closer to Mom. I don't think she's going to forgive me for defending Dad."

"She will," Louella insisted. "When the grief passes and she calms down--"

"I think I need to see Dad again," I cut in. "Will you

arrange that?"

"Right away," she answered. "I'll call a car for you."

Disconnecting the call, I looked again at the message, wondering if I should call Demi right away or wait until I had seen my father again. I decided on the latter and went to apply fresh makeup.

Dad seemed to have shrunk in just the few hours since I had last seen him. He slouched on the other side of the same table, the orange jumper looking baggy and ill-fitted to his frame. The manic expression was gone and I saw deep sorrow in his gaze as I entered the room.

"You should stay away, darling girl," he said as I sat down across from him. "This will be bad for your career."

"You're my father," I said, taking his hand. "I care more about you than about acting."

He smiled sadly. "You've worked so hard...don't let this be your ruin."

I squeezed his hand in my own. "Dad...what happened?"

"I killed her. I killed your mother." Tears spilled down his cheeks. "And I am so sorry. If I could undo it, I would. I just...I don't know what happened."

"It sounds like you went crazy."

He nodded. "But I'm still guilty. Even if I was...crazy, as you say, I still sta..." His eyebrows bunched together as his mouth drew down.

"But you didn't mean to, Dad! You were angry--"

"Don't offer excuses for me, Diana. Her first husband hit her so hard he shattered one side of her face -- because he was angry. Anger is never an excuse for violence. What I did was wrong, and I need to be punished for it."

"You just need treatment, Dad. Doctors who can help you--"

"That's not what I want. I'm pleading guilty. I want to go to prison...where I belong."

"But Dad!"

He pulled his hands free of mine. "I want you to go tell your sister I love her and that I'm very sorry for what I did. And then both of you need to get on with your lives." He threw one leg over the bench he was sitting on and motioned toward the guard, who prepared to unlock the door. "I love you more than anything, my precious girl. I'm so sorry for what I did to you. Please don't come back. Just remember the time we had in Europe." He smiled. "I know I'll never forget it."

As he walked away, I said, "I love you too, Dad."

I had the car drive me directly to my sister's house from the jail. Ranice answered the door of their small central-Phoenix bungalow. She stepped outside and pulled the door shut behind her. "Now isn't a great time, Diana," she said. In the sunlight, her chocolate skin gleamed and her eyes seemed lit from within. My sister had excellent taste in women -- not only was she gorgeous, she was devoted to and protective of Demi.

"I'm here to apologize."

"I don't think she's ready to kiss and make up just yet. I've never seen her so upset."

"I've been to see Dad, and he wants me to convey a message to her. Do you think I could just see her for a moment?"

"I don't think it's a good idea, honey. I don't want another homicide in the family," she said with a humorless laugh.

"Will you tell her, then?"

She pursed her lips and let her gaze slip away from mine for a few seconds. "Okay," she said finally. "What do

I need to tell her?"

"Dad is very sorry about what he did. He's pleading guilty and going to jail in penance. He knows he can't fix it, but he wants to be sure that she and I are okay. He doesn't want us to lose each other."

"You're not hiring an attorney for him?"

I shook my head. "That's not what he wants."

She gave me a warm hug and kissed my cheek. "Go to your hotel. I'll talk to Demi when she's calmer and I'm sure we'll see you soon."

I let the car take me back to the hotel, where I invited Louella to come to my room for dinner. When she arrived, we ordered room service -- a couple of cheeseburgers with fries. Not the best for us, but definitely comfort food after a stressful few days. We each took one end of the sofa and looked at each other.

"So?" she prompted. "How's your dad?"

"He's pleading guilty. He doesn't want a lawyer."

"He can't be in his right mind, Diana. You need to protect him from himself." She folded her arms across her chest.

"He was perfectly lucid and his reasoning was sound. He knows he killed Mom and he understands why Demi isn't coming to see him. He wants me to reconcile with Demi and let him take his punishment."

"I can't believe you'd let him talk you into that! He's your father, Diana. You have to do something to help him. You know he isn't a violent man."

"He stabbed my mother a dozen times," I said quietly.

"In a moment of insanity, yes. But--"

"I have another reason." I pulled my phone out of my pocket and opened the email I had received earlier in the day. "Read this," I said, passing her the phone.

As her eyes scanned the short message, she frowned. "What is this, some kind of joke?"

"I don't think so. I got it right after Demi and Ranice left today -- after we fought."

"Someone in the press trying to get a rise out of you?"

"That's my personal email account, Louella. Only you, Paul, Demi, and Dad have that address."

"Why isn't there a sender? And what's with the date? Twelve-thirty-one-sixty-nine? That makes no sense."

"There's never a sender and the date is always December 31, 2069."

"How do you know it's 2069 and not 1969?"

"Because Joe told me."

She narrowed her eyes. "Joe? Your college boyfriend?"

"Yes."

"How many of these have you gotten?"

"This is the fourth one."

"All of them since Joe first told you about them?"

"Yes."

She balled her hands into fists. "You mean he's been controlling you through these 'emails' for a decade? That's just sick! What kind of perverted bastard--?"

"It's not him."

"It has to be! Because what you're saying...Diana, it doesn't make any sense."

"The emails are from the future. More specifically, they're from me in the future."

"Why would you think that? You're a smart woman -- you know that the simplest explanation is almost always the correct one."

"It's not him. The first email told me to leave him...right after he asked me to move to California."

"Maybe he got cold feet and that was his way of getting rid of you."

I reached over and retrieved the phone from her. "There's no way it could be him, all right? Whoever sent those notes...they knew things that no one else could know."

"Like what?"

"The role in *The Prophet's Wives*. Whoever wrote the second note knew I was about to be offered the part of Zoe."

She bit her lip and thought silently for a moment. "And the third one?"

"Told me to take Dad on vacation."

She snorted. "And that worked out so well."

"As you just pointed out, Louella, I'm a smart woman. If I'm sending the emails to myself, maybe taking Dad on vacation averted something even worse than what happened."

"Worse than your father killing your mother?" she asked, one eyebrow raised in doubt. "I can't imagine anything that would top that."

"And maybe I didn't want to imagine anything worse than whatever happened to prompt the email that sent Dad and me to Europe."

She crossed her arms over her chest. When room service knocked on the door, I answered it and retrieved our dinners. When the server had retreated, I sat down at the small table and said, "Come eat."

She unfolded herself from the couch slowly, apparently still thinking about the emails. Sitting down across from me, she said, "Okay. Let's accept -- for the moment -- that the emails are from you. Why do you think you would tell yourself not to hire a lawyer for your father?"

"I didn't tell myself that," I pointed out, slathering ketchup on my burger. "I told myself to apologize to my sister."

"But in doing that, you acknowledge that you must let your father go to prison."

"True. Which is why I went to see Dad."

"But he has clearly lost his mind!"

I shook my head. "I think he's sane. And I have to let him do what is right."

97

Louella stared at her plate without taking a bite of the burger.

"Eat," I cajoled. "It's getting cold."

"It's already too cold in here." She looked at me with disapproval. "If you allow this to happen, you aren't the person I thought you were."

"Louella! What else can I do?" In all my years as Louella's protege and friend, I had never seen such anger in her expression. A sound of intense frustration seemed to rumble from the depths of her soul and out into the room. "You're in love with my father," I whispered, knowing it was true as soon as the words hit the air.

Tears rolled down her face. "He deserved...so much... better than your...mother," she sobbed. "I would have...given him...happiness."

"You stayed close to me because of him."

She didn't say anything else. Instead, she nodded as she sobbed into her hands.

I reached out to hug her, but she pulled away from me and left the room.

The media stayed on my side, running report after report portraying me as the heartbroken daughter orphaned in tragic circumstances. Pictures of Demi and I huddled together at our mother's graveside were featured prominently on dozens of news websites. Memes floated around the internet with words of condolence printed beneath our mournful faces.

Louella silently decamped a few days later. She left me a letter expressing her sorrow as well as her embarrassment. I will never understand how she could just leave after so many years at my side. I felt as if half my body had been amputated.

After a few weeks had passed, I received a call

from my agent Paul. "How you doin', kiddo?"

"I've been better."

"Yeah, I'm sure you have. Look, I wouldn't bother you, but you've got a few offers to look at."

"Paul, my mother's dead and my father just went to prison for the next twenty years. I'm not really interested in working right now."

"I know, I know...but, sweetheart, these are some of the best offers you've ever gotten! Listen, I'll just pop them in the mail to Louella, and she can brief you."

"Louella's not here."

"When will she be back? One of these--"

"She's not coming back."

Silence buzzed across two-thousand miles. "What happened to her?"

"She quit, Paul. She's not my assistant anymore."

"That doesn't make any sense, Diana," he said sternly. "No one is more devoted to you than Louella...except me, of course."

"It turns out she had ulterior motives for sticking close to me."

"Well," he said briskly, "you need to replace her right away. Have you started interviewing?"

"I don't think I'd be comfortable with just anybody living with me and helping me make career decisions."

"Of course not. But, at the very least, you need a fast reader who can give you synopses of the scripts and offers you receive."

I glanced around my empty California home, wondering if I even wanted to be here anymore. "Are any of the offers in New York?"

"Of course not! You're a movie star!"

"What if I just want to do a little Broadway play or something?"

"Absolutely not. Baby doll, you are a hot commodity right now in California. You don't backtrack to the theater when you have a career in Hollywood!"

He was right, of course. I didn't need him or Louella to tell me that. "My dad thought he was raising a singer," I said quietly.

"A singer? You want to sing? Is that what you're telling me? When you have multi-million-dollar acting roles thrown at your feet, you want to become Bette Midler all of a sudden?"

"Actually, I'd rather be Barbra Streisand," I said with a laugh.

"I'll tell you what, sweetheart...if you want a record deal, I'll get you a record deal. But you have to do some acting too, all right?"

"Okay."

"Call your sister. Get her and Ranita--"

"Ranice," I corrected him.

"Whatever. Get the dykes to come and help you out."

"Paul! Jesus!"

He chuckled. "I thought political correctness was out of fashion."

"You are a pig, you know that?"

"Of course, baby doll. All good agents are. Take care of yourself. I'll call you in a few days."

I hung up the phone and stared out the window at the blue sky reflected in my swimming pool. He was right -- I needed someone, if only for the company. Ranice had just announced that this would be her last season as a professional basketball player, and I knew Demi didn't really enjoy the commentator role she'd been playing for the league in the last few years. I couldn't make my sister and her wife move to California, but I could certainly extend an invitation for them to visit me for a while.

"That sounded good, Di, but you were a little pitchy

on that last note. Can you give it to me stronger?" My producer -- the first man to give me palpitations in a decade -- smiled at me through the sound-booth window, his green eyes twinkling like emeralds.

"Sure, Ferris," I said.

"We'll take it from the last line, okay?"

"Okay." The music swelled in my headphones again -- a big-band sound that had slipped in and out of favor over the past hundred years or so. We were trying to bring it back. Ferris Bodeen, the dark-haired musical prodigy who made my heart go pitty-pat, was nearly seven years younger than me and had already earned a platinum reputation in the music industry. He had worked with some of the most famous names in the industry -- from P!nk (on a successful comeback album) to Dirty Linen (the latest Indian-punk band out of Bangalore). I belted out the last line of the song and felt myself blush when Ferris's head rocked with satisfaction.

This album, a compilation of classics and standards, would be my second. My first -- a collection of show tunes from hit musicals -- had been a surprise hit. According to Paul, the success of that album proved that I was golden. My fans would buy anything with my name on it. As he put it, "You're Barbra fucking Streisand, baby doll!"

Ferris Bodeen had approached Paul about the possibility of working with me -- not the other way around. The first time I met him, I think we were both on the verge of passing out. He was starstruck; I saw stars, too, but they had more to do with his angular features and fading Irish accent. The first time he placed his hand against my abdomen -- a completely innocent gesture on his part -- I felt a shock of electricity run through me, warming and enlivening parts of my body that had nothing to do with singing. I don't know how I kept from throwing myself into his arms, but somehow, I resisted.

When the recording session was over, Ferris walked

into the acoustically balanced room and gave me a warm hug. "That was marvelous, Di -- incredible."

"Thank you, Ferris," I said, unable to move under his touch.

He pulled away and looked at me with a half smile. "Are you okay?"

"I'm fine," I said, pushing the headphones off of my ears and down around my neck. I had an urge to smooth my hair, but resisted it. Why should he care if my hair was a mess? "So, what's next?"

"That's it for you. I'll mix the sound and we'll get it out there. I expect it will go live by the end of the month -- just in time for Christmas."

"Great," I said, attempting to curve my lips into a passable excuse for a smile. "That's good news."

"Then why do you look like I just killed your puppy?"

"Do I? How horrible!" I clapped my hands over my face and shook my head to clear it. "I'm so sorry," I said, dropping my hands into his in what I hoped was a friendly manner. "I can't believe we're already done working together! I'm going to miss hanging out with you."

"That doesn't have to end," he half-mumbled.

"It doesn't?"

He cleared his throat. "No, not at all. The thing is, Di--" He looked toward the booth and motioned to his sound guy to cut the tape. The overly hairy man just folded his arms and leaned away from the board, a smarmy smirk playing across his face. "Limp dick," he muttered. "The thing is...I fancy you a bit. I was rather hoping you and I might...spend some more time together... as non-collaborators."

I smiled -- a genuine cheek-pinching, toothy grin -- and said yes.

#

We went on our first date that night and Ferris received a crash course in being recognized. His name may have been well-known among artists, but the general public had no idea who he was...except that he was the man on my arm. The internet exploded the next day with picture after picture of Ferris and me eating dinner, strolling on the beach, and sharing our first kiss.

He was at my gate the next morning. I buzzed him through immediately, anxious for him to avoid the two photographers who practically camped across the road from my estate.

"Have you seen the news?" he asked, panic in his eyes.

"Yes. Come in."

He strode through the door and raked his longish hair back with his bony hand. I could read the concern in the lines around his eyes. "Is it always like this? With the cameras and everything?"

I nodded. "Too much for you?"

"It'll definitely make me think twice before leaving the house with my hair mussed," he answered, bemused. "How do you stand it?"

"Do you know how to boil a frog?"

"Why? Are you craving frog's legs?"

I took his hand and led him to the sofa, pulling him down behind me. "Being a Hollywood star is a lot like being a frog."

"I've never heard that comparison before. But...go on. I love to listen to you talk."

His words puzzled me. "Wait a second...you're the one with the lilting accent. I'm just...you know...American."

"Don't you know that an American accent is the most alluring accent of all? Why do you think I came to your fair country?"

I laughed. "Now you're just being silly. Millions of women sound just like me."

"Maybe so," he acknowledged. "Though I've noticed a few different accents in this country. Nevertheless, your voice -- speaking or singing -- is the most beautiful one I've ever heard. Now, go on with your frog story."

I leaned toward him and touched my lips to his, feeling his warm, sweet lips give a fraction of an inch under mine before he kissed me back, placing one of his hands against my back and pushing a moan out of me.

He moved his mouth to my ear and whispered, "You even moan sexier." I felt his tongue trace my earlobe and I shivered with delight.

A door opened somewhere in the distance, but I couldn't be bothered to warn whomever was about to stumble across us. I only hoped that she would retreat as soon as she glimpsed us on the couch. He pulled me into his lap; I could feel his desire against my thigh. Despite all my resolutions to take things slowly, I wanted to lead him to my bed.

"Ahem."

Ferris broke off our kiss and practically threw me to one side like a startled teenager. His wide-eyed gaze told me he knew exactly who was leaning against the archway less than ten feet away.

My sister, her fuzzy purple robe tied tightly around her middle, was looking at me as if I were a naughty child. "You lettin' strangers in for nookie these days, Diana?"

Before I could regain my composure, Ferris was on his feet and headed toward Demi. "Demi Mogens...what a pleasure," he said, his hand extended toward her.

She glanced down at it, but didn't unfold her arms. "Just because you recognize me don't make us friends, son."

I knew this was my sister's version of tough. I tried to stand up and come to his rescue, but one glare from my older sister kept me glued to the couch and watching the slow-motion catastrophe, hoping disaster would be averted.

"Forgive me," he said smoothly, bowing slightly. "Ferris Bodeen, Ms. Mogens. I am producing your sister's album."

"Irish, huh? You don't look particularly Celtic to me."

"Me mum was Spanish," he said. I thought I detected a thickening of his brogue and hid my smile behind my hand.

"I suppose that makes you a black Irish."

"Something like that."

She gave him a slow once-over and looked at me. "Be careful of this one, Diana. He's smooth as cream. And no more making out on the couch at eight o'clock in the morning -- that's a shock to the system that I can't handle anymore." She shrugged past him and headed for the kitchen.

Ferris turned and looked at me, his eyes twinkling.

"You follow American women's basketball?" I whispered when I thought Demi was out of earshot.

"Of course he doesn't, you dummy!" she yelled. "But everyone knows how to use the internet, girl!"

An impish grin appeared as he nodded once. "I couldn't sleep, so I did a little online digging."

"Which is how you saw all the photos of us together so early."

"Yes." He sat down on the chair to one side of the sectional sofa where I remained. "So, tell me how to boil a frog."

"You put it in cold water, and then heat it up slowly."

Having been sufficiently cooled by Demi's sudden appearance, Ferris and I both decided that falling into bed was ill-advised. With regret, I told him to go home and think about how important his anonymity was to him. I doubted I'd hear from him before the album was ready for distribution.

Less than a week later, he was on my doorstep again

-- this time with a bouquet of fall-tinted flowers and my album on a microchip. "May I come in?" he asked, his face half-obscured by the blooms.

"If you'd like." I stood aside and welcomed him inside.

"Is your sister at home?"

"No. She and her wife are at Lamaze class."

"Ranice Jackson, right?"

"You've done some more homework, I see." I took the bouquet and walked toward the kitchen, leaving him to follow or stay behind as he chose.

"I have," he answered. I heard him behind me, though his pace was considerably slower than my own. "So, we're alone?"

"Just the two of us. Why?"

"No reason," he answered casually from the dining area.

I heard music fill the house and realized that he had located my sound system. I didn't immediately recognize it -- then my voice, singing an Ella Fitzgerald swing standard, reached my ears. I dropped the bouquet on the counter and walked back to where he stood, my eyes wide. "Wow."

"Great, isn't it? The song really suits you."

"Is this the final mix?"

"Of course." He looked offended. "Why would I bring you an unfinished version?"

"It's just...I...thought it would take longer," I stammered.

"Something so near perfection as your voice requires little in the way of production." He stepped toward me.

"I thought you would give me up when you realized how little of my life is truly my own."

"I considered it. After all, I've been famous in the music business for a few years now, but never had the amount of coverage I got in one night with you. I'm so unknown to the world at large that it took the reporters three days to put a name to my face. Three days! I might as well be anyone!"

"Not anymore," I said ruefully.

"No," he agreed, "not anymore. The boys at your gate greeted me by name and asked what we had planned for tonight."

"What do we have planned?"

He stepped closer and took me in his arms, clasping one of my hands in his. He began to sway to the music, pulling me along with him until I smiled and swayed in rhythm with him. "I thought we'd start with a dance," he said softly against my ear as he whirled me around the dining table.

"If you stop seeing me, you will get your privacy back."

"Of all the things I value, I think privacy might be the most overrated." His cheek was against my head, and one hand was against the small of my back. "I would rather live my life in front of cameras with you next to me than be without you."

I pulled back and met his eyes. The sincerity I found there made me well up with tears. Every other relationship I'd been in since college had been about gaining more fame -- for me, for whomever I was with.

"Don't cry, Di," he said, pressing his lips to my forehead. "I never want to see you cry."

Bracing myself against him, I raised onto my tiptoes and kissed him, feeling again the soft give of his lips as they opened under mine. He released my hand from our dance position and wrapped his other arm around me, squeezing me to him as our lips remained locked together. In all my years as a romantic lead in movies, I had never felt the flow of passionate electricity that I felt standing next to my dining room table that night. I knew, without a doubt, that Ferris Bodeen would be with me for the rest of my life if I had anything to do with planning my future.

And, of course, if there was one thing I had the ultimate, infinite control of, it was my future.

After her initial reaction, Demi gradually warmed to Ferris. It didn't hurt that he took every chance to ingratiate himself with her. He even watched some highlights from her days in the WNBA and spent a few hours talking to her about her glory days.

Ranice liked him immediately. Implanted with Demi's fertilized egg, she was round and glowing with her pregnancy that Christmas. Despite Demi's insistence that she should take it easy, Ranice still insisted on serving him a real Southern-style holiday meal, complete with pecan pie -- something Ferris had never eaten before. He was enjoying his first bite when Paul called to wish me Merry Christmas.

"Baby doll! How did Santa treat you this year?"

"I can't complain, Paul," I answered, stepping away from the table. "What about you? Did you get anything good?"

"Mrs. Foster bought me a copy of your new album. Bodeen is a magician, sweetheart! You sound like a damned angel on those cuts. I hope you don't mind working with him again."

I smiled back at the table, where I could see Ferris pushing away two-thirds of the pie and rubbing his stomach as if he were about to explode. "I think I could do that."

"Good to hear. I can feel it, kid -- this one's going to go platinum by the end of January."

"Platinum?" I repeated. Ferris, Demi, and Ranice all stopped talking and looked at me.

"Absolutely," Paul said. "Listen, in the meantime, I sent a script to your house last week. Have you read it yet?"

"What was it called?"

"*An Unassigned Life.* It's a ghost story with a comedic bent. There's a good score, too."

"It's a musical? Let me ask Ranice." I covered the receiver with my hand and asked, "Have you read *An Unassigned Life*?"

"I'm almost done with it. I was planning to talk to you about it after the holidays were over."

"Paul thinks it's a winner."

"Really? I was kind of on the fence about it. The opening sequence is a suicide -- grim stuff. But it has a few good names attached to it."

I took my hand off the receiver. "Paul? Ranice isn't sure about it. She says it's grim."

"Only at the beginning," he answered. "Listen, sweetheart, it has a great message -- very uplifting in the end. No pressure, though. Give it a read and let me know what you think. The producers want an answer before the new year."

"Sure, no pressure," I said, laughing. "Have a good holiday, Paul."

"You too, baby doll." He disconnected.

When I sat back down at the table, Ranice was detailing the plot of the script as far as she knew it. "...and then the ghost starts to actively pursue the wife of the guy he's controlling. It's really dark...and I don't even know which part the producer wants Diana to play."

"The female lead, probably," I said. "I don't think Paul would be pushing me to play a supporting role. He says the music is great."

Ranice shrugged. "I don't know what it sounds like. I haven't listened to it. Was it on Broadway first?"

"I've never heard of it. Where's the script?"

"On my bedside table."

I excused myself again and went to the bedroom to retrieve it. Flipping it open, I found the music microchip in a small envelope taped to the inside cover. Extracting it, I returned to the dining room and pushed the chip into the music system. Immediately, an ethereal overture featuring harps and flutes filled the room.

"That's a good start," Ferris commented.

I sat down next to him and took his hand under the table. Together, the four of us listened in near-silence to the entire score. When the last song -- a piece about everyone finding inspiration and a home on Willow Street -- finished, we seemed to exhale as a group.

"You need to do this movie," Ferris said with certainty.

"Yes," agreed Demi. "This movie is for you."

"Really?"

Demi, the only one who really knew how deeply I identified with Barbra Streisand, said, "This is your *Funny Girl* moment."

Ferris, who was less familiar with 20th-century movie musicals, frowned. "I don't think I understand what that means."

"You don't need to," Ranice answered for us. "It's a sister thing, apparently."

An Unassigned Life opened with box-office numbers that hadn't been seen in decades. My career flourished, both in Hollywood and in the music business. Not only that, but Ferris's new-found visibility brought his career to a higher level than he ever imagined.

After a few years of living together, we decided to marry. Together with Demi, Ranice, and their little girl -- whom they named Charity after our mother -- we flew to

Hawaii, ostensibly for a vacation. Once there, we had a spur-of-the-moment ceremony on Hulopoe Beach, the sand squishing up between our toes and my niece running away from the surf as it rolled in and out. Demi, who had become ordained with an "internet church," performed the ceremony before the press even knew what was happening. They thought we were touring the pineapple fields.

Our life together was a fairy tale -- a dream from which I never wanted to awaken. He looked at me as if I were the sun and the moon and all the stars in the sky. I must have looked at him the same way. We decided to wait before having children. I say "we"...but what choice did I give him, really? I stayed on birth control until I was thirty-seven, not wanting to interrupt the most productive part of my career with childbearing.

When I became pregnant at thirty-nine, we were overjoyed. After years of sharing our home, Demi and Ranice found a home of their own. Ranice, who would remain my assistant for the next several decades, explained that we would need more space when the baby came, and I believed her. In truth, Ferris and I both breathed a sigh of relief when they left. We picked out names and began redecorating Charity's old bedroom as a nursery.

I bowed out of two roles I had previously accepted because my pregnant belly would be impossible to hide when it came time to film my parts. Instead, Ferris and I began planning a new album to record in the coming months -- something I would be able to do without risking myself or the baby.

But I miscarried at seventeen weeks, waking up in a puddle of blood that nearly scared Ferris to death. We cried and held each other at the hospital, taking comfort in each other. We vowed to try again, and we did. But I lost baby after baby -- five in all.

The last one was the hardest. She was a girl and I

was six months along. Ferris was working when I felt the first contraction. I called him right away.

"Call an ambulance. I'll meet you at the hospital."

"I can't do that, Ferris," I said as reasonably as I could. "You know that will put the paparazzi on the scent."

"So what? You and our daughter are more important than a little publicity."

"I don't want our personal business splashed across the internet."

He breathed out loudly. "It will take me forty-five minutes to get home."

"I'll be okay until you can get here."

"I'm leaving now."

We disconnected the call and I sat down on the bright-blue sectional to wait for him to show up.

I don't remember him arriving or the panicked drive to the hospital. I don't remember our daughter's birth or the doctor telling us that she had only hours to live.

She had black hair and blue eyes and was so small that the blanket seemed huge around her. We named her Lola and I held her as she died.

Ferris has never said that he blames me for our lack of children. He never mentions the five years of birth control that ate up my childbearing years. Whenever the news and entertainment sites put together a list of the solidest or longest marriages in Hollywood, we're always in the top ten. The older we get, the closer we get to number one. I can't imagine my life without Ferris; he claims to feel the same way.

It must be hard for him, though. I wonder sometimes if he wishes I would just die so that he could find a fertile young woman to give him a son or a daughter. Old male celebrities have been doing that for years: waiting until their first wives die to marry someone younger. Oh, I know...they're not marrying the young hotties for their ability to procreate; yet somehow, they always seem to.

Of course, I'm a ridiculously healthy old woman -- eighty-one and not on a single pill. That's what years of keeping in movie-star shape will do for you. At this rate, I may outlive Ferris.

I've lived an incredibly happy life, despite my mother's murder and my father's incarceration and death. Ferris and I have been together nearly fifty years. My career has been remarkable and varied, and people still trip over themselves to get my autograph. Generations of music and movie lovers think of me as a personal friend -- the one who sings at their wedding, sits with them when they are heartbroken, and keeps them company through their days.

But as the day approaches, I wonder what exactly is the right amount of happiness? At what point should I accept my life as it is and be grateful for it? Surely, everything that happened prior to that last email I received is as good as I could make it. I wouldn't change a thing about my life with Ferris -- except if I could give him children. That would be perfection, wouldn't it?

Sixth

I cuddled up next to Ferris as the ocean breeze fluttered the sheer curtains hanging in front of our open veranda doors. My wedding dress -- a gauzy white spaghetti-strap number -- lay crumpled on the chair where it had landed during the passionate undressing of the night before.

I studied the contrast between my skin and his -- my ivory, almost-translucent tone made his flesh look tanned and robust in comparison. Sighing, I dropped my head into the cradle of his shoulder.

"Happy?" he asked, his voice sounding rusty and dull from sleep.

"Very. You?"

"Ridiculously."

I propped myself up on one elbow and stared down at his calm expression. "We didn't have to get married, you know."

"Yes we did. I couldn't have you besmirching my honor anymore. Half the world thinks I'm a wanton slut."

I laughed and slapped his smooth chest playfully. "No one ever accuses the man of being a slut."

"Not true!" he protested. "In Ireland, easy men are just as disdained as easy women."

"Really?"

His eyes sparkled as he pulled me toward him for a kiss. I heard my phone vibrate against the nightstand as our lips locked together. When I came up for breath, I said, "Hold that thought. I need to check my phone."

"It can't be that important. Leave it."

"You never know. What if it's Demi or Ranice?"

"Then they should know better than to interrupt a honeymooning couple." He tried to pull me back down to him, but I slid away, ducking under his arm.

"Just a sec." Checking my messages, I saw a new

email from 2069. "I'm going to the bathroom to freshen up," I said, palming the phone.

"You're perfect just the way you are."

"Give me a break, baby! I need to pee!" I giggled as I closed the door behind me. Sitting down, I opened the message.

Don't wait to start a family.

Ferris and I hadn't really talked about kids yet, but we both knew that my career was hot right now. The idea of giving that up made my stomach flip-flop uncomfortably. If I walked away from acting now, wouldn't that mean all my hard work was for nothing?

I turned on the water in the sink to buy myself another minute. Children. I guess I always thought there would be time to think about them later -- after the first crow's feet appeared and nullified my appeal as a romantic lead. Every female star knew that the best decade to spend at home was the one after the first wrinkles appeared. Women who weren't ready to stop working invested in minor touch-up surgeries: a lid tuck here, a lip plumping there. If they didn't go overboard, they could extend their ingenue shelf life by five to ten years. My mom's skin had still been wrinkle-free at the time of her death. With my genes, I anticipated reaching forty or better before my middle-age break.

I ran my toothbrush over my teeth and returned to the bed to find Ferris asleep again. I crawled in on the opposite side and stared at him while he slept. He was seven years younger than me. Maybe the idea of children hadn't even occurred to him yet. Resolving to let the matter rest until he brought it up, I allowed my eyelids to close.

Ferris mentioned children for the first time over dinner on our first anniversary. He had grilled steaks and baked potatoes and lit candles for our table. He had also sent Demi, Ranice, and our niece Charity to Disneyland for the weekend; the house was silent, dark, and aromatic when I arrived home from the set that evening.

"Welcome home, Mrs. Bodeen," he said with a playful smile. No one ever called me that but him.

"Why, thank you, Mr. Bodeen. What's the occasion?"

"It's our anniversary. And you wonder why I feel like I'm the woman in this relationship."

"Oh, my God. Ferris, I'm so sorry...it totally slipped my mind."

He chuckled as he hugged and kissed me. "I'm not surprised. I would have been more shocked if you had remembered. Come on," he urged, pulling me toward the table, "eat your steak before it gets cold. I understand red meat is good for women -- lots of iron."

I allowed him to seat me and drop a napkin across my lap. I was tired -- emotionally drained. We had filmed two major dramatic scenes that day and all I really wanted to do was crawl into bed and veg out watching bad television. When I cut off my first bite of steak, though, I was glad he had cooked. I leaned back in my chair and savored the taste as my long day slipped away.

"I've been thinking..." he started, looking at me with soft eyes.

I sipped the red wine he had so thoughtfully poured for me. "Mm. What's that?"

"I've been thinking. I know we never really talked about it, but do you want children?"

"Shouldn't this have come up before we were married?"

"Ideally, yes. What can I say? I missed a plot point."

I reached across the table. "Yes, of course I do."

"When?"

"I don't know exactly. When my career slows down, I suppose."

"When do you think that will be?"

"Are you trying to ask me something specific?"

"I suppose I am."

"Let's rip the band aid off, then."

"I think we should start a family."

"But--"

"I'm sorry," he said hastily. "I know I'm being ridiculous here. I just...I want a child or two or three. We have loads of money between us."

"But I've spent my whole life working towards this."

"It's just fame, Di. It's fleeting. It doesn't mean what you think it means."

"What do I think it means?"

He broke eye contact with me and sighed. "I love you. Aren't I enough?"

My phone chimed letting me know I had messages waiting. The sound jogged my memory, taking me back to that first morning of our marriage and the message I received. I squeezed his hand and smiled. "You're right. You are more than enough for me. Let's start our family."

The hurt I'd seen in his eyes melted away as he picked up his glass. "Let's drink to that."

I didn't become pregnant immediately. When I worried about how long it was taking for me to conceive, my doctor soothed my nerves by explaining that all my years of birth control would take a while to leave my system.

In the meantime, I stuck to my schedule. I had roles lined up a year out and Ferris was compiling a collection of songs for my next album. As we made plans for the future of our family, our marriage grew stronger. I stopped fearing that we were just another temporary Hollywood couple and started to believe that we were meant to be together.

Ranice was the first to suggest that she, Demi, and Charity should move out.

"You don't have to do that." I was scooping peas onto my plate one evening that summer. Charity, only four, was busily stabbing at the round green vegetables with her fork, creating an uneven beat of clanks against her plate.

"I think we should. You and Ferris don't get any time alone together, really. Your sister and I have been present for your entire relationship. Don't get us wrong -- we love you both. And we know that you love us and are attached to Charity. But you're on the verge of starting your own family now. You should spend some time alone before you do that."

"Don't be ridiculous," Ferris protested. "You're like my own sisters--"

"Exactly." Demi set her knife and fork down and squared her shoulders. "You can't have a real marriage when you're still living with family."

"But you two--"

"Doesn't count. We were together for years before we moved in with Diana."

I tried again. "This house is plenty big enough for all of us."

"No, it's not," Ranice answered. "Honey, you're going to need a nursery and probably a room for the nanny too. You need our bedrooms."

"We're not having a nanny," Ferris said.

"You say that now, but you're both busy. You have careers to attend to. You'll need someone to look after the child when you're both at work or too exhausted to think straight."

"Where will you go?" I asked.

"We found a house in the neighborhood. Don't worry -- we'll be close by."

"This is more than a theory."

"Yes," Demi confessed. "We close on the house next week."

"Why didn't you tell us sooner?"

"You've both been busy working. We just figured we would duck out as quietly as possible. There's no reason our move should cause you any inconvenience."

I knew she meant it in a nice way, but her words still felt like a slap in the face. "You know I love you -- all of you -- more than just about anything in the world! How could you think that I would see you as an inconvenience?"

My sister, gruff under the best circumstances, practically growled in frustration. "Geez, Diana, not everything is about you. We can't live together forever. Ranice and I need our own space just as much as you and Ferris do."

"I'm sorry, you're right. I just didn't realize that things were tense around here."

"It's not that," Ranice hurried to say. "I miss having a place that is really mine, that's all. With Charity getting bigger, I'd just like to be somewhere that feels more like my own home."

"Of course," Ferris piped up. "We understand."

The rest of the meal was eaten in uncomfortable silence.

The first time I came home after my sister's family moved out, the house felt colder -- not just in a metaphorical sense, either. Checking the thermostat, I was surprised to see that the temperature was set at seventy degrees. Of course, I had nothing to compare this temperature to -- the house had always felt comfortable enough to me.

"Ferris?" I called. "Are you home?"

He stumbled out of our bedroom, stretching his arms and then rubbing his hands in his hair, giving himself the boyishly charming look that first drew me in. "Hello, sweetheart," he said, smiling widely.

"Is it cold in here?"

"No. Feels good to me."

"Okay...is it colder than usual in here?"

His eyes twinkled. "Maybe a little." He shrugged.

I went to my closet and found a sweater.

A lot of little things began to change. The next time I got up early and wanted to fix myself a cup of coffee, I nearly tore the kitchen apart looking for the grounds. I finally found the individual cups directly over the coffee machine -- a logical spot, but not where they had been kept for the majority of my time in the house. As I searched for them, I also found the spices, silverware, and canisters had been relocated, as well. When I turned on the television, it was almost always on sports; before, it had been perpetually tuned to a children's channel. Ferris left music playing most of the time; I came home to my voice pouring through the house more often than not. The house was cleaner, too. The bedroom that had been Charity's was repainted a pale green, and Demi's room was a mellow blue. Without Charity to drip popsicles across it, the floor gleamed.

Then, one day, I came through the door and found a fluffy white thing bounding around my feet and whimpering excitedly.

"What's this?"

Ferris, his deep green eyes serene with contentment, answered, "That, my dear woman, is a dog. I presume you've seen one before?"

"Yes. On television and in pet stores. Never standing in my living room. Where did it come from?"

"She," he said pointedly, "came from a breeder. Corkie is a Wheaten Terrier."

My nose twitched. "Corkie?"

"After County Cork. Why?"

"So, is it too much to hope that she's just visiting?"

"She's perfectly wonderful! Why would you want to pretend she was a guest?"

"Don't people -- I mean, regular people -- don't they usually talk about buying pets before they actually buy one?"

"We've talked about it."

I thought over the conversations we had shared in the last few months. "No, we haven't."

"Yeah, we did. When we first got together, I told you I wanted to get a dog someday and you said that sounded like a great idea." He looked down at the puppy and waved his hands like some two-bit magician. "Ta da!"

"Seriously?"

"Trust me, Di, you're going to love her. Watch this." He got down on his knees and called the ball of fluff with legs over to him. "Corkie, sit!"

The puppy bounced her butt against the ground before standing up excitedly again.

"Sit," he said again, drawing the word out.

Fidgeting, she dropped her butt to the floor three or four times in succession.

"Good sit, Corkie!" Ferris exclaimed, whereupon the dog jumped up on two feet and proceeded to slurp a sloppy trail across his cheek.

I laughed.

"You like her, right?"

"She's cute," I conceded. "How big will she be when she's grown?"

"She'll come to your mid-thigh or thereabouts."

"What happens when we have a baby?"

"Most dogs are good with kids. We'll train her to be gentle."

"She's a puppy! Puppies aren't gentle -- they're rambunctious and wild."

"Look, you aren't even pregnant yet. By the time

we actually have a baby, she'll be calmer."

I doubted it, but I still knelt down to pet the ball of fur and energy. She rolled onto her back immediately, offering her belly for a rub. "Okay. We'll give it a try."

My husband grinned from ear to ear. "You're going to love her."

"Corkie, though? Is that--"

"Non-negotiable," he said firmly. "I've always wanted a dog named Corkie."

I lay down right in the foyer and propped myself up on one elbow as I continued to rub her belly. When she noticed me at her level, she rolled back to her paws and belly-crawled toward my nose, her tongue licking the air as she approached.

"I think she likes you," Ferris observed.

"What's not to like?"

"Good point." He dropped to the floor and crawled toward me as well. Soon, the three of us were huddled together in the middle of the floor, a family for the first time.

Even though I remained busy with my career, I never forgot that we were trying to have a baby. If I had, Ferris would have reminded me. He took my temperature every morning; he tracked my cycles; he controlled my diet. When my fertility was at its peak, he made sure we made love -- even if I protested that I was exhausted. His desire for a child was twice as strong as mine, but I told myself that was okay -- when I held our child in my arms, I would be glad he had taken the lead.

One day in my thirty-seventh year, he called me at work -- something he never did.

"Ferris! Is everything all right?"

"Di, have you started your...has Aunt Flo come for

her monthly visit?"

"My God, Ferris...you take my temperature every time I stand still and you can't ask if I've started my period?"

My hairdresser, a tattooed and pierced middle-aged woman, chuckled and rolled her eyes.

"It just seems so personal."

"You're kind of ridiculous, you know that?"

"Yeah, whatever. Have you?"

"No. But it doesn't seem like it's been a full month--"

"It's been six weeks."

When I thought about it, I knew he was right -- I hadn't had a period since production started on my current film nearly five weeks before. "Wow. I hope nothing is wrong."

"Why would you say that?"

"I just...I mean..."

"Seriously, Di, why? We've been trying to get pregnant for years now -- why would you assume something is wrong?"

"I didn't! I just--"

"Never mind," he said irritably. "Send one of your flunkies out for a pregnancy test. Call me when you have the results."

"Don't you want to--"

"I did. I'm not in the mood now." He hung up the phone abruptly.

"Everything okay?" asked my stylist.

"Yeah. Fine. Do you know how many scenes I'm in today?"

"Two, I think -- both of the evening-wear scenes."

"I need to find Mick." I started to push myself out of my seat, but she pressed down hard on my shoulders.

"Not yet, you don't. In case you haven't noticed, this is a pretty intricate hairdo I'm putting on you, and we're still half an hour from finished."

She turned me to face the mirror and I saw what

she was talking about. My hair was piled so high it could have been a condominium for birds. A quarter of my tresses were on my shoulders as she wove in additional extensions. That was the problem with space operas -- the writers always assume that the hairstyles will become more intricate, not less. I relaxed back into the seat and pulled out my phone again. I sent a quick text to Dawn, the assistant the production team had assigned me.

A moment later, the perky blonde girl with her straight eyebrows and aquiline nose was beside me. "What can I do for you, Miss Mogens?"

"I need to speak with Mick."

"He's busy filming a scene right now." She smoothed her short pleated tartan skirt. I was pretty sure the studio head had a secret fetish involving Catholic schoolgirls -- all the female pages wore the skirts, along with matching knee socks.

"This is important. When do you think he'll be done?"

"I don't know exactly. It could be a while."

"Who is in the scene?"

She named the male lead and a couple of the minor stars who I knew thought they deserved more screen time. They had already spent a good portion of our time lobbying for more lines in scenes where they were simply on the outer edge of the overall picture.

"That's at least an hour...maybe two, if Abbott and Costello won't shut up."

Dawn stifled a laugh. "May I do anything else for you?"

I studied her for a moment. "Can you keep a secret or do you supplement your income by sharing with the paparazzi?"

"If I did, would I tell you?" she asked with a skeptical half-smile.

"Right answer. I need a pregnancy test. Could you

run to the drugstore and buy me one?"

She shrugged. "No problem. Any particular brand?"

"I don't know...is one better than another?"

"I doubt it."

"Bring me whatever you would buy for yourself if you needed to be sure."

She put her hand out, apparently waiting for a tip.

"I'll catch you later," I said, though I thought she was a bit of a mercenary.

"So you want me to use the production credit card to pay?" she asked, arching her brows.

"No! God, no. Sorry about that." Selecting my cash account on my phone, I handed her the device. "Use this to pay. The security code is 1231."

"1231. Got it. I'll be back in a few minutes."

"Trusting, aren't you?" my hairdresser said, her fingers still deftly weaving in extensions.

"She's trustworthy."

"How do you know? You've barely talked to her before today."

"Because if she intended to sell me out her answer would have been a quick no."

"How do you know I won't?"

"Janice, you've worked with me on half a dozen films. If you were selling my secrets, I would have known it by now. I say things while sitting under your hands all the time. I talk to my friends, my sister, my agent...everyone. You have been privy to more 'secrets' than I can count on two hands."

She laughed silently. "I suppose you're right. And not just yours, you know. Everyone talks like no one is listening when they're in the chair. The stories I could tell you..."

"But you won't, and that's the point."

She smirked. "I know which side my bread is buttered on. But someday, I'm going to write one hell of a tell-all book!"

Though I was tempted to ask her for a few juicy tidbits -- names withheld, of course -- I managed to bite my tongue and pick up my script. I was relatively certain I knew my lines, but a few more minutes reviewing them was never a bad idea. I hated working with actors who couldn't be bothered to learn their parts, so I always made sure I was prepared. The common excuse was that filming didn't require theater-style preparations -- crowding your brain with so much information could actually inhibit your performance. Besides, what would the cue-card holders do if everyone knew their lines without prompting?

Because of that attitude, I usually found filming to be a tedious experience. I knew and spoke my lines correctly, while my co-star required multiple readings of his or her lines. That inevitably led to what amounted to hours of sitting on the sidelines, waiting for my co-star to finish the scene I completed on the first or, rarely, second take. However, my co-star on this movie was quick-witted and theater-minded like me. When we were the only ones in a given scene, the crew practically cheered us on. Because of that and our natural chemistry, we had been cast opposite one another in five films, including this one.

Dawn reappeared, carrying my pregnancy test in a double-wrapped plastic bag. She handed it and my phone to me. "Anything else I can do for you, Ms. Mogens?"

I smiled at the young woman. "How long have you worked for the studio, Dawn?"

"Just a couple years. I started as an intern during my senior year of college."

"You're still pretty young. Tell me, is the movie business everything you hoped it would be?"

She put a hand on her hip, and suddenly I could see all the attitude she hid under a layer of blonde pertness. "Is anything ever all one expects it to be?"

"You're very cynical."

She didn't respond.

"What is your ultimate goal here in Hollywoodland?"

"I'm a writer."

"Scriptwriter?"

"Someday, I hope."

I looked her over again. Something made me trust her, and I truly needed a full-time assistant. I knew that Ranice didn't enjoy the job anymore, though she continued to show up when I needed someone around. "Would you be interested in being my full-time personal assistant?"

"You want me to be your fetch-and-carry girl? Look, I know an English degree is practically worthless these days, but I'm worth more than a slave. No thanks."

"The job is more than just errands. I get something like twenty scripts a week. I need someone who can read and summarize them, as well as provide their opinion as to the workability of the project."

"Script reader? And what else -- babysitter?"

"My husband works from home, so even if you did babysit occasionally, it wouldn't become your full-time gig. I'm looking for an assistant, not a nanny. Besides, we don't even know if I'm pregnant yet."

She smiled at that. "How much would you be willing to pay?"

"What do they pay you here?"

"Oh, no...I'm not that stupid. You tell me what you think I'm worth, and I'll tell you if that's enough."

Years before, I had paid Louella almost nothing to do the job I was proposing to Dawn. But Louella had been a friend, and she had all but volunteered for the duty. Ranice wouldn't let me pay her at all. At a loss, I added up what I'd made in the last twelve months on films alone. I offered her five percent of the total, annually.

Her jaw dropped.

"Not enough?" I asked.

"Um...yeah, that's plenty. Are you sure...?"

"I'm not going to lie to you, Dawn -- the job is probably a lot tougher than it sounds. You would be my assistant, my script reader, my friend, my dog walker, and, sometimes, my babysitter. You will see me at my worst. You will be privy to a thousand secret details of not only my life but also my family's lives. And I'll probably make you miserable on top of it all. I've been told that when my mood turns sour, I suck all the joy out of the room."

"Who told you that?" Janice asked. She was still working on my hair, though it seemed she was nearly done.

"Ferris, of course."

"Brave man."

"He gets away with more than most."

"I get it," Dawn said. "The job is mostly about keeping you happy. I think I can do that."

"Yes, but are you sure?"

"Of course not, but I'm willing to try. Especially if it means I can wear something other than this perverted studio page outfit."

"Fantastic. Welcome to my team!"

"I'll have to submit my resignation."

"Filming wraps in two weeks, so that shouldn't be a problem. You can officially start as my assistant after that."

"Wait...that figure you quoted -- is that the live-in wage?"

"Ideally, yes."

"I have a lease on an apartment that doesn't expire for a few months. And I don't know if I really want to live with you. That might be a little too...close for comfort."

"Well, then, you have a few months to decide." I turned to Janice. "Are you done yet? I really need to pee on this stick."

"Just a sec...." She picked up her can of spray again

and plastered the last bit of hair to the huge pile atop my head. "Done. Just be careful with it -- you're about eight inches taller than normal with this hair."

"Great. How am I supposed to get into my trailer, let alone the tiny bathroom?"

"Follow me," Dawn said.

She led me through a maze of buildings and into a cinder-block structure that looked a lot like a sitcom setting from a few decades before. A coffee bar was on the first floor, and a number of men and women dressed in the Catholic-school garb were lounging there. This was the pages' building, I realized. Most of the group stopped talking and looked up as I walked through the door, but they quickly returned to their coffees and conversation.

"Why are we here?" I whispered to Dawn.

"There's a large bathroom upstairs," she replied quietly. "Plenty of room for you and your hair."

Sure enough, the second floor had what amounted to a locker room with a large women's restroom. It wasn't the cleanest I'd ever seen, but it was certainly serviceable for my current needs.

"You know how to use one of those?" Dawn asked, indicating the bag that held the pregnancy test.

"It can't be that hard, right?"

"It's not rocket science, but then actors aren't generally known for their quick wits."

"Ouch. Do you really think you know me well enough to judge my intellect?"

"No," she said, smiling. "But you should know you're not just getting a pretty face for an assistant. I can give as good as I get."

"Then you're pretty much perfect. I don't need another kiss-ass in my life."

"You have a lot of those?"

I went into the handicapped stall and opened the box. A page of instructions fell out. A quick glance told me everything I needed to know. "I have more of those than I do real people around me."

"I'm sorry to hear that."

"Yeah, well, it comes with the job."

"You want me to step outside for a minute?"

"Not necessary. Besides, I'd kind of like someone with me when I find out if I'm going to be a mom or not. Just turn on the faucet."

She did, and two minutes later, I was out of the stall with the test.

"Now we just have to wait for the results." I washed my hands and turned off the faucets.

"Do you want to be a mother?" she asked, leaning against the wall.

"Ferris wants to be a dad," I answered, deflecting her question.

"Not really what I asked."

I frowned. "I always planned to have kids...someday. I just thought -- after my career took off -- that I'd wait for the sweet spot before I did."

"You mean the years between ingenue and serious actress?"

"You know about that?"

She laughed. "Everyone in the business knows about that -- even the lowly pages. Isn't it strange that, even today, men don't really have the sweet-spot experience?"

"They don't need to take a few years off to have children."

"Neither do most women in the business these days. Most of them hit those years and their marriages take a dive, because they are Hollywood marriages anyway -- fantasies destined to crumble at the first signs of age."

"Wow. How long have you been in California?"

"Raised here. Why?"

"You're so cynical for someone so young."

"My parents were actors."

"Really? Who are they?"

"They were just character actors -- they never got far."

It finally clicked that she was speaking about them in the past tense. "What happened to them?"

"Something like what happened to your parents, just a lot quieter."

"I'm sorry."

"Don't be," she said, pasting that page-smile back in place. "Bad things happen all the time. But you should know I asked to work for you."

"I didn't know the pages were allowed to make assignment requests."

"Let's just call it a case of quid pro quo."

I didn't want to know whose back she had scratched, so I turned my attention to the test. "You think I should check the results yet?"

"Flip it over," she said, pushing off the wall and walking to the sinks where the test rested.

Biting my lip, I picked it up and saw the plus sign. My stomach rolled. For a moment, I thought I was going to lose what little food I had in me.

As I leaned over the sink, I felt Dawn rubbing my shoulders. "It's okay," she cooed. "Everything will be fine. Do you want me to get you anything? You don't have to go through with the pregnancy, you know. I can get you a Mother's Choice."

Mother's Choice was the pharmaceutical pregnancy remedy that was outlawed in the United States. If a citizen was caught even carrying the pill on their person, they could be charged with attempted murder, thanks to the Christian extremists who had controlled our country for the better part of twenty years now. The only way to get it was to go to Canada. Vancouver had become a popular vacation destination in the last five years. "How? Are you going across the northern border?"

She laughed. "There are other ways to get the stuff, you know."

"No, I didn't know that."

"Are you saying you want a pill?"

Suddenly, I was suspicious of my new assistant. Maybe she wasn't a tabloid informant, but that didn't mean she wasn't a political or criminal-justice spy. Only a few years before, the FBI had swooped down on a television star who was accused of taking a Mother's Choice. They sentenced her to ten years, but then granted her leniency for doing a series of public service announcements where she claimed that her unborn child haunted her dreams and that regrets were eating her alive. It was pathetic, really. "Why would you even ask that? I told you Ferris and I want children."

She shrugged. "Just offering." Her phone beeped and she pulled it out of her pocket. "Mick's ready for you on the set."

When the shoot was over, Dawn became a regular fixture around the house. Ferris and I both liked her -- she was quick and funny and seemed to know instinctively which roles and songs were right for me. She went through scripts rapidly, reading faster than anyone I'd ever met before. I forgot about my moment of doubt and accepted that she was a friend.

The pregnancy left me tired most of the time, and I found myself nodding off in the middle of the day. Dawn cleared my schedule for me, officially bowing out of or putting off projects as we deemed necessary. She decorated the baby's room, locating gender-neutral furnishings that featured zoo animals. She went with me to the obstetrician's office when Ferris was too busy. And she kept Ferris company whenever I took a nap.

By my sixth month, Dawn had moved into the spare room originally intended for a nanny. She had become a part of our family. When Ranice brought Charity to visit, the little girl called her Aunt Dawn.

One afternoon, while Dawn and Charity were swimming, Ranice said, "She certainly seems to have made herself at home."

We were sitting in the living room, watching the two of them splash around through the plate-glass windows. "We wanted her to be comfortable."

"That girl is so comfortable I think she'd claim squatter's rights if you wanted her out."

"She's a lot of help, Ranice. She more than earns her place in our world."

"Ferris seems...affectionate...with her."

I felt an angry bolt of electricity straighten my spine. "Are you trying to cause a problem here?"

"No! I just...I don't want you to risk your future by ignoring your instincts." She shifted uncomfortably. "I'm not here all the time, so I don't know for sure. But if I were a frog, I wouldn't like the temperature of this water."

That night, I watched the two of them together with new eyes as they bantered across the dining table.

"I think I've got a good plan for your next album, Di," Ferris said.

"Really? What is it?" I asked.

"You're going to love it," Dawn put in. "Ferris has a completely brilliant lineup of lullabies."

"They're not lullabies," he reprimanded, laughing. "They're songs written to children."

"I don't understand." I put my silverware down and looked directly at Ferris.

Dawn answered me: "You know: 'Hey, Jude,' 'Baby Mine'...songs like those."

Ferris shot her an appreciative smile; our baby kicked me in the ribs and I grimaced.

"Are you all right?" Dawn asked.

"Fine. The baby just decided to sucker-punch me."

"Not too much more of that left -- you're in the homestretch now."

"Now you've got me thinking we need to do a sports-themed album," he joked.

Dawn laughed.

"I'm not feeling well tonight," I said, pushing away from the table.

"You should eat some more, Di," Ferris said, looking at my half-full plate.

"I'm not hungry."

"But the baby--"

"I said, I'm not hungry." I took a deep breath and tried to relax. "I'm going to bed now."

"Let me help you," Dawn said, shooting out of her chair and around to my side.

I pushed her away. "I'm not an invalid. I'm just pregnant. In a few months, I'll feel better." I looked at Ferris. "You'll have your damned baby and everything will go back to normal -- at least, as normal as we can be." I cut my eyes at Dawn.

"She's just not feeling herself," Dawn said by way of excuse.

I let out a cackle that sounded insane even to me. "You're damned right I'm not myself! I'm not even the only me in my own body! I'm never alone anymore, yet I'm more alone every day." My knees buckled at the thought. Dawn, unable to support me entirely, managed to lower me to the ground.

Ferris, who had seemed paralyzed when my outburst began, suddenly shook himself awake and rushed to my side. "Diana, sweetheart, what is wrong with you? Are you in pain?"

"My heart hurts," I moaned, clutching my hands against my chest. "I'm breaking in two."

"Let me help you to your bed," Dawn begged. "Please, let's just get you someplace comfortable."

"No! Stay away from me!"

"It's okay," Ferris said. "I'll take care of her. You go to your room." He slipped his arms around my back and under my knees, lifting me off the ground. I let my head fall against his chest as I continued to sob. When we reached the bedroom, he lay me down and crawled into bed alongside me, wrapping his arms around my heaving chest. "It's all okay, Di," he soothed. "Everything will be okay."

I concentrated on breathing -- in, out, in, out. Deeper and slower with each breath. I could feel Ferris's breath on my neck, warm and soft and calm. When I no longer felt like my heart was ripping in two and the world was spinning away from me, I said, "I think Dawn should go."

Ferris took care of it. He gave Dawn a generous severance package -- the rest of what she would have made for a year as my assistant -- and helped her pack her things up. He even called a friend of his and found her a new position. He didn't understand why I wanted her gone, but he did as I requested and made her disappear. Ranice stepped back into the role of my assistant without missing a beat.

The rest of my pregnancy progressed smoothly, and, when the time came, I was able to deliver our baby boy at home. We named him Paul Seamus, after my agent and Ferris's father. Together, we interviewed a dozen young men and women to be Seamus's nanny, finally settling on a young college graduate named Petronella Hart. Pet, as she preferred to be called, had gotten her Bachelor degree in Early Childhood Education, but wasn't sure she wanted to be a teacher after all. Though she was sweet, she wasn't much to look at -- her nose was hooked and her waist was thick. She had some unfortunate scarring across both cheeks, due to chronic acne that her family had apparently chosen to ignore rather than treat. The baby took to her immediately, and I found her to be pleasant and non-threatening.

While I worked toward returning my figure to perfection, Ferris and I spent a few weeks in the studio recording the new album of classic lullabies. Ferris was right about the collection -- the songs seemed to flow together naturally. The finished project was soothing and melodic. At my insistence, the album art was a drawing of our little family -- Shay (as we called him) in my arms and Ferris behind me, one hand on my shoulder and the other on our child's head.

Before long, my life felt exactly the way it always had. I was back on movie sets -- sometimes in California, sometimes other places -- and Ferris was at home, now with the child he had wanted so much. Seamus, like Corkie, seemed to prefer him to me. He smiled at Ferris and at Pet. He learned to pet Corkie gently.

In the beginning, Ferris would swoop Seamus into the air and carry him to the door, greeting me with, "Look! There's Mommy!"

Seamus would giggle and look at his father with delight. But as soon as I took him in my arms, he would begin to squirm and whine, and before long, a full-throated wail would pierce our eardrums. Corkie would growl at me and Pet would come running.

When he was a toddler, I caught that little boy looking at me as if he were trying to work out just exactly who I was. He was still too young to know that he shouldn't stare; his gaze would cut through me until I forced myself to look away.

Through some stroke of luck, I never had a lull in my career after Seamus was born. I consistently starred in three films a year, which meant I spent all of three months total at home for the first ten years of the boy's life. I was never home long enough to feel like I wasn't a stranger, especially when Ferris, Seamus, and Pet shared inside jokes and daily rituals.

I was sitting in my room, brushing my hair one night when Seamus peeked shyly around the corner of my doorway.

"Mom?" He looked like a miniature version of his father, only with paler skin.

"Yes, Shay?"

"Can I talk to you?"

I set my brush down and looked at him directly. "What would you like to talk about?"

He frowned, and his small, dark eyebrows drew together. "Are you really my mom?"

"Of course! Who else would be?"

He shrugged. "Other kids have moms who aren't really their moms."

"You mean like stepmothers?"

"Yeah...and adopted moms."

I smiled at his words. "No, you aren't adopted. You are all mine."

"Then why don't you love me?"

I felt a lump in my throat as I searched for the right answer -- one that wouldn't make him feel like my poor skills as a parent were his fault. Finally, I pulled him onto the bench where I was sitting. "I love you very much, Seamus. I'm sorry I'm not good at showing you that love. You see, my mommy wasn't a very nice person. She always made me feel like she didn't like me at all. My daddy tried to make up for her attitude, but there's only so much a daddy can do."

His frown etched more deeply into his little features. "So you don't love me because of your mom?"

I put my arm around him and tried to relax into the

gesture. If I had been on set, I could have acted like I loved him; in my home -- where I am supposed to be a real person -- I couldn't. I felt like a mannequin someone had positioned to look like a mother. "I'll try to do better, Seamus. I'm so sorry."

He looked up at me and said, "If you really loved me, you would let Daddy and Pet be happy."

"What?" I exhaled, the wind knocked out of my lungs.

"Daddy and Pet love me more than anything else in the world."

"Why aren't they happy?" I asked slowly.

"They want to go away and take me with them, but you won't let them."

I caught a glimpse of someone in my vanity mirror at that moment. She was sickly pale and looked as if she were about to pass out. A moment later, I realized that the woman was me. My mouth was dry and my lungs were crumbling inside my body. "Where do they want to go?"

The boy shrugged. "Away is all they say."

I willed my arm to squeeze his body to mine and kissed the top of his head. I stuck a smile on my lips and said, "Thank you for coming to talk to me. Remember, Mom loves you."

"Okay." He slid off the bench and walked slowly out of the room as my organs turned to dust. I dragged my empty hull of a body to the bed, where I sobbed silently into the pillows until I fell asleep.

When I awoke, I had a course of action to follow. "Pet," I called out, hoping that she was nearby. "Pet!" I yelled more loudly.

"Yes, ma'am," the nanny finally answered. I heard her scurrying down the hallway like the ferret I now recognized her to be.

As soon as she was in my doorway, I said, "I think Ferris and I could use some alone time. Would you be a dear and take Shay out to a movie tonight?" I watched her face contort through half a dozen expressions before settling on one.

"Of course, ma'am."

"One more thing, Pet. How long have you been sleeping with my husband?"

"I would never!" she exclaimed too quickly.

I curved my lips. "Of course you wouldn't. Where is Ferris?"

"He had a meeting with a client today."

"So he's out of the house?"

"Yes, ma'am. Until six or so, he said."

"Make sure you and Shay are gone before he gets home."

She stood in my doorway as stiffly as a cigar-store indian.

"You should go now," I prompted, and she fled down the hall.

Corkie padded into the room and looked up at me with her sad, intelligent eyes. I reached down and petted her, wondering how much longer she could possibly survive...wondering how much longer my marriage would survive.

I cooked that night, something I rarely did. I lit candles and placed them on the table. I turned the lights down low and put on the first album we made together. I slipped into the same simple white dress I had worn on the beach when we said our vows so many years before. I may have been rapidly approaching fifty, but I was still a beautiful woman.

When Ferris walked through the door, I swept him into a passionate kiss and was gratified to feel his hands pulling me close, not pushing me away. When we broke our lip-lock, he whispered, "What have I done to deserve this welcome?"

"I just thought we could use some time together -- without Pet or Seamus."

"How romantic of you! Are you all right?" He mockingly touched my forehead with the back of his hand.

I brushed him off with a girlish giggle. "Can't a woman just want a little time with her husband?"

"I suppose so."

I'd never thought of him as an actor -- or even a good liar -- and yet I saw no signs of guilt in him. I took his hand and led him to the table. "I'll be right back," I said.

"You cooked too? My God...where is my wife?"

I smiled and walked to the kitchen. I put a generous portion of pot roast and potatoes on his plate and a little less on my own.

"Smells wonderful," he said as I walked toward the table with our food. "What inspired this?"

"I thought you could use a break. You do so much around here...and I don't say how much I appreciate it, do I?"

"Not often," he admitted, cutting a small piece of meat and putting it in his mouth. "Mm. This is wonderful, Di."

"My father taught me how to cook. Did I ever tell you that?"

"I guess it's never come up before."

I dropped my napkin in my lap and watched him savor the food. "I'm glad you like it." He smiled at me with his sparkling green eyes. "We should get away -- just the three of us. Maybe a trip to Hawaii? We had such a wonderful time there."

"That was a long time ago, wasn't it? Sometimes it seems like yesterday."

"You'd be okay with that? A trip for just the three of us?" I pushed.

"Of course. Pet could probably use a vacation herself."

I took a deep breath, knowing this could be the last moment of our marriage. "Do you think maybe Shay is too old to have a nanny at this point?"

He frowned as if he were deep in thought.

I rushed on. "It's just that, at ten, a nanny seems too...babyish, don't you think? Pet has been great, and, of course, if we'd had more children...but we didn't. I think it might be time for us to just be a family. I've never really been the mother I wish I had been. I think I let Pet do too many of the things I should have done. I want to try to fix that--"

"A lot of the kids in his school still have nannies," Ferris interrupted.

"And that makes it okay?"

Ferris chewed his food thoughtfully, looking off into the corner as he did so. "No," he answered finally, "it doesn't. I guess I've let this kaleidoscope view of the world change me. I never would have thought I'd let a nanny do most of the work with my own kid."

This wasn't the answer I was expecting. "So you agree that we should let Pet go?"

"Yes. You're right. It's time for her to go."

I reached across the table and took his hand in mine. "You still love me?"

His face spread into a smile that set my heart ablaze. "Of course I love you, you silly girl! Who else but you?"

"I'm going to retire, I think...at least for a few years."

"Lovely! You can practice your mum skills and we can travel as a family. Maybe we could even hire a private tutor for a while and take Seamus out of school."

"Oh! How wonderful would that be? We could rent a condo on one of the touring ships for a year and see every port!"

"How better for our son to learn geography?" He finished his food and set his plate to one side, reaching across the table for my other hand. "It's settled then. How many more films are you committed to?"

"Just the next three. After those, I can bow out gracefully."

"Should we hold off on letting Pet go? I don't want to traumatize Shay."

"I think a clean break would be best. I'll tell her tomorrow."

"I could do it, if you'd rather."

Either he was a better actor than I was, or he really didn't care about Pet at all. I couldn't discern any falsehood in his expression. I remembered the quickness of Pet's response earlier. Could it simply have been triggered by her own desire for Ferris rather than the guilt of an adulterous liaison? I had no way of knowing for sure. "No," I said decisively. "I'll let her go."

"Be sure to give her a decent severance package, Di. She has been extremely faithful to Seamus -- we've never had to worry as long as she was with him." His stern expression relaxed into a smile. "Now that this is settled -- did you make any dessert?"

I thought about the individual servings of panne cotta chilling in the refrigerator. I would have to come out later and dispose of them. "I'm dessert," I said, standing and allowing my shimmering white dress to fall to the floor.

Ferris walked to me and took me in his arms, a second later sweeping me off my feet and carrying me to the bedroom, where we made love like newlyweds, our fingers exploring each other's bodies greedily. I couldn't remember the last time we touched like that -- the last time we had taken it slow and tantalized one another with gentle caresses.

Afterward, we lay face to face and whispered about

our new future until we drifted off to sleep.

When I opened my eyes the next morning, Ferris was still beside me, sound asleep, a smile on his lips. I sighed contentedly and stared at him for a few moments before rolling out of bed. I grabbed my pink-satin robe from the bathroom and padded silently down the hallway. I needed to dispose of the panne cotta before anyone in the house got a sweet tooth.

Something was wrong. The house was silent. In the living room, I checked the clock -- seven in the morning -- and glanced out the plate-glass windows to see if they were already in the swimming pool. The water was still.

Corkie was laying in her bed, still sleeping. I walked over to pet her. Her body felt cold and stiff. I buried my eyes against her neck and sobbed. No one heard me -- no one came to console me. I rocked against the floor and the tears gradually subsided.

Suddenly, a new fear rose up: what if Pet took Seamus and ran? Nannies did that sometimes, didn't they? They became convinced that the child they were caring for was actually their own -- sometimes, they even convinced the child that their delusion was the truth. Seamus already wished that Pet were his real mother -- she wouldn't have to work very hard to convince him she was!

I stood up, but couldn't decide what to do. Finally, I realized I should check Shay's room. I opened the door onto a scene from a horror movie: Pet and Seamus curled together, their faces forever frozen in a paralytic rictus of pain, their bodies gray and cold. Stifling a scream, I sank down on the floor next to the bed and waited for tears to fall anew. I'm not sure how long I sat there, but I couldn't feel anything like the sadness I'd felt upon finding Corkie. I must have been numb or in shock or--

143

The scene in the bedroom grew brighter as the sun came up and then seemed to fade into sepia tones as I worked out what I needed to do next. There was no coming back from this -- I had murdered my son and my nanny. When Ferris woke up, my marriage would be over. Ferris -- he would never look at me the way he had last night...never again. What had I done? Why hadn't I washed the dessert down the drain the night before? Why had I even cooked up the poisonous stuff in the first place? What was wrong with me? An unhappy marriage was nothing to kill over -- certainly nothing to die over! Especially when I could fix it. So what if I couldn't fix it for another thirty years? It could still be fixed. Even this could be fixed...someday.

Finally, I walked toward the kitchen to dispose of the panne cotta. One ramekin was in the sink and filled with water. The ramekin from which Corkie had taken her death was on the floor, empty, no doubt licked clean by our beloved dog. Opening the refrigerator door, I took out the last two ramekins. I spooned the contents of one of them into the disposal. I grabbed a spoon for the other and carried it to the bedroom.

Demi and Ranice sat behind me as I recounted my crime to the judge as part of my plea agreement. Demi, stoic as always, never let her disappointment or horror show. Ranice sobbed openly.

I confessed that, after Seamus informed me that Ferris and Pet were a couple, I went for a hike with the express purpose of locating hemlock, which grew near the trails around our neighborhood. I knew this because of a film I had starred in just a few years before. In it, my character murdered her husband with hemlock tea. I returned home and ran the root through my food processor. I made panne cotta, adding the hemlock to the mixture of cream, sugar, and gelatin and allowing the ingredients plenty of time to meld before pouring it through a sieve and allowing it to gel. I made four doses -- one for each of us. I told the court about finding my son and his nanny dead in his bedroom and my dog dead in her bed. I confessed to carrying the lethal dose of poisoned panne cotta to my husband and caring for him through five long hours as his body slowly, painfully shut down.

"Why did you kill him?" the judge asked.

"Because I loved him so much I couldn't stand for him to look at me with hatred."

"Why didn't you kill yourself as you originally intended?"

My reason for living flashed through my head, but outwardly I only shrugged.

The judge shook her head and I sat down, my allocution complete.

The plea agreement did nothing but keep the death sentence off the table -- and that was all I needed. Citing the heinous nature of my crimes and my evident premeditation and current lack of contrition, the judge gave me life without parole -- no less than I deserved.

Because of who I was, my fellow inmates were surprisingly kind to me. Most of them were more than a little starstruck by my presence -- something I had never considered. Even the warden was sensitive to my needs. I suppose I was sort of like Al Capone -- I've read that his needs were catered to, as well.

Of course, by the end of the 2050s, internet was considered a basic human right. Every prisoner received a computer tablet for their own use. The tablets did more to humanize the penal system than just about anything else. The prisoners weren't shy about posting videos of guards or inmates behaving badly, and, as a result, prisoner-on-prisoner and guard-on-prisoner violence has all but disappeared. I wouldn't say the last thirty years of my life have been ideal, but they haven't been impossible to bear, either.

Ranice and Demi are both long gone, but my niece still visits me. Charity is a gorgeous woman, even at nearly fifty years old. She was a teenager when I killed her cousin and uncle, and she was angry at me for a long time. When her mothers were in a fatal car crash on a California freeway a couple of decades ago, she only came to tell me why they weren't going to be visiting anymore -- she never intended to pick up where Ranice left off.

"Why did you do it?" she asked as she sat across from me in the visiting room.

All around us were people who had committed horrible and not-so-horrible crimes for reasons that would never provide a satisfactory answer to their victims, yet their families gathered around them and offered them comfort and hope. Here was a young woman who was both my family and the family of my victims -- in that moment, I realized how confusing that must have been for her. I told her the truth. "I thought Pet and Ferris were sleeping together. I thought he was going to leave me, and I went out of my head."

"But you were wrong. Pet's diary proved that you were wrong."

"I know." The diary showed that, while Pet did have a crush on Ferris, she had become engaged to a young man with whom she went to college just days before she died. The story that Shay told me was completely from his imagination. "I can fix this, Charity. But I couldn't stand to have your uncle hate me. It would have been too much...too painful. It might have stopped me from making the right choice -- from sending the email that will change the past."

She looked at me as if I were crazy. "Aunt Diana,

nothing can change the past. It's over and done with."

"That's not true! I have already changed the past five times just in my lifetime! All I have to do is send an email on December 31, 2069, and everything will be okay."

She squinted at me. "Did you tell my mothers this?"

"No. They wouldn't have believed me anyway." I smiled at her. "You don't believe me, do you?"

"No. But I think I can help you now. Aunt Di, you're mentally ill! You don't belong in here at all!"

"Yes, I do. I killed three people and a dog, Charity. I belong right here."

She shook her head again. "Listen, I can get you a psychiatrist--"

"Don't you dare. I won't tell anyone what I've told you today. This is just between me and you."

My rational niece, with all her medical training, studied me. "You have to trust me. I'm a doctor...we can make you better..."

"I'm fine just the way I am, sweetheart."

She leaned forward. "How do you know you've changed the past?"

"I've followed my own advice in five different emails over my lifetime. What happened in this lifetime was new, otherwise I would have changed it before. That means I can change it with my next email."

"You don't belong here," she repeated.

What should have been a one-time visit turned into monthly, and later bi-monthly, conversations. She was just here a few days ago -- her Christmas visit. She brought her kids and her husband with her. One of her daughters looks almost exactly like me, only with dark brown hair. It's funny how strong my mother's genes were, even if her character was weak.

Tomorrow, I will change the past and our lives will be different. Maybe I'll be lucky enough to be a bigger part of Charity's family; maybe I'll have grandchildren of my own. At the very least, I'll have my husband.

Seventh

Ranice had only just left the house when my phone vibrated, telling me that I had messages waiting. Unsettled by her suggestion that Dawn and Ferris were too close, I ignored the device as I pondered Ranice's words. No matter how much help she was, Dawn would have to go if she were flirting with Ferris.

"You okay?" she asked, emerging from the hallway as she rubbed her hair dry from swimming with my niece.

"Fine."

"You sure? You seem distracted."

"Just thinking."

She spotted my phone on the coffee table, its light blinking to remind me I had unanswered messages. "You should check those. I think Paul was sending you some contracts via email." She carried it over to me and plopped down on the other end of the blue sectional.

I frowned as I took it from her. Instead of checking the messages, I concentrated on her profile. She had a sharp nose and a big mouth, but she was definitely pretty in a wholesome way. "Do you have a boyfriend, Dawn?"

She looked at me with a big smile. "Why do you ask?"

"I just realized that you never seem to go anywhere. My family can't be your whole life!"

She laughed. "Of course not. I can't believe it took you five months to wonder, though. Pregnancy must really make you forgetful."

"I suppose it does. So?"

"The boyfriend thing? Yeah, I have one. It's not very serious, though."

"Why haven't we ever seen him?"

"He's in the Navy. Right now, he's cruising around Africa, looking for trouble." She grinned, apparently enjoying an inside joke.

"Ah."

149

"I have some scripts to read," she said, bouncing to her feet. "Can I get you anything right now?"

"No. I'm fine. Go on...do what I hired you for."

I must have sounded as hostile as I was feeling because she looked at me strangely. "Okay." She smiled uneasily and disappeared.

Grinding my teeth in irritation, I picked up my phone and scanned my messages. There was nothing from Paul, but I did find a note from December 2069. It had been years since my last email, and yet I knew what it would say before I opened it. "Don't fire Dawn."

What the hell was the matter with me that my judgment was so poor I had to continually nudge myself into course corrections? The thought occurred to me that perhaps the course corrections themselves were making a mess of my life, but I dismissed it. The evidence clearly pointed toward improvements, not disasters. From leaving Joe to pursue my career to agreeing to start a family as soon as Ferris wanted to, everything seemed better with the advice of future-me. Maybe the answer was simply to figure out what I would most like to do and then do the opposite. I smiled to myself at the thought.

That night, I watched Dawn and Ferris with new eyes as they bantered across the dining table.

"I think I've got a good plan for your next album, Di," Ferris said.

"Really? What is it?" I asked.

"You're going to love it," Dawn put in. "Ferris has a completely brilliant lineup of lullabies."

"They're not lullabies," he reprimanded, laughing. "They're songs written to children."

"I don't understand." I put my silverware down and looked directly at Ferris.

Dawn answered me: "You know: 'Hey, Jude,' 'Baby Mine'...songs like those."

Ferris shot her an appreciative smile; our baby kicked me in the ribs and I grimaced.

"Are you all right?" Dawn asked.

"Fine. The baby just decided to sucker-punch me."

"Not too much more of that left -- you're in the homestretch now."

"Now you've got me thinking we need to do a sports-themed album," he joked.

Dawn laughed.

"I'm not feeling well tonight," I said, pushing away from the table.

"You should eat some more, Di," Ferris said, looking at my half-full plate.

"I'm not hungry."

"But the baby--"

"I said, I'm not hungry." I took a deep breath and tried to relax. "I'm going to bed now."

"Let me help you," Dawn said, shooting out of her chair and around to my side.

I pushed her away. "I'm not an invalid. I'm just pregnant. In a few months, I'll feel better."

"It's okay, Dawn. I'll help her." Ferris came around the side of the table and wrapped his arm around me.

I leaned my head into his chest and felt the first tears fall. "I don't know what's wrong with me," I said.

"You're six months pregnant, sweetheart. You've got hormones surging through your body. It's okay that you're a little emotional."

I thought again of the email message I'd received. Maybe that was why I needed future-me this time: my emotions were too raw to be trusted.

In the bedroom, he helped me pull off my shoes and my dress. I sat down on the edge of the bed and looked up at him -- my handsome Irish music man. "Do you have feelings for Dawn?"

He sat down next to me and took my hand in his. "What sort of feelings? Romantic ones?"

I nodded.

"No. I'm not attracted to her. She's a nice girl, but I have you."

"What if something happened to me? What if I died in childbirth or something like that? Would you be attracted to her then?"

He smiled as if I'd said something adorable. "No, I wouldn't. She's like my kid sister, Di. I look at her and all I see is a smart, ambitious young woman who wants to be just like you. She's not much more than a starstruck kid who can't believe she fell into such a great job. Where is this coming from?"

If he was lying I couldn't tell. "Ranice. She thought you two were flirting with each other."

"I wouldn't. You and our baby are the two most important people in my life. I would never jeopardize our future for a fling with a teenager."

"She's closer to your age than I am."

"Maybe physically," he acknowledged. "Mentally, though, you and I are a match made in heaven. I will never find anyone better than you -- and that's a promise."

I tipped my body sideways, resting my head against my pillow. Ferris slid in behind me, wrapping his arms around us -- me and the wriggling child sharing my body. We drifted off to sleep with the sound of distant clattering dishes coming from the dining room as Dawn put away the leftovers and moved the plates to the kitchen.

Paul Seamus was born on a blustery L.A. day after twelve hours of labor. The first time I held him in my arms and felt Ferris's hand on my shoulder I knew that we were complete -- like an electrical circuit suddenly coming to life. The warmth surged through us and we became a single unit: a family.

For the first six months, neither Ferris nor I could bear to leave the house. Dawn ran all of our errands -- bought our groceries, picked up our contracts, even answered our incoming phone calls. Eventually, though, we had to break out of our cocoon of love and begin to fly again.

We started slowly. Ferris and I went into the recording studio and came out with the album of songs for and about children. We called it *In His Eyes*. A lot of people thought we had been swept up in some kind of religious cult, and the album's title didn't help matters. We caught a lot of flak for what people assumed was true.

Just a year before, the National Science Advisory Council had declared that "God," in the traditional sense, didn't exist. The most recent election had swept much of the old guard from office. The new Senate majority leader -- herself a scientist -- called for hearings regarding the influence of religion on terrorism. More than one expert witness declared that belief in any god was a major factor in the creation of terrorist organizations. Before long, the President was signing a new bill into law: Religious Emancipation. As citizens of the United States, we were declared free of all duty and guilt associated with religion. The South had seceded and renamed themselves Zion a few months ago. Most of Utah was empty now, as the Mormons fled this new science-favoring society for the religion-focused South. The president of the U.S. and the Bishop of Zion had jointly agreed to give all citizens of the United States a full year to decide whether they wanted to remain in the U.S. or move to Zion.

Every gossip site on the internet was speculating about when Ferris and I would be making the trek to the newly formed country. Every time either of us got on a plane, the news blasted that we were scoping out new homes on the Floridian peninsula or considering settling in New Orleans. We were derided as "flaky Hollywood types" who "needed a god in order to give their lives meaning."

The truth, of course, was that neither of us had given any thought at all to God. Besides, even if we did decide that we needed to worship a supreme being, there were still temples and churches in the U.S. -- they were just required to pay taxes now.

The album was a huge hit in Zion, but it didn't get much play in the U.S. Likewise, the scripts slowed to a trickle. Shay was walking before Dawn found a movie role she thought was suitable for me. She brought the script to me in the nursery, where I was watching Corky and Seamus play together.

"This is a good one," she said, holding the script out to me.

"What is it?"

"It's biographical. Hillary Clinton."

"I don't look a thing like Clinton."

"This is your Meryl Streep moment, Diana. You can play this role."

I smiled and shook my head. "I thought I was Barbra Streisand."

"You can be both." She thought for a moment. "Correction. You can be better than both...you can be better than all of the stars put together!"

"Dawn..."

"Seriously, Di! You are more talented than any other actor in Hollywood today. The only reason the scripts have dropped off is because you haven't made a film in a while. All you have to do is remind them that you're still here. The scripts will start pouring in again."

Ferris appeared in the doorway behind Dawn.

"What's up?"

"Dawn thinks I should play a president's wife."

Dawn turned to face him. "Not just any run-of-the-mill First Lady. Hillary Clinton, Ferris. Hillary Clinton! The woman who changed politics!"

"Personal heroine, I take it?"

"Hell, yes! She was fucking amazing!"

"Hey, now!" I said sharply. "Little ears in the room. We don't want his first word to be that one."

"Sorry, Di. But yes, Hillary Clinton would be an amazing role."

"What do you think?" I asked Ferris. "Should I go back to work?"

"You were going to eventually. Where are they planning to shoot?"

"Part of it they want to shoot in Arkansas before the border closes," Dawn said.

"But the border closes in six months." Ferris frowned. "This is just going to add fuel to the fire about us choosing God over science. We'll be seen as backwards by most of Hollywood."

"Until they realize she's just making a movie down there!" Dawn exclaimed. "I'm telling you, this role will make Diana the go-to actress for every meaty female role. She won't just be nominated for an Academy Award, she'll win an Oscar!"

Ferris picked up Shay and felt his bottom. "He's wet."

Dawn held out her arms. "I'll change him. You two, go discuss this." Handing the script to me and taking the baby from Ferris, she shooed us out of the room.

With his free hand, Ferris pulled me toward our bedroom. We lay down, the script open between us, and read the first few pages. It opened with the first time Bill and Hillary met on a college campus.

After half an hour of reading, we were up to Hillary's 2008 run for president. "I would have voted for her," I sighed. "She was inspiring."

"Obama had the momentum, though."

"Yeah. That was inevitable."

"I wasn't here yet, you know. I was still living in County Cork. Ireland was in an economic upswing -- for the first time, it looked like we were going to be a power."

"The world was a lot different then, wasn't it?"

"Yes, it was. And Hillary Clinton played a huge role in changing our future."

"Is it too soon to do a movie about her? You know how history rewrites what we believe to be true. In ten years, it might come out that she was--"

"You can't think about what might tarnish her image in the future. Play her as the heroine she is today, and Dawn is right -- you'll win an Oscar."

I accepted the role; three months later, Dawn and I were in Little Rock. Ferris stayed in California with Seamus, causing the gossip sites to proclaim that our marriage was over because we didn't share the same beliefs. No matter how many statements of denial we issued, the tabloid press seemed determined to stick with their story.

"Maybe you and Shay should come down here." I was sitting in a beautiful condo overlooking the Arkansas River. The owner, an older actress who had found some success as a vampiress during the supernatural craze a few decades earlier, had rented it to us. She herself had fled Zion, unwilling to spend what was left of her career playing biblical heroines at the Florida film complex located in the recently renamed Holywood, Florida.

"Don't worry about what the sleazemongers are saying, Di. We know that we're not splitting up."

"I miss my baby so much, though!"

"Hey, what about me?" he said, laughing.

"You too, of course. But mostly Shay," I teased.

"Lovely. Thanks for that."

The doorbell chimed. "I've got to go, sweetheart. Jager's here." Jager Easterbrook was a dead ringer for a young Bill Clinton. He had spent the last several years playing a series of nice-guy roles on television. He was always the best friend of the female lead, never the female lead's love interest. Though I had never met him in person before filming started, I recommended him for the role of Bill.

"Again?"

"He just needs a little more rehearsal time."

"This is the fourth night this week, isn't it?"

"We're just getting more comfortable with each other. We want to give the performances of our lives in this film -- we're trying to get deep into our characters." I squirmed a little, suddenly uncomfortable with the amount of time Jager and I were spending together. But I wasn't attracted to him -- he was like the goofy brother I never had.

"Maybe we'll come down for the weekend, okay?"

"That would be so great!"

"Okay. I'll see you then."

As I hung up the phone, Dawn knocked on my door. "Yes?"

"Jager's here, Diana."

I heard the vague note of disapproval in her voice. "Tell him I'll be right out."

"Okay."

"Why don't you go to the movies or something, Dawn? You've been practically tied to my hip since we got here. Take some time off."

"I don't mind. Besides, there's not much of a selection of films around here. Only the Gs and PGs, you know."

"Take a book and go to dinner then," I answered irritably.

"Are you angry with me, Diana?"

"No, of course not. I just think that Jager and I will make more progress without an audience."

The door opened and Dawn looked at me with serious, evaluating eyes. "That's what I'm afraid of."

"You are not the keeper of my marriage. You don't need to worry about me."

"Someone should!" she whispered harshly. "You are looking at him like you are falling in love."

I shrugged. "I'm not even attracted to him!"

"I believe you -- you aren't attracted to Jager. You're attracted to the character he's portraying. That's even more dangerous, Diana."

"You don't understand...you're not an actress. We have to build this bond, or we won't make a convincing couple in the movie!"

"Bill and Hillary didn't have a romantic relationship -- they had a political one!"

"Really? Then how do you explain Chelsea?" I knew my voice was getting louder -- Dawn's was too. I consciously brought my volume back down to a conversational level. "You don't need to worry," I repeated. "This is just a movie role. I'm not going to risk my family for a part."

"Better women than you have done just that."

"Maybe you'd be happier back in California," I suggested.

"No. I'm your assistant."

I took a deep breath. "Ferris and the baby are coming to visit this weekend. Could you have a crib delivered?"

"Of course." She relaxed and smiled. "I'm so glad they're coming -- I've missed them both so much."

"Well, they're going to run you ragged once they're here. Ferris loves museums, and since I won't have time..."

"I'll be on tour-guide duty. Understood."

"I insist you take the night off, Dawn. I promise -- I

won't do anything you wouldn't do."

She rubbed her shoulder and eyed me pensively. "If you're sure..."

"One-hundred-percent certain."

"Okay."

She left my room and I went back to practicing my Hillary expressions in the mirror, giving her time to excuse herself from the condo. When I heard the door close, I walked down the long hallway to the living room, where I found Jager standing at the window, his hands clasped lightly behind his back. I took a deep breath and slipped into character. Jager had suggested that an evening of improvisation would help us to more fully embrace our characters. "Bill?"

"Hillary," he drawled. "You look lovely tonight."

"Don't give me that line. I know what you've been doing...whom you have been doing."

"I don't know what you're talking about."

"The girl...that cheap little tramp masquerading as an intern."

"She's nothing at all. No woman can hold a candle to you, Hillary." His blue eyes sparkled and for just a moment I was sure that I was Hillary and he was Bill and we were the most powerful couple in the world.

When filming wrapped, Dawn and I took the train back to California. Jager, whose next project was starting in just a few weeks, headed for New York. I thought that as soon as I was away from Jager and my characterization of Hillary dropped out of my mind, my unexpected and not-entirely-unwelcome sexual attraction to him would disappear.

Our on-screen chemistry was as palpable as that of Brad Pitt and Angelina Jolie a generation before us. We burned up the celluloid, whether we were kissing passionately or wounding each other with words. The director, a notoriously harsh critic of his own work, proclaimed the film to be his masterpiece. The tabloids speculated -- without evidence -- that I was on the verge of leaving Ferris, the nice-guy equivalent of that sweet Jennifer Aniston Pitt dumped to be with Jolie.

Dawn, ever faithful, reassured Ferris that nothing had happened between Jager and me other than a perfect meshing of talent. Privately though, she questioned me about the phone calls I was still getting from "Bill."

"It's nothing, Dawn. We're just friends."

"Are you being honest with me, Diana?"

"Of course."

"If you're just friends," she said, dropping onto the sofa beside me, "why does he still call himself Bill when he phones you? Why doesn't he call you by your real name?"

"He's a goof, you know that." I dropped my eyes to the book I was pretending to read.

"Do you love him?" she asked point-blank.

I hesitated a moment too long. "No--"

"You fucking liar!"

"Quiet! You'll wake the baby," I whispered urgently. "Why do you care so much?"

"Goddamn you! I've tied my life to you and your family. Ferris is like the brother I never had. Seamus might as well be my nephew. You're on the verge of--"

"I'm not leaving. This is just a little infatuation. It will fade."

"It's been months, Diana! What's going to happen when the press catches you two making moon eyes at each other at the Oscars?"

"They won't. We're actors, remember?"

"Oh, yeah, and you actors are so good at hiding your emotions." She rolled her eyes.

My phone rang. Glancing down, I saw that Jager

was calling. "I need to take this."

"Don't."

"What?"

"I said don't. Prove to me that you are just friends."

"Why is this so important all of a sudden?"

She held a script out to me. "This is why."

"What's this?"

She shook her head and sighed. "This is the next movie you should make. But Jager is already signed on to play the male lead."

I pressed the "ignore" button on my phone. "Who sent it?"

"It came from Paul. Don't worry -- Jager didn't handpick you for the part."

"You're sure?"

"As sure as I can be. But I'll tell Paul to turn it down if you have anything other than platonic feelings for Jager."

"He's just a friend," I said, telling myself it was true -- Jager and I were friends. Bill and Hillary were the lovers.

"Leave Ferris," Bill whispered against my cheek as we lay in his Parisian hotel suite. A sheet covered my thighs, leaving my breasts exposed. They weren't as pert as they once had been, but they were certainly fine for a woman of my age. My age: fifty. I had played Hillary to Jager's Bill for a decade now -- through half a dozen movies, three Oscars (two mine and one his), and two failed marriages (both his).

"I can't, you know that. Ferris loves me and Seamus is still a child."

He let out a single disbelieving guffaw. "You really think Ferris doesn't know what we're doing?"

I froze. His hand gently caressed my belly; my stomach heaved violently and a sat up, pushing away from him. "You don't know anything about my marriage. I love him, not you."

"Don't you mean Diana loves him?"

"Hillary isn't a real person, Jager!" I screamed, breaking the first rule of our relationship. "Hillary and Bill don't really exist." The words I had meant to injure him took the wind from my own lungs instead. I couldn't breathe, couldn't catch my breath. I leaned forward, bracing my hands against the bed as I struggled for air.

Jager didn't seem to notice. "You are unbelievable, Diana! Do you not see the shambles you have made of my life? I've tried to leave you -- time after time..."

His voice seemed to fade away, though I knew he was still talking -- no, yelling -- at me. All I could hear though was my heartbeat and my rasping attempts to pull in oxygen. I hung my head down and tried to slow my breathing. My mind wandered.

He pushed against my shoulder hard enough to knock me onto my side. "Are you even listening to me?"

I'm not sure how long I had been in my own world, but I was breathing normally now. Jager, his face red with anger, waited for my response. "I should have broken this off a long time ago." My voice sounded older and more tired than I had ever heard it sound before.

"You can't do that."

"I can. And I will."

"I'll tell. I won't stay quiet."

I looked at him and knew that he would do just that -- he had no reason not to. "Please," I said, trying to keep the whine out of my voice, "please, Jager, don't do that. I have a son--"

"You should have thought of that ten years ago. You can't play with my heart like this -- I'll ruin you. You, with your perfect life and perfect career...let's see how many of your fans stand by your side when I start talking about your infidelity."

I shrugged and laughed. "No one in Zion sees my films anyway," I bluffed. "Our country doesn't care about fidelity anymore."

"Oh? You think all that talk about how evolved we are as a society will give you a free pass on sleeping around?" He shook his head. "I guess we'll see who is right."

Biting my lip, I tried to come up with an argument that would defuse the situation. I slipped back into Hillary. "Come on, Bill, let's not fight. All those other people -- they don't know us like we know each other."

Warily, he answered, "I don't want to play anymore, Diana."

"Who's Diana? Another of your little acolytes? Does she give a better blow job than I do?"

He fought against a smile and lost. "No one is better than you, Hill," he drawled.

I let him pull me back to the bed and hoped that the crisis had been averted as I kissed a trail down his still-taut stomach.

The photos of Jager and I strolling through Paris arm in arm were hard to explain.

"I'm not stupid, Di," Ferris said, his face taut. In the background, I could see Dawn and Seamus splashing in the pool.

"You're inside, right?" I asked him, suddenly afraid that our son was hearing this conversation.

"Of course I am."

"Ferris, I swear to you, those pictures aren't what you think they are."

"I read the script. I know that you and Jager aren't

romantically involved in this film." His voice was quiet, resigned.

"We're friends! We've been in how many movies together? We aren't just the roles we play anymore. We spend time together when the cameras aren't rolling--"

"Obviously."

"But we're just friends. That's all I'm trying to say here."

"Everyone thinks I'm a fucking cuckold, Di. The whole world knows you're sleeping with him -- everyone but me, apparently."

"Listen, you're not...are you really going to throw away nearly twenty years because of what you think you're seeing in those pictures?"

"I know what I'm seeing."

"Filming is almost over. I'll be home in two weeks. Once I'm by your side again, you'll see that you're getting jealous over nothing."

"Come home now."

"You know I can't do that. We're on a tight schedule--"

"Get on the next flight, or so help me, you'll come home to an empty house."

"It's just a picture of us strolling on a street, Ferris!" I heard the door to my suite open.

"What's wrong?"

"Nothing."

"I saw that look. What's going on? Is he there now?"

"No. It's just the maid."

"Jager!" he screamed.

"He's not here."

"Jager! God damn it, be a man!"

Despite the plea in my eyes, Jager walked around to stand behind me. "Yeah, I'm here."

I dropped the videophone and walked away. Jager

picked it up.

"Are you sleeping with my wife?"

"Yes."

"That's all I needed to know. Tell her the water just got too hot for this frog." The tone indicating that the call had been terminated sounded.

"You hear that?" Jager asked with a big smile on his face. "We can be just Jager and Diana from now on. No more hiding, no more pretending." He wrapped his arms around me from behind.

I dug my nails into his wrists; in the split second of his surprise, I broke away from him, throwing one elbow behind me violently. "Never touch me again. You have just ruined my life! How can you think that I would want to be with the man who killed my family?! You think I don't know where those pictures came from?"

"What do you mean?" He delivered the line poorly.

"You set it up. You told the paparazzi where we would be and when."

He laughed. "You really think you wouldn't have noticed a pack of photographers dogging our steps?"

He was right; that would have been obvious. Besides, the Parisian press had strict rules when it came to following celebrities, including staying at a respectful distance. Whomever had taken the photos had been able to get close enough to capture our faces clearly. "How, then? I know you did it."

"I didn't. And when you realize that, I know you'll come crawling back to me, begging for my forgiveness."

I could see right through him -- he was playing another character, a cocky, son-of-a-bitch gangster. I wondered if I had ever met the real Jager at all. He wasn't the charming politician or the honorable cop or even the sleazy lawyer he was playing in our latest film. He was an empty vessel who thought I was the only thing that could fill him. "I'm going home."

"You can't do that. You have a contract--"

"Fuck the contract."

"He'll be gone before you get there."

I yanked my suitcase out of the closet and began throwing clothes into it haphazardly. "You don't know that."

"Even if you get a flight today, you won't be home until tomorrow. You really think he's not already moving out of the house?" He smiled smugly. "Let's face it, sweetheart -- he probably didn't even call you until he was packed. I wouldn't have."

I turned on my heel and found him standing directly in front me. Rearing back, I let my hand fly at his face so fast he didn't have time to duck. I felt more than heard his nose break under the impact. Blood gushed from his nose as he backed away from me, shocked. "Whatever this was, it's over now. Get out."

"You don't mean that." His eyes had turned to black coal.

I stepped backwards away from him, bumping my calves against the bed. "I do. Leave."

He stopped, one hand over his nose, which must have hurt like a son of a bitch, and his other hovering between us as if he were deciding whether I was worth the effort to choke. Finally, he let it drop. "I divorced two women for you."

"I never asked you to do that. You used me as an excuse to end two marriages. What are you so afraid of?"

His eyes widened and he backed away from me as if I had uttered a curse against him. Never taking his eyes off me, he left the suite, pulling the door closed behind him.

My attorney, a thirtyish woman with a practical brunette bob and too-thick eyebrows, sat next to me at the conference room table. Across from me, Ferris's attorney, a similarly coiffed blonde, waited for me to answer a question. "Well, Ms. Mogens?"

"The house was mine long before I married Ferris. I would prefer to keep it."

"I'm sure you would, but since you are away much of the time and Mr. Bodeen is the primary caregiver for your son, doesn't it make sense for him to retain the house?" Her smoothly reasoned argument sounded like nails on a chalkboard to me.

"It's my house," I argued stubbornly.

"What is more important to you? Your house or your child?"

My attorney -- Brown Betty, as I had dubbed her in my mind -- laid a calming hand over my nearest wrist. "Seamus is going through a lot of upheaval, Diana."

I looked pleadingly toward Ferris, but his eyes were glued to the table. He hadn't looked at me once. "I'd like to reconcile."

Ferris shook his head sharply.

"I'm afraid that's not on the table, Ms. Mogens," Blondie said.

"I'd like Ferris to say that, if it's true."

"I think you can take my word for it."

"If he says it, he can have the house."

The room fell silent as we waited -- the two lawyers and I -- for Ferris to speak. His fists clenched and his head slowly raised until his eyes were even with my neck. I imagined his hands going around my neck and squeezing -- the thought was less painful than my current reality. "I don't want to reconcile. I would never reconcile with an adulteress." His head sagged between his shoulders.

I exhaled in unison with the lawyers. "Fine."

My eyes glued to the same spot as Ferris's, I sat in silence as the rest of the details were hammered out between Brown Betty and Blondie.

Another woman might have been surprised when Ferris and Dawn married less than a year later, but I wasn't. Dawn was a good woman. She had sacrificed her youth working as my assistant, trying to be the glue that kept my family together. When Ferris and I divorced, she continued on as my assistant, though she remained in my former home with Shay and Ferris. When I made the decision to take a break from Hollywood and instead put together a song-and-dance act in Vegas, I suggested she remain in California. She could take care of most of what I needed her to do with a tablet computer.

I was just a few days from opening night when Dawn called me unexpectedly. Paul, my agent of thirty years, had been in the hospital recently, so I stopped singing and took the call. "What's wrong?"

"It's not Paul, Diana. He's fine for now. As a matter of fact, his son called to say he was moving up the liver transplant list."

I sighed, my relief transmuting to irritation. "Then why...?"

"I need your approval on something, and it couldn't wait."

"Geez, Dawn, you know me well enough to predict my answers. Just do what seems right."

"This seemed like something I should get your actual okay on."

I signaled the sound technician to start the song over. "You have thirty seconds."

"Ferris wants to marry me."

To my credit, I didn't drop or throw the phone. "When?"

"Soon. Maybe next week."

"Why?"

"I'm pregnant."

"His?"

"Yes."

The music swelled around me. "Fine. You're fired."

"But--"

"It's for the best, Dawn. Have a happy life." I ended the call and handed the phone off to a young man who had been playing the physical part of Dawn for the last few months. "Carl, you've been promoted. Call Dawn for the details." Another deep breath and it was time for me to sing.

Vegas has been good to me. My one-woman show has been going strong for decades now. I bought a condo just off the strip after the first few years. I always intended to go back to Hollywood -- or maybe even New York -- but after Paul died, I lost the will to fight for a bigger career. Besides, every American and most Zionists know who I am.

Do you know who really cuts loose in Vegas? You guessed it -- the Zionists. They really go crazy here. It's fun to watch, especially from the stage. When I first started, I had a big venue, the kind of place where the people can't get near the star. It didn't take me long to realize that a more intimate setting would make for a better show experience. As soon as my contract was up at Caesar's Palace, I moved to a small theater in the Paris. My audience went from over a thousand a night down to two hundred and fifty, and the price of a ticket tripled. But -- almost instantly -- I became the queen of the Strip.

Ferris and Dawn did their best to raise Seamus. I only saw him on holidays, and then only because of the court order. He didn't want to be with me at all, and I couldn't blame him.

Ferris called me when he found our son's marijuana license. "Did you tell him this was okay?" he screamed at me. It was the first time I'd seen him in nearly a decade; he looked so much older than he had when we divorced. Behind him, one of his and Dawn's daughters had stopped, jaw hanging open, to see at whom her dad was yelling.

"Of course not," I answered. I wondered if he saw the new crow's feet and the frown lines that had developed on my face in recent years.

"My god, Di, Dawn and I have been trying to raise him to be a decent, respectable young man--"

"And, of course, you never smoked weed."

"That's beside the point."

"Ferris, he's twenty-one years old. If he wants to try drugs -- especially legal ones -- we don't have a lot of say in the matter."

"Did you know he was? I mean, did you see him smoking when he was in Vegas last week?"

"He was here?" My heart quickened.

"He said he was visiting you."

I shook my head. "He never called. I didn't see him."

He pushed out a snort of irritation. "I should have known that was bullshit." He disconnected the call, and my glimpse into his life disappeared.

When Shay slipped away from them -- from all of us, really -- and began experimenting with unregulated, "retro" street drugs, we knew we had failed him completely. I only saw him once after that, when he showed up backstage at the end of one of my concerts. If he hadn't known my assistant Carl by name, he never would have gotten past security.

"Mom?" He didn't look like himself -- he was gaunt and his skin was ravaged. He looked older than I did.

"Shay?" Carl took the bouquet of roses from my arms before I dropped them. "Is it really you?"

"Yeah, Mom," he said, his smile flickering on his face.

Feeling the tears well in my eyes, I wrapped my arms around my once-handsome son. "Where have you been?"

"Here and there. I was in Thailand for a while."

I wasn't sure if he was telling me the truth, but I took him at face value. "That must have been exciting. What were you doing there?"

"Heroin, mostly."

My anger stopped my tears and I pulled back, taking his head between my palms. "You are so much more than you allow yourself to be! You are the son of two talented people! You carry more talent in your genes than--"

"Suri Cruise?" he said with a disdainful smile, pulling the name of a long-forgotten starlet out of his mind.

I pursed my lips, willing myself not to fight with him.

"Diana," Carl said prissily, "You've still got an encore to do."

"Can't you skip it, Mom? We haven't seen each other in years."

I shook my head. "No. These people paid a small fortune to sit in a room and listen to me sing and talk. I need to give them what they paid for."

He smiled disbelievingly. "They'll always come first, won't they? Over everything and everyone else, it's the audience that matters most."

I opened my mouth to refute his words, but no argument came.

"Diana!" Carl cajoled.

"Not tonight, Carl." I threaded my arm around Shay's and led him toward my dressing room. Once we were there, we each sat down in a corner of the antique red sofa that looked like it had started its life at one of the whorehouses just outside of Vegas.

Seamus wore a puzzled expression.

"What's wrong? Isn't this what you wanted?"

"I always thought what was wrong with me had everything to do with you. You left me. You didn't want me. You abandoned me."

"Dawn and your father loved you so much. I didn't

think you'd feel my absence."

"You're my mother! Of course I felt it!"

"But I was never there. I was gone all the time -- on movie set after movie set. I couldn't take you with me and I couldn't just leave you with a nanny. Ferris and Dawn -- they were settled."

"You moved to Vegas, Mom. Why would you do that?"

"It was close to California. I thought -- if I were settled -- you would come and stay with me more often. I have always kept a room for you. You're my son; I just want what's best for you."

"You have a room for me? Still?"

I nodded. "We can get you into rehab. There are some great treatment centers here--"

"'Dry out in the desert?'" he said, referring to one of the better-known programs located in Henderson. "Are you really suggesting that if I get clean everything will be okay?"

"Maybe not perfect, but better. You could stay with me...take up occupancy in that room I've been saving for you all these years. There are lots of job opportunities--"

His laughter cut me off. "Why should I work when I can bum around the world? Haven't you heard, Mom? You and Dad are loaded. All I have to do is stay off the radar and the money keeps rolling in."

"What are you talking about?"

His ravaged body almost seemed to collapse inward. "I always thought you and Dad were on the same page when it came to me."

"How could we be? He hasn't spoken more than a hundred words to me in fifteen years."

"He said it. He said that I was an embarrassment to both of you. That I was nothing more than a career-ending mistake and the best thing I could do would be to disappear!"

"I never felt that way!" I scooted close to him and cradled his head against my body. "You are my son. No matter what else is important, you are my child, first and foremost."

His body relaxed and I felt his chest heave against my side as tears began to flow.

I heard the door creak open and Carl's too-pretty face peered inside the room. I held a finger to my lips and waved him away.

I don't know when I fell asleep, but when I awoke the next morning he was gone. He scrawled a note on the mirror using my lipstick: "I love you, Mom. I'm sorry."

Anger welled up in me again as I recalled my conversation with Seamus. I wanted to call and confront Ferris, but I knew it wouldn't do any good. I fell back on an old habit: I called Dawn.

"My gosh! Diana! Long time, no talk!" Dawn said brightly. Her face was a little rounder -- more matronly -- than it had once been. Though I had fired her long ago, she remained my most natural confidante. I knew she would never spill my secrets -- not even to Ferris.

"Shay was here last night."

Her face registered brief surprise and her voice stiffened. "How nice. How is he?"

"Still alive...for now. Have you seen him lately?"

"Not personally. I understand he stopped by and spoke with Ferris a few days ago."

"He told me Ferris was paying him to stay away," I said bluntly.

Her eyes shifted away from her tablet.

"Is someone with you?"

Ferris appeared over her shoulder. "Yes, Diana, I'm here." Dawn disappeared from the screen and Ferris's face filled it. "I saw him a few days ago. I gave him money to go away. I guess he didn't think I gave him enough if he went to Vegas to bother you."

"He's our child, Ferris. What could he possibly have done--?"

"He's a drug addict. He's a bad influence on our girls."

"Give me a frickin' break!"

"I'm running for governor!" he blurted. "I can't have him wandering around California, making me look like an ass!"

I laughed. "You're Irish!"

"So? Schwarzenegger was Austrian. Besides, I've been American since we were married."

"Schwarzenegger was an actor. You're just a music producer."

He frowned angrily and rolled his eyes. "Thanks for your support."

"Our son doesn't need to help you look like an ass...you've already got that covered on your own." I turned off my tablet and slid it across my dressing table. I had loved that man once, less than half a lifetime before. He had gazed at me with his green eyes and melted every bit of ice I'd built up through years of being an actress. Even after more than fifteen years apart, the layer of ice had yet to become as thick or as sheltering as it once was for me. I felt nauseous and achy.

Carl opened the door just in time to see me reach for my trash can and lose what was left of my dinner from the night before. "Diana! Ohmigod! What are you doing here! Were you here all night!"

"Relax, Carl. I'm just a little nauseous."

"Where is Shay?" he asked.

Silently, I watched his eyes scan the lipstick message on my mirror.

He came over and sat beside me on the small bench, supporting half of his body on one leg while draping the rest of himself around me in comfort. "I'm so sorry."

"You didn't do anything wrong, Carl." I felt the warmth of his body against mine and, for the first time in years, wished I had a lover. Not that Carl would fill that purpose -- I definitely wasn't his type. He was always more fond of-- "Carl, is Shay gay?"

He pulled his head up and looked at me, frowning. "No. Not at all."

"How do you know?"

He rolled his eyes. "It's not like we have a secret handshake. We just...know."

"Gay-dar? Wait...do they still say 'gay-dar'?"

"Delightful Di, I wish you had been my mother." He took the trashcan from my hands and set it as far away as he could reach. "Shay doesn't know how lucky he is."

"I wasn't a good mother to him. I left him with his father and my former assistant."

"Because you thought it was best."

"I'm so tired, Carl. Sometimes I think I should just stop. I could do nothing, don't you think? Retire? It's not like I need--" Another dull pain passed through me and I tensed against it.

"What's going on with you? Are you sick?"

"It's nothing. I just think I'm emotionally upset. I spoke with Ferris before you found me."

"Why?"

"Something Shay said -- about Ferris paying him to stay away." I winced as the pain struck again.

Carl broke away from me and felt for my pulse on my wrist. "Something is wrong, Di. You're pale and clammy. I'm calling an ambulance."

I must have fainted after that, because the next time I saw Carl, I was looking up from a hospital bed. He looked like he hadn't slept in a week. "You look terrible," I said. My voice was raspy.

"You're one to talk," he answered, squeezing my hand. "You gave me one hell of a scare."

"What's wrong with me?"

I had been in the hospital for more than a week,

according to Carl. I had a massive heart attack brought on by stress and what the doctor called "lifestyle factors": namely, my fondness for cheese and my two-a-day scotch habit. The doctors built me a new heart and a new liver and sent me on my way, but not before strongly advising that I skip the cheese and the booze in the future.

Carl didn't tell me that Shay was dead until I had fully recovered. I couldn't blame him; he was fond of me and didn't want to look for a new job if I suddenly died. If he had never told me, I still would have known in my heart. I'd like to say that I had some sort of coma dream where he came to me and told me that he was okay -- he was with God or whatever really happens when that internal bulb burns out. I didn't though. It was more like how it feels to walk into a home when the power is out -- as if I suddenly couldn't hear the buzzing that meant he was alive. I had already adapted to the idea before Carl managed to say the words.

Up until my heart attack, I'd always taken for granted that I would live to send an email on the last day of 2069. After all, I had already sent six of them! Now, I wonder if there will come a lifetime when I won't live to fix my mistakes. Considering how completely I screwed up my son in this life, that is a horrible thought. Every day I live is a gift -- a present I plan to give to Seamus.

But what should I fix? Clearly, Ranice was right when she warned me that Ferris and Dawn had chemistry. After decades of watching Dawn, though, I know that she would never have been so disloyal as to have an affair with Ferris if we had stayed together. The Hillary Clinton biopic where I first worked with Jager had made my career -- if I had never met him, where would I be today?

Eighth

"Don't do another film with Jager -- ever." The email was short, sweet, and to the point. I was in the middle of reading the script for a movie in which Jager had already signed on to play the lead. The part was good -- meaty and dramatic. It was just the sort of role I should play, especially coming off the Hillary Clinton role, which called for a kind of quiet aggression. I wanted it -- and I wanted more role-playing with Jager, or "Bill," as I called him in our regular texts and emails.

If I didn't win for playing Hillary, this part was guaranteed to clinch it for me next year. Dawn had all but said so when she handed me the script.

I deleted the email from the future me.

"And, for the second year in a row, the Oscar for Best Actress goes to Diana Mogens!"

By the time the pretty young thing on stage got my name out of her mouth, I was halfway to the stage. Why hesitate? I knew it was me as soon as she announced it was my second win in as many years. The audience applauded politely, if not enthusiastically, as I mounted the stage. The man, a former co-star with whom I had, many years ago, romped naked for the better part of six months, handed me the statuette with a smirk.

"Thank you so much," I said smoothly, smiling at the audience. "It is such an honor and a privilege to hold another of these fine awards in my hands. I have reached the pinnacle of success that each of us, as actors, seeks to attain. And to do it after playing such powerful characters -- Hillary Clinton and Dido Chronis -- is a double honor. I would like to thank, first and foremost, my husband Ferris Bodeen and our handsome son Seamus for sharing me with the world. Paul Foster, thank you for taking a chance on an unknown all those years ago. And a special thank you to all of the academy members -- I couldn't have done it without you!" The red ten-second warning light flashed as I finished my speech. Raising the gilded trophy in my hand, I cued the swelling music that would wash me off the stage and back to my seat in the audience. As I passed Jager, who was sitting near the front with his latest "public" girlfriend, he winked his congratulations. I ignored him.

Jager sidled up to me at the *Vanity Fair* party a few hours later. "Congratulations. Where's the better half?"

I turned my shoulder to him. "Getting drinks. Do you mind? You're in my space."

"You didn't seem to have a problem with that a few months ago," he drawled.

I felt like one of Pavlov's dogs as my body had a physical response to his Bill Clinton impression. I steeled myself to remain calm and not quiver like some silly fangirl. "It's over, Jager."

"It's not over until I say so. And I don't say so."

I glanced around, hoping no one was listening in on our whispered conversation. "Stop it. Now. I am happily married and I intend to stay that way."

"I'm getting married, too."

I whipped around to look at him directly. "What?"

"Yep." He raised his glass and indicated toward the vapid-looking young woman he had been sitting next to at the ceremony. Her face brightened when she saw him and she gave us a finger wave. "What do you think?"

"She's a little young."

"Nineteen. Jealous?"

"You can do what you want, Jager. We're not a couple."

"Jager! Sorry about the award, buddy," Ferris said jovially as he handed me my drink. "You were robbed."

"It's fine, really. I knew that our Diana's performance would steal the movie right out from under me."

"Yeah, she's a dynamo, isn't she?" He wrapped his free arm around my shoulders possessively. "What's this I hear about you tying the knot?"

"Don't tell me...it's all over the gossip sites already."

"You're a hot commodity these days, my friend. You'll not be able to take a shit without everyone knowing from now on."

I stiffened a little as it occurred to me that Ferris may already have been aware I had cheated on him. He always kept his eye on the rumor mill. "Don't worry," I said laughingly, "the paparazzi get it wrong more often than they get it right."

"That's funny," Ferris said in a humorless voice. "They were so accurate when we first met. It was like they had microphones planted under our tables and in our bedrooms."

I waved a hand as if he were being droll. "You know how it is, darling. When there is nothing interesting to say about a given star, they make it up."

The raven-haired beauty whom Jager had claimed as his own appeared at his side. "Introduce me?" she asked him, flashing an overly sweet smile.

"Of course. Antonina Helberg, may I introduce Diana Mogens and Ferris Bodeen? Diana and Ferris, this is Antonina -- the love of my life."

I held out my hand and she shook it lightly. "Lovely to meet you, my dear. How long have you and Jager been together?"

"A few months now, isn't it, baby?" Her voice was childlike in tenor. "I've only been in California since the summer. It's like some kind of fantasy! Jager just swept me off my feet!"

"Where did you meet?"

"Antonina worked in the Starbucks near my apartment," Jager said, flashing his white teeth at me like a barracuda.

"Like I said: a fantasy!" She gripped one of his hands in both of hers and gazed at him like the starstruck teenager she was.

I let my eyes wander over her body, evaluating its elasticity as compared to my own. She had more than two decades in her favor -- and that was a good thing. If I simply made myself unavailable, Jager might really be satisfied with her and allow me to resume my role as a faithful wife and mother.

She caught my roving eyes and took them to mean something else. Smiling invitingly, she said, "I like to think of myself as a sexual adventurer. I'm out to conquer new territories and plant my flags in new places, if you get my meaning."

Glancing at Ferris, I saw his eyebrows disappear beneath his hair and his cheeks go red. "Um, we're not really...into that."

"Oh! Sorry. I was getting a vibe--"

I saw Jager squeeze her hands reflexively as she took a step backward. "Antonina is part of the Genderless Love movement."

"I'm not familiar with that." I shifted my weight to one foot and took a long sip of the scotch Ferris had brought me.

"They believe that love should be spread equally among all human beings."

"Won't marriage put in a crimp in that?" I asked.

"Not at all," she answered. "Marriage is a union of the minds, not the bodies."

"So, you don't think fidelity is a necessary factor in a successful marriage?" Ferris squirmed. I knew his Catholic upbringing was showering him with guilt for just talking to this woman who would have been labeled a blasphemer by the Pope -- if there were still a pope in Rome. All of our government's proclamations about science trumping God couldn't wash away his basic religious programming.

"Marriage is about finding someone to share life's journey with."

Jager smiled and rubbed Antonina's back. "It's more important that we share intellectual compatibility than sexual fidelity. At least, that's how I understand it."

I understood why he would marry someone like Antonina -- he would have a socially acceptable marriage and still be free to pursue me. The emailed advice I had failed to heed had been right -- I needed to stay as far away from Jager as I could.

Rolling over in bed a few weeks later, I stared at Ferris, my handsome Irish rogue, and smiled. He was starting to show his age now. A few crow's feet and smile lines had lightly embedded themselves in his face. If anything, they made him more appealing. I hoped that our son would look more like him than my own family as he grew.

His eyes opened. "Hey, there, beautiful. You're awake early."

"Couldn't sleep anymore." I used one finger to draw the sheet covering his chest away. Sprigs of curly black chest hair sprang beneath my hand.

He caught my wrist and arched one eyebrow questioningly. "I wouldn't continue down that path unless you're prepared to go the distance."

"Why not? Shay is still asleep and Dawn is away for the weekend..."

He grinned and flipped me onto my back, holding

both of my arms above my head with one hand as he used his other one to lift my short nightgown from my hips to above my breasts. His lips found my nipples and I shuddered with pleasure. His other hand released mine and I ran my fingers through his thick black hair. He came up to kiss me and a swell of passion within me wished to swallow him whole. I held his mouth against mine until we were both gasping for breath. Jager couldn't make me feel like this, even on our best days. "I want to leave Hollywood," I whispered against his neck.

He pulled back as if he had touched a live electrical current. "What?"

"I want to quit. I don't want to be famous anymore."

He sat back on his haunches. "Are you serious?"

Sensing that the moment had passed, I pushed myself up to a half-sitting position. "Yeah. I think I am."

"You think? What does that mean?" His erection was shrinking and I regretted my timing immensely.

"I want us to be a real family."

"We are! Just because we live in Hollywood--"

"Seamus isn't being raised like a normal kid. You and I spend less than half the year sleeping in the same bed. Dawn sees you both more than I do."

"That's the price of your career, sweetheart."

"Why do I even need a career anymore? If we left Hollywood, we could live forever on what I've already banked."

He sighed sadly. "What about my career goals? I'm only thirty-five, Di. I have a lot left to achieve."

"You can be a music producer anywhere. With your reputation, the artists will come to you!"

He glanced out the window. The palm trees swaying in the light California breeze weren't doing much to help my argument. "I don't know. Where would we go?"

Reaching up, I took his head between my hands and turned his face toward me. "Does it matter? Wherever

182

we are, we will be together."

"Then why can't we simply stay here? Just stop accepting parts."

"As long as I'm in California, I'm going to be tempted by scripts. If we're somewhere else..."

"What? You think no one will send you offers via email?" He looked at me like I'd lost my mind. "Sixty-five percent of actors working today live outside of California."

"Yes, but most of those live in New York. What if we moved to a fly-over state? Don't you think we could--"

"Disappear?" he interrupted. "You have one of the most recognizable faces in all of American film."

"So I'll have it altered."

Aghast, he let his jaw drop.

"Not a lot," I hastened to add. "Maybe just change my nose a little or lift my eyelids."

"And when someone who has seen all your films in Podunk, Iowa, recognizes you?"

"I'm an actress. I'll convince them that they are wrong."

"So you'll just be Di Bodeen, small-town housewife."

"Yes."

He shook his head, his eyes closed. "What about the paparazzi? Won't they blow your cover? I mean, all they have to do is track me, and they'll find you."

He was right, of course. If I really wanted to escape Hollywood, I couldn't do it as the wife of a well-known music producer. "What if we just...move to Oregon?"

"It's wet and rainy there. Too much like Ireland for my tastes."

"Arizona?"

He moved toward the headboard, sitting down next to me and shaking out his legs. "Just tell me why it's so important. Why do we have to move?" He lifted his arm and pulled me against him.

His cool skin felt good against my face. "I'm just

done, Ferris. Can't you understand that?"

"I wish I could, but..."

I felt the first tears roll off my cheeks. They splashed against his chest.

"Are you crying?"

"I'm sorry," I whispered.

"What is going on with you?"

"I've done something terrible, and I'm so sorry."

The morning I told Ferris everything, he came close to hitting me; he left me crumpled on the bed without ever touching me. He left the house before Seamus woke up. The only glimmer of hope was that he had, in fact, left our son in his bed. I believed that he would never abandon his son, and, therefore, would eventually return home. I managed to get up long enough to feed and bathe our son; then I planted my toddler in his room and closed the door. He was crying in the background when I called Dawn and begged her to cut her weekend short.

A few hours later, Dawn found me on the bed with Corkie, our sweet dog, curled up beside me. She sat down and began stroking the dog, who rolled over in response. "Where's Ferris? Isn't he supposed to be home today?"

"He left me," I said flatly.

"What?! He wouldn't!"

"He did."

"What's going on here? I just don't believe--"

"You were right," I cut in. "About Jager and me. You were right."

Her shoulders dropped. "You told Ferris."

"I didn't have a choice! It was either that or continue the affair with Jager indefinitely. He told me he would go public with our indiscretion if I didn't continue sleeping with him."

"This is going to destroy your career."

"I don't care about that. All I want is my family."

"Come on," she said, pulling me upright, "you need a shower and some coffee."

We heard Seamus stir in the next room, no doubt responding to her voice.

"Will you take care of him?" I asked as I stumbled toward the bathroom.

"Of course." She exited the room as I dropped my robe to the ground. I turned on the water full blast and as hot as it would go. Stepping under the punishing stream, I let the water pummel my body, each stream like a molten-iron fist seeking to burn the sin out of me. Though I didn't share Ferris's Catholic background, I knew I had sinned. I had failed the one man who meant more to me than anyone else in this world. I scrubbed at my skin until it was red and raw. An image from an old film flashed through my mind: a monk flailing himself until he was bloody. I wanted to see pink water run down the drain, but no matter how hard I scrubbed, I couldn't make it happen. Picking up the razor, I dug it into the flesh of my leg until I scraped away a piece of flesh. At last, blood welled. As it swirled away down the drain, the tightness in my chest subsided and I felt like I could breathe again.

"Diana?" Dawn called from just outside the bathroom. "You've been in there a long time. Are you all right?"

"Yeah," I answered.

"I have some hot tea waiting for you in the living room."

"I'll be out soon." As a show of good faith, I turned off the water.

"Great. See you in a few minutes."

I watched, mesmerized, as the blood flow down my leg until it had made a red stripe all the way to my ankle. I grabbed my towel and dried my hair and the rest of my body -- save my bleeding leg -- as the blood trickled toward the drain, gradually becoming redder as the water disappeared. I folded the towel and hung it over the top of the shower. I stepped out with my unwounded leg and reached for a wad of toilet paper to staunch the quarter-shaped cut. As I leaned back against the cold marble of the shower enclosure, I could feel the tension returning to my body. I hadn't bled enough.

Digging in the medicine cabinet, I found a bandage to cover the spot. The flesh-colored piece looked brown against my inflamed skin, though it was already fading back to its normal pallor. In my bedroom, I pulled on a pair of velour pants that I usually wore only on the coldest nights. They covered the spot and comforted me at the same time.

As I walked past Shay's room, I saw him playing on the floor contentedly, undisturbed by the turmoil of the household now that Dawn was back in the house.

My cup of hot tea was waiting on the end table near my corner of the blue sectional. I curled my legs beneath me and let myself sink into its soft leather. The wafting scent of oranges hit my nose as I picked up the cup. I breathed in deeply.

"Diana! What did you do to yourself?" Dawn stood a few feet in front of me, clearly dismayed.

"I took a hot shower."

"Scalding is more like it. You look like you're on fire."

I shrugged and sipped.

"Do you know where Ferris was going?" she asked. "I tried to call his cell phone, but he doesn't have it with him."

"Why do you say that?"

"Because I heard it ring -- it's over on the dining room table now."

Shaking my head, I said, "He didn't tell me where he was going. I suppose that would have been counterproductive to his goal of leaving me."

"He hasn't left!" she said, exasperated. "He'll be back. He didn't take anything with him -- he just needed some distance."

"Between him and his adulterous wife." I swallowed some more tea, and my stomach rumbled irritably. "I think I'm hungry."

"What do you want?"

"I don't know if I can really eat anything."

"When I was sick as a child, my mother always made me toast."

I nodded and she walked back to the kitchen. "Don't worry," she said over her shoulder, "I'm sure he'll call soon."

When Ferris didn't call or come home after twenty-four hours, Dawn insisted that we report him missing. By some odd coincidence, one of the officers who had told me about my mother's murder nearly a decade earlier arrived to take the report. She had been promoted; she no longer wore the blue uniform and cap of a patrol officer. Instead, she wore a black-silk pantsuit that made me wonder idly how much L.A. paid their detectives.

"Ms. Mogens, I am Detective Lautmann," she said in her raspy voice. She had lines around her mouth that suggested she had a pack-a-day habit, even though cigarettes remained illegal. Of course, she could have been smoking marijuana, I reasoned; that was legal, so long as you didn't drive under the influence. I'm sure doctors were liberal with their medical marijuana prescriptions when it came to the cops; it was the number-one stress reliever in the country.

"I remember you. You were here about my mother."

For a moment, her face wavered between the studied professional blankness of a cop and a warmer, more sympathetic expression. Finally, she smiled. "I'm surprised you remember me. That must have been a very stressful time in your life."

I nodded.

"Ms. Mogens's husband, Ferris Bodeen, is missing. I would say this is also a very stressful time for her." Dawn directed Detective Lautmann and her partner -- a stout, bald, and bored man -- to the dining table. "Please, have a seat. May I offer either of you something to drink?"

"No, thank you," Lautmann said as I took the seat across from her. "When did you last see Mr. Bodeen?"

"Sunday. We had a fight," I volunteered.

"May I ask what the fight was about?"

Dawn held up a hand to stop her. "Why does that matter?"

"It's okay," I said. "Everyone will know soon enough. I had an affair with Jager Easterbrook."

Lautmann's eyebrows shot up for a split second. She looked down and focused on her tablet to record the information I provided. Her previously bored partner was grinning lasciviously, as if I were a smorgasbord and he had a free pass.

"Were you leaving Mr. Bodeen for Mr. Easterbrook?" Lautmann asked, looking up.

"No."

"You have children, don't you?"

"Just a son. Seamus. He's in his bedroom."

She nodded slowly. "I imagine custody would be difficult to work out."

"We aren't divorcing."

"Yeah," the man laughed, "I'm sure you're not. Just like your parents--"

"Gronek," Lautmann said, cutting him off, "why don't you go check in with HQ. I've got this."

He sneered and pushed back from the table. "Yeah, whatever." He stomped out the door without another word.

I smiled at the detective. "I thought he was in

charge."

"That's what he thinks, too. Only one problem: I outrank him. I'm sorry about what he said. Though, to be honest, he's right: more often than not, children resolve issues in the same ways that their parents did. Since your father killed your mother..."

"Instant suspect -- just add motive." I laughed lightly. "I didn't kill my husband. Ferris is still alive -- I'm just not sure where he is at the moment."

"Whose idea was it to call the police?"

Dawn raised her hand off the table slightly. "That would be me."

Lautmann made another note on her tablet. "Did Ms. Mogens object?" she asked Dawn, who looked at me. "I'm asking you, Miss...?"

"LeSoeur," she supplied.

"French?"

"On my father's side, yes."

"A very discreet people. That must be an asset when it comes to working with celebrities."

Dawn blushed. I wondered what she was thinking.

"So, you weren't ready to call us in," Lautmann surmised, looking at me again.

"I didn't think it was necessary. He's only been gone a couple days."

She picked up the cell phone in the middle of the table. "But this is his, isn't it?"

I blinked at her. Dawn nodded.

"He left the house without his phone and hasn't been back for it. How will he contact you? If he's like most of us, he doesn't remember phone numbers -- that's what this is for, right?"

"I hadn't considered..."

"No, I'm sure you hadn't." She switched off her tablet and said, "I'll be in touch."

I waited at the table as Dawn walked the officer

out. When she didn't return immediately, I went to the window and watched a silent exchange between Lautmann and my ever-loyal assistant. I could only assume she was backing my statement. After several minutes, the detective nodded curtly and Dawn turned back to the door. Before going to her car, Lautmann met my eyes through the window and held them for a few seconds.

"What are you doing?" Dawn asked as soon as she saw where I was standing. "Get away from the window! You're acting guilty!"

"I just wondered what was taking so long," I said, stepping toward her and away from the thin glass that separated me from my accuser.

"She needed to question me away from you to be sure I wasn't holding anything back."

"Were you?"

She rolled her eyes. "Come on, Diana...what else could I have said to her? He was already gone when I got here. You looked like you needed a shower, but not because you were dirty. You had obviously been lolling in bed, feeling sorry for your damned self, not burying Ferris in the garden."

I smiled weakly. "Thanks."

"Not a problem," she answered briskly. "I'm going to call Demi and Ranice. It's time to show a bit of that family solidarity you and Demi are known for."

"We are?"

"Of course! Everyone remembers how you two held each other up during that mess with your parents. Why don't you go play with Shay for a few minutes? Maybe get him dressed in something adorable to remind any lurking photographers that you are a devoted mother."

"I should take him outside, in other words."

"It's time to put your best foot forward, Diana."

I had plenty of time to regret my decision to ignore my future self's advice. If I had only made the one movie with Jager, perhaps he would have let me go. Our affair would have been sloughed off as part of developing our characters -- more of a working relationship than anything else. The police certainly wouldn't have had a reason to go poking around, talking to crew members and actors from my recent films. Jager and I had been discreet in Hollywood terms -- our relationship was an open secret. No one had actually seen us in bed together (except when the scene called for it), but everyone suspected we were more than just co-stars. So, when Detective Lautmann asked around, she found more than enough circumstantial evidence to suggest I wasn't the worried spouse I appeared to be.

The stories spun around quietly and slowly at first, picking up speed with each "anonymous source" and leaked detail of Ferris's mysterious disappearance. I worked to shelter Shay from the storm -- to keep the eye of it as calm and normal as our lives had been previously. Dawn, Ranice, and Demi formed the outer layer of protection for us. Dawn took the phone calls from the press, Ranice handled the day-to-day details that could have intruded on Shay's and my self-built cocoon, and Demi kept the vultures -- the paparazzi -- at least a hundred yards from my property.

The only good thing in my life was Shay. I hadn't spent much of the previous year with him, but now I held him in my arms morning and night, fed him, played with him, and regained the strong bond of motherhood with him. At first, he asked for Ferris every day, but children have short memories. Soon, it was every other day, then only once in a while. He stopped reaching for Dawn when he fell down and instead sought me for comfort. If only Ferris would have returned, we would have been a happy family once more -- I was certain of it.

One night, as I rocked Shay to sleep, Ranice came and stood in the doorway of my son's room to watch us. She folded her arms under her breasts and sighed. I raised a finger to my lips to let her know not to talk -- Seamus was on the verge of sleep.

As soon as his eyes slid shut and stayed that way, I stood and lowered him into the crib. I froze as he stirred for just a moment before allowing himself to slide back into his dreams. I tiptoed out of the room; Ranice backed up to give me space. "I thought you and Demi would already be gone."

"Demi is at home with Charity. I came back to talk to you."

"About?"

"Don't be dense, Diana. You know what about."

"Would you like something to drink? I'm going to fix myself some tea."

"That sounds good." We walked together toward the kitchen. "Where's Dawn?"

"She had the evening off. I think she has a boyfriend."

"Since when?" Ranice asked sharply.

"A few weeks now."

"What if she's cooperating with the police?"

I shrugged. "And why would I care about that?"

Ranice grabbed my shoulders and spun me around. "Did you do something to Ferris?" she asked, her eyes boring into me.

"No. I swear to...whatever we're supposed to swear to these days, I didn't do anything to him."

"Well, it looks like you did."

"I can't help that. I want him to come home."

"What if he can't?"

I shook my head. "I don't understand."

"What if he's already gone?"

"He is gone...he's missing."

She grabbed my chin with one hand and, frowning, held my gaze. "I mean dead, Diana. What if he is dead?"

My knees softened and tried to buckle, but my sister-in-law was a strong woman. She held me upright as she guided my feet toward the sofa and lowered me into a sitting position. "He can't be," I said under my breath. "He promised..."

"What?" she asked, sitting down next to me.

I remembered a vow from our wedding. "He promised he would always be by my side."

"Sometimes we can't keep our promises."

"I did something wrong," I confessed.

Ranice pulled away as if I had just jabbed her with a poison dart. "How could you--?"

"Not that. I didn't hurt him. But I got some advice from...a reliable source...and I ignored it. If I hadn't..."

She shook her head. "You aren't being rational. You couldn't have done anything--"

"The tabloid sites are right -- I did sleep with Jager."

"I know. Dawn told me." She sighed again. "I was wrong to ever suggest that Dawn would try to take Ferris away from you. She thinks of you two as the big brother and sister she never had."

"Yet you think she could be working with the cops?"

"If I thought my brother or sister had done something wrong, I'd help the cops...no matter how much I loved them. No one is above the law. Not even celebrities."

My leg muscles had regained their strength. "Time for that tea."

"I'll get it," she said, pushing herself up.

"I'll go with you."

In the kitchen, I filled the teapot with fresh water and placed it on the stove to come to a boil. Ranice found the teabags and pulled two out, opening each package in preparation. We leaned against the counters as we waited for the water.

After a few minutes of silence, Ranice said, "Maybe she thinks if she works with the cops, she can help prove your innocence."

"How could that work?"

"I don't know...but it's a possibility."

"We don't even know if she's working with them." I pulled the honey pot out of the cabinet. "Do you want milk?"

"No," she answered.

"One thing is certain: my career is over."

"Not if you're innocent!"

I shook my head. "Why should I keep making movies, anyway? I have more money than I could spend in twenty lifetimes, especially if I move back to Arizona or up to Portland. If Ferris really is gone, then Shay is going to need a full-time parent -- not someone like Dawn to pick up the slack."

"But you've worked so hard for so many years--"

"Now is a good time to give that up."

"You sound like you know he won't be back."

"It's been more than a month, Ranice. Even if he's okay, he's not coming back. We're never going to be a family again."

A hiker found Ferris's skeleton on a gray morning in November. The police didn't know who it was immediately, though Detective Lautmann did call to let me know a body had been found. Along with everyone in the Los Angeles area, I learned that most of the flesh was gone, as well as the bones of one arm, on the evening news. Because the body was within a reasonable walking distance from my home, even the news anchors speculated that this could be Ferris.

Lautmann came by to confirm Ferris's death and apologize for suspecting me; I sat silently at the table as she talked. Dawn called Ranice and Demi, and then sat next to me at the table, holding my hand.

"The body was found under some brush in a ravine. We believe he wasn't located sooner because he was so far off the established path that no one could see him. The hiker who found him was actually attempting a wilderness hike, using only a GPS as his guide."

"So he wasn't buried?" Dawn asked.

"No. It appears that he crawled under the bushes to shield himself from the weather. If you'll remember, we had a number of severe rainstorms in the days after he disappeared."

I didn't remember much from those first days, but I nodded as if I did.

Dawn grasped the detective's underlying meaning before I could. "He was still alive...down in the ravine?"

"I'm afraid so."

Dawn gasped; I closed my eyes against the image of his suffering.

"You have to understand -- there wasn't much left for the medical examiner to work with. We believe he survived the fall because none of the injuries to his body were immediately terminal. It appears he stumbled on the trail above the ravine and tumbled down the steep hill. You said he left the house that Sunday morning at about seven, correct?"

I nodded.

"That's the only mystery. The trail is normally quite busy on weekend mornings. Someone should have seen him fall, yet no one reported it. If he had been carrying his phone, we suspect he would have been able to call for help. At the very least, we could have triangulated his phone's signal." She shook her head. "It's no one's fault, Ms. Mogens -- just a series of little details that ultimately led to his death."

The front door opened and my niece ran in and threw her arms around my neck, sobbing. She had been very attached to her uncle -- the only male authority figure in her life. Demi and Ranice followed, quietly taking seats at the table. Demi, who sat on my other side and took my free hand, asked, "What happened?"

"She just finished explaining," I said.

"I can go over it again," Detective Lautmann offered.

"No. I'll tell her...later."

"Ms. Mogens, on behalf of the entire police department, I would like to offer you our sincerest condolences on the loss of your husband."

"Why don't you save your condolences and offer her a decent apology?" Ranice huffed.

"You must understand -- in cases such as this one, the spouse is always a person of interest."

"Between you and the press, Diana is as much a victim as Ferris."

"The department will be issuing a statement tomorrow clearing Ms. Mogens of all involvement in this terrible accident."

Ranice snorted. "Hell of a lot of good that does. You can't undo what you've done with a few contrite words."

Lautmann, her lips pulled into a straight, tight line, stared at my sister-in-law. "Yes. Well. Some things can't be helped."

I stood, pulling away from both Demi and Dawn. "Thank you, Detective Lautmann. I appreciate you coming to see me personally."

She stood as well, and I watched the relief of my releasing her flood across her face. "It was the least I could do."

"The very least," Ranice muttered.

I shot her a withering look and she had the good sense to slump, ashamed.

Dawn escorted Lautmann out. As nice of a woman as she seemed to be, I sincerely hoped I would never see her again.

"I'm--" Ranice started.

"Please excuse me," I interrupted. "I need some time alone." Pushing away from the table, I brushed past Dawn as she was returning to the dining room.

"Do you want anything?" she asked.

I shook my head as I felt Corkie brush against my knee. She followed me into the bedroom and pressed her warm body against mine. Funny how this animal -- a dog that Ferris had wanted so much more than I ever did -- was the only creature to provide true comfort in his absence. I hugged her more closely to me. Ferris wasn't coming back. Was this what had happened to future me, too? It must have; otherwise I would never have willingly surrendered my film career.

Our new home in Portland was bigger than the one we left in California. Dawn, who refused to leave my employ despite my all but firing her, occupied a completely self-sufficient apartment with a side entrance. Though the weather was gloomier than Ferris might have preferred, Oregon was a perfect fit for Shay and me; the frequently gray sky matched our frequently dark moods.

Demi and Ranice had been sorry to see us leave, but weren't inclined to follow. Charity loved her school and her friends too much -- at least, that was the argument my sister and her wife presented. They acted like they weren't hurt by my shunning them in the days immediately following Ferris's confirmed death.

I didn't cry until we had moved into our new home.

197

There was so much to do before then: arranging for Ferris's funeral, packing up the house, convincing Paul that I no longer had any desire to be a star. But the new house was quiet -- as silent as death, in fact. Every time I closed my eyes, I saw Ferris. I imagined him, his body broken, pulling himself along to where he could at least protect himself from the weather. I imagined him, freezing cold, shivering through the night in wet clothes, cursing himself for forgetting his phone...praying that I would come looking for him. In his last thoughts, he must have been cursing me -- and I didn't blame him. I sobbed into my pillow for months.

Shay didn't understand death yet. He was too young to grasp the concept of forever. Every week or two, he would ask, "When is Daddy coming back?"

"He's not, sweetheart. He's gone forever."

"Hasn't it been forever yet, Mommy?"

"No."

"I want him to come home. Can we call him?"

"No. He doesn't have a phone."

"Where is he?"

At times like these, I wished for the comforting lie of Heaven. "He's dead, Shay."

"But where is he?"

When I couldn't answer him, he would break things: his toys, my statuettes, anything he could get his hands on. Dawn would have to calm him; I couldn't do it. I didn't care what he broke.

Dawn met her husband at an art show in one of the arts district galleries. The moment she brought him home and introduced him to me, I knew she would marry him. In fifteen years at my side, that was the first time she ever bothered to introduce a man to me.

"Diana, this is Borden Sulsbacher. Borden, this is Diana Mogens."

"Sulsbacher? As in the artist?" I asked. He had been featured on a Portland news website only a few months before.

"Yes," he said, blushing slightly under his beard. "I'm a big fan of yours, Ms. Mogens. I grew up watching your films, and my mom loved your music."

I realized then that he was much younger than Dawn, who had recently turned forty. "It's nice to know I still have fans," I answered, smiling. "Shay, come meet someone who remembers your mom."

My son, now just a few months shy of fifteen, came out of his room. He was as handsome as his father had once been, with his dark hair and sparkling eyes. The Oregon weather kept him as pale as I was. He came over and gave me a quick hug. "How did you know I was home?"

"I'm old, not deaf. I heard the door." I turned him to look at Borden. "Shay, this is Borden, a friend of Dawn's."

"Hey."

"Hey," Borden answered.

Neither extended his hand. I still wasn't completely used to this generation that seemed to eschew physical contact. It seemed rude.

"Would you like to stay for dinner?" I asked. Since my retirement from show business, I had become quite a good cook. In fact, I was making chicken Cordon Bleu for dinner that night.

"No, thank you," Borden said. "We have reservations downtown."

I looked again at Dawn and realized she was wearing a dress and a pair of heels. I hadn't seen her in a dress since we came to Portland. I hadn't even known she still owned one. "How romantic. How long have you been seeing each other?"

"Diana--" Dawn said warningly.

"About six months," Borden volunteered.

He didn't have to say anything else; the slight bulge in his pants pocket told the tale. The next time I saw Dawn, she had an engagement ring on her hand and an apology on her lips. "He's moving to France, Diana," she said, her eyes imploring me to forgive her.

I wanted to be petty and selfish and insist that she stay with Shay and me, but I couldn't. "It's okay, Dawn. You've given me nearly half your life. I want you to go with Borden and be happy."

"Why don't you and Shay come with us? You could buy a chateau or something."

I gave her a hug. "I don't think so. You need to be free to be his wife, not my confidante and assistant. Besides, what do I need an assistant for at this point? How many fan letters do I get? One a week? Two?"

She shrugged. "That's about right," she said, smiling wistfully. "You've been so good to me over the years, though."

"You were better. You could have had a real career as a screenwriter; instead, you followed me through hell and out the other side. Go on -- reach your full potential. You're marrying a rising art star, you have plenty of money after years of working for me...you have no excuses. Go write something."

"I don't know what it would be. I haven't had a real idea in years."

"Then start with a biography."

She laughed. "Whose? The only person I know anything about is..." she stopped talking and blinked at me.

"Me. Write my biography, Dawn."

"But I promised you I would never tell any of your secrets."

"I'm giving you permission to do it. You will do right by me -- you always have."

"I'll think about it," she said, worry creasing her forehead.

Nearly two years after she and Borden left for France, I received an email from her with a manuscript attached. "Thank you for everything," it read. "I hope you'll read this and let me know if I've captured the right portrait of your life."

She wrote about everything -- the good and the bad. She must have kept journals the entire time she was my assistant -- from the first day to the last. Even the conversations we had were accurately recorded. She examined my relationship with Jager Easterbrook. The details of Ferris's life were there, too. Some of her words upset me, but all of them were true. I sent her a note to let her know she had my blessing to publish it.

When Shay came home that day, I sat him down on the porch outside.

"What's going on, Mom? You look worried." He was only months from graduating high school; he had already been accepted to several colleges. He was leaning toward the University of Portland because of its excellent business program. The fact that it still maintained loose ties with the Catholic church also attracted him; like his father, he found comfort in the rich history of one of the oldest organized faiths. No one worshiped openly anymore, but I suspected he and a few of his friends were practicing Catholicism in secret. I didn't understand it, but I didn't try to stop him, either. And I certainly didn't report him. Ever since the Zionist terror attacks in Chicago, all suspected religionists -- no matter the denomination -- were arrested and held indefinitely. The lucky ones eventually landed in Zion, where they were able to contact their families via email. The others...no one knew for sure.

"Dawn wrote a book about us."

He gasped and fell into the padded patio chair.

"She wouldn't!"

"It's okay. I gave her permission to do it."

"Why would you do that? What were you thinking?"

"Someone would have written about us eventually. I thought it would be better if that person were someone who actually knew and loved us."

He looked away from me, toward the trees and flowers that bordered our property. Finally, he nodded. "You're right. If our story had to be told, Dawn was the right person to tell it. But why now?"

"Because all of the scandal will have faded away before you have to start your career."

"May I read it?"

"Yes. I want you to. And when you do, remember that I loved your father very much. I made mistakes that I wish more than anything in the world I could take back -- but wishing won't fix the past." Only emails can do that.

He started reading it that day and didn't put it down for the whole weekend. On Sunday night, he came and woke me up.

"What's wrong, Shay?" I asked groggily.

"Please don't call me that anymore." His words were spoken softly, yet I detected steel beneath them. "My name is Paul from now on. Just like Saint Paul, I once was blind but now I see."

His mention of religion brought me to full consciousness. My eyes widened as I said, "Careful with that sort of talk, son. You never know who might be listening in."

"I turned off all of the electronic devices before I came to talk to you."

I sat up straight in bed. "Okay. Let's talk."

He stood and moved to the green recliner I kept on the other side of the room. Sitting down, he placed both of his long arms flat against the chair. "Before you get the wrong idea, Mom, I want you to know that nothing in the book came as a complete shock. There have been rumors for years that you and Jager Easterbrook had an affair. I didn't know exactly how Dad died, but, again, there was plenty of speculation on the subject."

"I'm so sorry, Sh--Paul. I was trying to guard you against the words of strangers by moving you here."

He smiled and shook his head. "Don't you know that this world offers no true protection? The only security I've found is in the words of God."

"But you can't pursue God in the United States. You'll end up in prison!"

"That's why I'm leaving. I have been accepted to a Catholic seminary in Brazil."

I didn't fight him on his decision, even though I could have: he hadn't finished high school yet. I knew that once he left the United States, he would never again be let back into the country. He would belong to God's army, and I would be alone.

Correction: I am alone. As I write these words, I am sitting in my Portland home while Paul ministers to a group of Russian believers. Dawn and her husband have never returned to the U.S. either -- Borden's artwork put the two of them on the no-fly list, as well. Having no faith in God has killed our faith in mankind in this country.

I sometimes fantasize about making the trek south and east of here to Zion. They may rely more heavily on the Word of God than I would personally prefer, but being gathered in His arms must be a better way to live.

It's Christmas again -- though you'd never know it if you looked outside. Not a single string of lights on any of the houses! They were banned a few years ago for two reasons: electricity usage and religious sentiment. Someone "high up" suspected that the covert Christians were using the lights to send each other messages. My guess is that it was just another case of an urban myth being blown out of proportion. Even the electricity reason was bogus; most lights were solar-powered anyway.

I've made it to 2069 -- again. I find myself laughing about it so frequently that my caregiver, Astrid, keeps giving me strange looks. I hired her myself; if I hadn't, I fear she might have already turned me in as a nut job. Luckily, she seems more inclined to receive a salary -- especially considering how much I'm paying her -- than to do what is, most likely, right by me.

I must be crazy, right? My son is off saving souls for a God I don't believe in, and the only soul I want to save may never forgive me for my betrayal. I heard once, a long time ago, that the definition of insanity is doing the same thing over and over again and expecting a different result. Am I not doing just that? If I had any real courage, I would end the cycle now -- send a note to that college boyfriend and tell him to keep his trap shut about the loophole. What was his name? Jim...Jack...Joe...something like that. I guess I'd have to look him up to know for sure. I wonder if he's still alive.

So I'll just do what I've always done: try to fix what I broke. In this case, I'll fix Ferris. Even if he doesn't love me anymore, he deserves his life.

Ninth

My phone buzzed on the pillow next to me where I lay sobbing. I could hear Dawn moving around in the house, though she hadn't yet come to find me in the bedroom. I picked up the phone, hoping to find a message from Ferris. What I found instead was an unintelligible list of numbers and letters from an unknown sender. The sent date was 12/31/69. "Dawn." When she didn't respond, I called out more loudly, "Dawn! Come here!"

A minute later, I heard her hustling down the hallway. "What's wrong?"

I showed her the screen. "Does this mean anything to you?"

She studied it for a minute. "This reminds me of a hobby of my uncle's. I think he called it 'geocaching.'"

"What does that mean?"

"It's sort of like a scavenger hunt, only with directions. Who sent this to you?" she asked, studying the message carefully. "There's no sender's name, and the date is obviously hacked."

"I don't know," I lied. "Are these directions, then?"

"Sort of...they're called coordinates."

What kind of stupid game was future-me playing? I took the phone back, frowning.

"What happened between you and Ferris? Where is he?"

"I don't want to talk about it right now. Could you take me to wherever this is?"

She looked at me doubtfully. "Not the way you look right now. What if someone saw you? You look a wreck."

I smiled. My assistant was never off-duty. "I'll shower first and put on some makeup. Can you take me then?"

Pensively, she nodded. "I'll go call up a map. You get ready."

"We'll need to take Shay with us," I said, almost as

an afterthought.

"I know. Don't worry. We'll be ready when you are."

I stepped into the shower and rinsed off quickly. I didn't wash my hair, I only wet it down. I quickly combed my locks into a low ponytail and applied the bare-minimum of makeup necessary to render me attractive: lipstick and a bit of eyeliner. Stepping back from the mirror, I noticed that my eyes were ridiculously red. Thankfully, Ferris kept some eye drops in his side of the vanity. I treated both my eyes and, using a bit of tissue, kept the eyeliner from running.

In the bedroom, I retrieved a pair of jeans and a sweater from the closet. Looking out my window, I could see the clouds gathering for a storm. I shivered, though I wasn't cold, as I slid my phone into my front pocket. In the living room, I found Dawn, with Shay on her lap, waiting. He shrank back against her and watched me suspiciously. In her hand, Dawn held a tablet with a map on its screen. "You found it?"

"Yes. It's not far. Walking distance, actually. But maybe we should go tomorrow. It looks like rain."

I shook my head. "We need to go now."

"Are you all right?"

"As well as I can be, under the circumstances."

"I only ask because...well, that message might not even be for you! There's no sender and the date is wrong and--"

"It's for me. Let's go."

She pressed her lips together, stopping herself from continuing the pointless argument. Balancing Shay on one hip, she stood and handed me the tablet. "I think you should go alone. Shay doesn't need to be out in this weather," she said firmly.

"Okay."

Her expression of surprise was quickly replaced with triumph. "Great. If you aren't back in an hour, I'm reporting both of you missing."

I gave her a quick hug and headed for the door.

The map led me to a hiking trail in the nature preserve near our home. I knew Ferris sometimes hiked here to clear his head or to get inspiration. I breathed deeply, certain that I would find him meditating at the exact coordinates future-me had provided. I walked all the more quickly, anxious to reach him and beg his forgiveness.

The clouds continued to gather; to the west, I saw a flash of lightning followed quickly by the low, threatening rumble of thunder. The first few raindrops hit the dirt and the pleasant, dusty scent of a desert storm filled my nose. Looking down at the map, I could see that I was close to the spot the coordinates had indicated. Looking up the trail toward where the red dot said he should be, I saw only a few bushes and a steep drop-off to one side. I turned slowly around, scanning the area for any signs of life -- maybe he had already left. I knew I hadn't passed him, yet I still searched behind me hopefully. If he went further up the mountain with this storm coming, he could be in real danger.

The rain was gathering intensity. I felt the drops penetrate my sweater as I continued toward the pinpointed location. The trail narrowed slightly at that spot. I'd never been afraid of heights, but with the storm gathering force, I was uneasy. I looked for some sign that Ferris had been here, but the place seemed undisturbed -- until I looked down. Something had left a trail through the brush down the side of the mountain. The rain was starting to blur it, but my eyes could still follow it all the way to the bottom of the ravine. My heart pumped frantically when I spotted the body. I knew it was Ferris.

207

Desperately, I paced the edge of the trail, searching for a route down the steep incline. Not finding one readily accessible, I took out my phone and dialed for emergency services. When the operator answered, I said, "I need help! My husband fell off a hiking trail and he's at the bottom of a ravine!"

"Ma'am, where are you?"

"I...I don't know exactly. Can't you track me?"

"With your permission."

"Do it! Permission granted."

There was a brief pause. "Okay, Ms. Mogens, we've got you on-screen now. Where is your husband?"

"At the bottom of the ravine."

"We have an emergency crew en-route. Would you like me to stay on the phone with you until they arrive?"

"No. Wait! Yes. Please. I'm so scared."

"It's all right. The crew will be there soon, and they'll be able to help him. What happened?"

"I don't know. He went out for a walk earlier...we had a fight. He didn't come home, so I went looking for him."

"It's lucky that you knew where to look."

"Yeah...lucky." I let the phone drop away from my ear as I thought about the message. Just coordinates. That wasn't going to look good if Ferris died. Coming back to myself, I remembered the operator on the line and raised the phone.

"Ms. Mogens? Are you still there?"

"Yes. Sorry."

"Ms. Mogens, I think you may be in shock. I want you to sit down and put your head between your knees. Can you do that?"

I looked at the muddy ground around me, not wanting to get wet and dirty. I took a deep, relaxing breath. "No."

"I think you really should--"

"I'm fine. I'm just worried about Ferris."

"All right. The firemen are nearby. You should see them coming toward you in a minute."

I turned back in the direction from which I had come; sure enough, the first fireman was cresting a low hill. "I see them. Thank you."

"You're welcome, Ms. Mogens. I'm going to hang up now, all right?"

"Yes. Goodbye." I ended the call and stuck the device back into my pocket. Waving my arms in the air, I waited for the firemen to reach me.

Ferris was wrapped in casts from his neck down. The doctor explained to me that he had multiple fractures. Due to the extreme trauma and a few blood clots that needed to be dissolved, the hospital was keeping him in a medically induced coma. They reassured me that he would be fine and set up a cot in the room so that I could stay beside him.

I dialed Dawn's number as soon as I was alone.

"Holy crap, Diana! I thought you'd never call!"

"I'm sorry. I've been busy with the paramedics, doctors, and cops."

"I heard the sirens earlier. I had a feeling that was about you."

"I found Ferris."

"Oh, my god! Is he all right?"

"Not really. He's in a full body cast and the doctors are keeping him asleep for at least a day or two."

"Has he been awake at all?"

"He passed out almost as soon as the paramedics reached him. He was soaking wet from the storm and in serious pain from all the injuries."

"I'm so sorry."

"I'm going to stay at the hospital...at least for now. I don't want to leave him. Will you watch Shay?"

"Of course."

"The police may be by to talk to you. They were asking me all kinds of questions earlier...."

"Wait. You need an alibi?" she asked, sounding worried.

"They say it's no big deal. They always have to check on the spouse first when something like this happens."

"They don't think it was an accident?"

"Since there were no witnesses, they have to investigate it as a crime first. I'm sure once Ferris wakes up--"

"What if he doesn't?"

I sucked in my breath as my stomach bottomed out. "Don't even think that! He'll be fine. I found him, and he'll be fine."

"Who was that email from?"

"What email?"

"You know which one...the coordinates?"

I paused. "Best we don't mention that to the cops," I answered finally.

"I know I promised to keep your secrets, Diana, but this..."

"I swear, Dawn, I didn't do this to Ferris."

"Just tell me who sent the message. Call it a good-faith gesture."

I remembered how Louella had reacted when I'd told her my secret. I couldn't afford to lose Dawn...not right now. "If I could, I would."

"I won't say anything about it unless they ask me directly. That's the best I can do."

"I understand. Take care of Shay. Tell him Mommy and Daddy love him."

"I will." She ended the call and my phone went silent. I set it on a small table near the cot and lay down.

Closing my eyes, I waited for sleep to take me. Every muscle in my body ached. I felt as if I had hiked down the Grand Canyon and back up the other side. Nevertheless, my brain refused to shut down and give me the sleep necessary to feel better. Taking out my phone, I deleted the email with the coordinates. I knew the email would still be out there, floating around, until I got to my tablet computer at home, but there was nothing I could do about that.

I practiced the deep-breathing exercises I had learned from years of yoga, counting slowly and trying to clear my mind. The policeman who questioned me had seemed to disbelieve every word I said. If I had gotten to the coordinates sooner, would I have been there to stop Ferris from falling? Why did I think I needed to look good before I left the house? The thoughts and questions rolled through my brain, each one following close on the heels of the last. What if Ferris died? How would I live with myself? What would I tell Shay?

My phone vibrated against the table and I snatched it up quickly, relieved to be distracted from my own mind. "Hello?"

"Hilary, my darling." Jager's smooth Southern Clinton impression trickled into my ear like molasses.

"Jager."

"Not in the mood to play?"

"Not at all. What do you want?"

"I haven't seen you for a while. Maybe I should just have a word with Ferris."

"That's not funny." I couldn't catch my breath as the tears began to fall.

"It's not meant to be. I told you I would tell him--"

"Good luck with that."

"Are you challenging me?" His voice swung upward in disbelief. "You think I don't have the balls--?"

"Have you checked the news in the last few hours? I'm sure it's all over the place by now."

"What are you talking about?"

"Turn on your computer, Jager. I'll wait."

He sighed irritably. "I'm putting you on speaker." I heard the phone land on a table with a clunk. "Antonina! Where's the tablet?"

In the distance, I heard her answer. "I have it. There's something going on with that friend of yours..."

"Who?"

"Diana Mogens."

His footsteps landed heavily enough that I heard him move through his house to retrieve the device. A few minutes later, I heard him sit back down with another sigh. "What the hell did you do?" he asked.

I stayed silent.

"I'm talking to you, Diana. What did you do?"

"Brilliant," I said. "You know me so well and love me so much that you assume I could try to kill my husband."

"That didn't sound like a denial."

"You moron. Of course I didn't do this!"

"But the cops are saying--"

"They've got it all wrong."

"Wow. You sound just like everyone who has ever been accused of murder."

"You've read too many scripts, Jager."

He was silent. I heard lighter footsteps approaching.

"Diana, is that you?" Antonina asked.

"Yes."

"I'm sorry, but I'm going to have to disconnect this call. I'm not willing to be polyamorous with a murderess. Murder is murder, no matter who the victim is. Best of luck!"

With that, the conversation ended, and I was left holding a silent phone.

Days passed. The doctors would come in, review his chart, and disappear, never saying directly how dire the situation was, though their expressions said plenty. I forgot about everything -- Dawn, Seamus, Jager, my sister.

Everything outside of the hospital blurred together in a whirl of indistinguishable refuse. Ferris was at the center of the shit storm, so to speak; therefore, he was the only thing I could focus on.

For days, I ignored my phone, allowing the calls to go to voicemail. Finally, one afternoon, the doctors took Ferris for some kind of test, leaving me alone in the hospital room without anything to focus on. I pulled out my phone and found a dozen messages from Jager. I listened to the last one.

"You can't ignore me forever, Diana. You'd best answer me before I take *People Like Us* up on their offer."

A lump grew in my throat. *People Like Us* was one of the biggest and most influential celebrity gossip websites. Whatever they were offering Jager, it was bound to be a fortune -- more than I could reasonably counter. The rest of his messages were similar in content. The web magazine wanted him to share his story of working and sleeping with a murderess.

I called him back.

"Took you long enough," he answered grumpily.

"Maybe you haven't heard, but my husband is lying unconscious in a hospital bed. I've been a little distracted."

"Watch the sarcasm, Diana. It's not very becoming."

"What do you want?"

"Nothing. I've decided to take *People Like Us*'s offer."

The lump that had been in my throat slid through my body like hot grease. "Jager, please! Don't do this! I'll do anything...if you talk to them, I'll just look guiltier!"

"That could be because you are guilty."

"What do you want?" I asked again. "How much?"

"You think you can just buy me off?" The fake outrage in his voice was nauseating. "The nerve! I'm appalled that you think so little of me--"

"Stop. Just stop. I know you don't want to continue our affair--"

213

"Why? Because my fiancée has a problem with it?" He laughed. "She doesn't have to know."

I retched at the thought of letting this pig of a man ever touch me again. "Name your price, Jager -- in cash. Nothing else."

"Fine. I'll let you off the hook for, say, a hundred grand."

"Where should I send it?"

"I'll send you the account number. Just wire it."

The small, greenish room to which the policeman escorted me was cold, especially with the air conditioner running. I had left my sweater in the chair next to Ferris's bed at the hospital. I didn't think I would need it. After waiting in this room for the better part of an hour, I knew I'd made a mistake.

"Ms. Mogens. So sorry to keep you waiting." The tall, gravelly voiced woman who came through the door looked familiar. "My name is Detective Lautmann."

"Have we met before?" I asked, standing and holding out my hand.

She ignored my gesture. "Please, sit down." She pulled out the chair across from me, dropping a file on the table. "I'm surprised you remember," she said as she sat. "It's been, what? At least ten years."

The image of her in a blue uniform at my door flashed through my mind. "You told me about..." I dropped my gaze and bit my lip to keep the tears in check.

"Yeah. I was surprised to find that you had a new assistant. Your old one -- Louella, wasn't it? -- she seemed like a lifer to me."

"We were close. But it was time for her to live her own life."

"Whose life was she living?" Her lip curled up on one

side.

I shrugged.

"Your new assistant was very helpful," she commented.

"She's not new. She's been with me for a few years."

"So she said. Which is why I think she was reluctant to say anything at first."

"About what?" My breath hitched in my chest.

"The email with the coordinates."

"I don't know what you're talking about."

She leaned back, lifting the front two legs of her chair off the ground as she did. "Come now, Ms. Mogens. You remembered my face after a decade, but you don't remember an email you received two weeks ago?"

"I think I should call my lawyer."

"Why? We're just having a little chat about an email." She shifted forward and the chair legs clanked noisily against the floor. I jumped. She smiled. "Nervous?"

"My husband is lying in a hospital bed comatose. I'd say my nerves are pretty well shot, wouldn't you?"

"No need to be hostile, Ms. Mogens. Let's talk about something else. Maybe you'd like to tell me what you and Mr. Bodeen were arguing about the morning he went for his walk."

"It's a private matter."

"It doesn't have anything to do with Jager Easterbrook's recent interview with *People Like Us*?" She slid a printout from the gossip website across the table.

One glance at the headline was enough for me to know that he had decided to capitalize on my troubles: "My Torrid Affair with Diana Mogens -- and Why it Drove Her to Attempted Murder." "Holy fucking hell," I muttered.

"I guess you know what he's going to say if this ever goes to trial," Lautmann smirked. "Why don't you just save us all some trouble and confess?"

"I didn't hurt my husband."

"I believe you. I know, for instance, that you were in your house all day. You made a call not long after Ferris left and asked Dawn to come home. One of your neighbors happened to see Ferris walking along the side of the road alone at about nine that morning. The time of the phone call and the distance to and from the site of Ferris's fall make it impossible for you to have pushed him into the ravine."

"I could have told you that."

"But you don't really seem like the type to get your hands dirty. So, that brings us back to my earlier question: who sent you the email with the coordinates?"

"I don't know."

"But you remember the email now?"

"Yes," I confessed.

"Why did you try so hard to erase it from your email?"

"What do you mean? I just deleted it."

"You didn't 'just' do anything. You emptied your electronic trash. Do you know how often you have done that?"

I shook my head.

"Exactly once. The day after you led us to your husband's body."

"Please...he's still alive."

"For now."

"What the hell is wrong with you?" I screamed. "Can't you see that I'm upset? I'm sitting next to my husband's hospital bed, just waiting--"

"For what?" she cut in. "Which scares you more, Diana? The idea that he might die or that he might wake up?"

"Don't call me Diana. I am Ms. Mogens. And I want a lawyer."

The state took temporary custody of Shay, but my sister and Ranice petitioned the court and soon had him in their safekeeping. I spent only a few hours in jail; my lawyer -- someone Paul got for me -- had me out on bail before the end of the first day. I went back to the hospital. A cop was stationed outside of Ferris's hospital room.

"I'm sorry, Ms. Mogens, but you aren't allowed within fifty yards of your victim," the blue-uniformed young man said as he blocked the entrance.

"But he's my husband! I need to be with him."

"I'm sorry, but he's a protected state witness now."

"What are you afraid of? Why would I hurt him? He needs to recover so that he can testify that this is all a big mistake! If he dies, I'll be the one in real danger!"

"I'm sorry, ma'am," the officer repeated.

Spent, I dragged myself home, not even bothering to shield myself from the photographers stationed at the hospital and at my front gate. Inside the house, I wasn't surprised to discover that Dawn had moved out. Why would she stay? She -- and most of the world now -- believed that I attempted to kill Ferris. Only Corky greeted me at the door. She followed me to the sofa and laid her sweet head against my thigh to be petted.

"I've really screwed up, Cork," I said, stroking her lightly. "I don't know if this can be fixed."

She whined lightly and jumped up next to me, leaning herself against my body. I continued petting her absentmindedly as I flipped through the television channels. I settled on an old movie that I had seen years before -- a romantic comedy made the same year I was born.

Before long, I was stretched across the length of the sofa, just aware enough to hear the movie, but not really paying attention to it. Corky had wedged herself between the back of the sofa and my side. When someone buzzed from the gate, she launched herself toward the door, leaving a bruise on one side of my body and barking furiously. Rubbing along my hip -- the point from which both of her back paws had launched -- I picked up my phone and answered the buzzer.

"Ms. Mogens, I am Katrina Snow, from KTLA Channel 5? I'm sorry about your husband? Would you be willing to do an interview?"

I remembered hearing Miss Snow on television. She was a bubbly bleach-blonde weather girl whose main assets had nothing whatsoever to do with meteorology. She forecast the weather exactly the way she sounded through the intercom: *It will be mostly sunny with a high of 82 degrees? Hurricane Deepak is expected to reach Los Angeles at three o'clock tomorrow morning?* I sighed and said, "No. I'm not giving interviews at this time."

"Please, Ms. Mogens? This is the first story my station manager has sent me out on and I'd really like to do something besides read the weather?"

"Then get some vocal training and a breast reduction," I snapped before muting my phone. If she answered me, I didn't hear her. My heart was thumping; I wasn't tired anymore. How dare these people knock on my door as if I were just some...common criminal! Didn't they know who I was? I was still a movie star, damn it. And they would have to treat me like one.

Full of anxiety, I decided to take a swim. In the bedroom, I changed into my red one-piece suit that Ferris said made me look like a pinup girl from the last century. I closed my eyes and remembered the last time I had worn it. Ferris had stood behind me, caressing my sides and kissing my neck. "Do you still love me, after all these years?" I had asked. "Yes," he answered, "always."

I pulled open the French doors that led from our bedroom to the pool and walked with determination toward the water. I knew the heater wasn't on -- we usually didn't swim after the start of September. Diving into the pool, I hoped that the cold would startle me out of this bad dream I had stumbled into. My heart skipped a beat and my blood instantly contracted, leaving my fingers and toes temporarily numb. But I didn't wake up. I surfaced.

"The Attorney General is filing to have Ferris removed from life support," the attorney said. I could never remember his name -- Janski or Janusai or something like that. Luckily, he had told me to call him Jay the first time we met, so I stuck with that. He looked like a Jay to me: slicked-back black hair and a hawkish nose, eyebrows that looked more like inchworms kissing. They made it hard for me to focus on what he was saying.

"What?"

He repeated his earlier words slowly.

"She can't do that! Can she?"

"Technically, she can. Since you are his presumed attacker, you no longer have the power to make life or death decisions for him."

"But I'm his wife!"

"We can file a counter-suit to try to keep him alive, if you'd like." He shrugged as if it made no difference one way or the other to him.

"What do the doctors say? Is there any chance that he will wake up?"

"A slight one -- about five percent. He's not brain dead, but the doctors have advised the state that even if he wakes up tomorrow, the chance that he will remember what happened to him and be able to vocalize it is less than one percent. If he dies, the state can charge you with murder. Therefore, the state is seeking to disconnect life support."

"This is the love of my life and the father of my son

we're talking about! You can't let them do this!"

"The state will argue that you are simply trying to keep him alive in order to avoid the death penalty."

"What machines are keeping him alive?"

"Currently? Just a feeding tube."

"So the state wants to starve him to death in order to kill me? That's sick."

"So I take it you'd like to fight the state's motion."

"Yes. Fight it."

He shook his head. "I just want you to know that you are making the state's case for them by fighting this. They don't have much to go on otherwise."

"You're saying a jury will convict me of attempted murder because I'm trying to keep my husband alive?"

He shrugged his inchworm-eyebrows. "I'm saying you're screwed either way. If you don't fight, the state will say you wanted him dead. If you do, they'll say you're only trying to keep him alive so that you can't be charged with murder."

"I don't understand...they don't have any evidence--"

"They have the text message. They have the cash withdrawal you made a few days after he fell. And you're the one who found him."

I jumped on the money issue. "That was for Jager Easterbrook. It was supposed to buy his silence."

Jay closed his eyes and shook his head. "Listen, sweetheart, if we tell them that, then we've just given you an excellent motive for murder."

"Save his life, Jay. Whatever you need to do. Find a way to keep him alive."

The trial was a short one. Just as Jay had predicted, the prosecutor used my desperation to keep Ferris alive as proof that I feared the death penalty more than I loved my husband. Expert witnesses swore that Ferris would never wake up from his coma. The bank account to which I had wired the $100,000 was untraceable; no one knew it led right back to Jager Easterbrook, and he certainly wasn't sharing that information. He testified gleefully against me in court, making it up as he went along. He even had the nerve to suggest that I had asked him to kill Ferris.

Dawn also testified, though she was considerably unhappier about it. She cried on the stand. Even as she shared the most damning information -- that of the anonymous email -- she argued that there must be a reasonable explanation. She mouthed the words "I'm sorry" as she passed the table where I sat. She didn't have to say that...I already knew it.

Jay put me on the stand, questioning me about every detail of my marriage and my affair. When the prosecutor cross-examined me, she put my profession on trial.

"You're an actress, aren't you, Ms. Mogens?"

"Yes," I answered, stifling my impulse to roll my eyes.

"A good actress?"

"My peers believe so."

"That's right. How many awards have you won?"

"A few."

She paced closer to the witness box. "Come now, Ms. Mogens. No need to be shy. How many awards have you won for acting?"

"A Tony, two Academy Awards, and three Golden Globes."

The attorney smiled conspiratorially at the jury. "I'd say she's a pretty good actress, wouldn't you?"

"Objection!" Jay shouted, jumping to his feet.

She shrugged. "Withdrawn. I'd like to draw the witness's attention to Exhibit 'H.'" She placed a laminated magazine article in my hands. "Do you remember giving this interview, Ms. Mogens?"

Of course I did. It was actually my first national

interview -- one I gave after being cast in *The Prophet's Wives*. I nodded.

"For the record, Ms. Mogens has nodded. I'd like you to read the highlighted section aloud."

I scanned the page until my eyes found the passage. "I have the best job in the world. I get to lie for a living."

"Objection! Relevance?" Jay called out.

"Goes to means, your Honor," the prosecutor answered calmly.

"Overruled. Please continue," the judge said, his voice as thick as his body under his black robe.

"As an actress, wouldn't you say that you were uniquely qualified to murder your husband?"

"Objection, your Honor!" Jay shouted.

"Withdrawn. I think we're done here."

The jury was out less than an hour. I was sentenced to twenty years, and Ferris remained in a hospital bed, unaware of the injustice around him.

Prison wasn't as horrible as I'd heard, but it wasn't a cake walk either. The women who would have liked to have seen me "put in my place" were outnumbered by my fans. On the outside, my cellmate had attacked another woman with a broken bottle for flirting with her boyfriend. They were both drunk at the time. The victim got a few jagged scars. Belle went to prison for assault. Unfortunately, her temper wasn't much better when she was sober. As a result, her sentence had gone from a couple years to more than ten in the time since I had arrived. I made an effort to get along with her.

Prison was full of opportunities to learn a new trade. I argued that I didn't need one, since I would still be able to act when I was released. That didn't matter, though; I learned to chop vegetables and wash dishes anyway. Sometimes, fear would overtake me as I stood with my back to the other women, many of whom also held knives. I fell into bed every night, mentally, more than physically, exhausted.

I wasn't completely abandoned. Demi and Ranice still came to see me. They brought Shay with them, at least until he was old enough to understand why his mother was living in prison. Paul even flew out once to see me, though it wasn't really a social call. He needed my signature on a few papers so that he could handle my "brand" while I was serving out my time. Apparently, there was a market for my life story.

Dawn didn't visit me right away. I heard through my sister that she was living on the few years of salary I had paid her while she wrote a book. I used my prison wages to buy a digital copy of her work as soon as it went on the market. It didn't take me long to realize it was a fictionalized account of her time as my assistant. She sold the film rights almost as soon as it was published. They cast an unknown actress in the primary role. I didn't understand why until I saw the woman's picture -- she could have been my double. Though I was happy that Dawn was doing well, I was thrilled when the film flopped. Apparently, there wasn't as much of an audience for tragedy as the studio had believed.

A couple years after that, I was surprised to see Dawn waiting for me in the visitors' lounge. A smile flickered across her face as I approached the table where she sat. I decided to play the hardened criminal for her -- I didn't smile back.

"You look well," she said as I sat down.

"Thank you. You too."

"I wrote a book," she said, fidgeting.

"I know. I read it."

"They made a movie out of it."

"Yeah, I heard."

"Didn't come out so well."

"Heard that too. Can we move on? This small talk is a waste of time. Why are you here?"

She swallowed nervously. "I've been thinking. About what I did. Testifying, I mean."

"You did what you had to do."

"Yeah, but...I don't know. I swore to keep your secrets."

"From the press. I never should have suggested you keep the email a secret from the cops."

"Where did it come from? Really?"

"From me, in the future. I have to say, future-me really didn't think that one through."

"You know that sounds crazy."

"Yeah. I'm aware."

She came back once a month for the rest of my prison sentence. We talked about other things, of course -- her writing, her boyfriends, my experiences behind bars -- but she never failed to ask where the email came from. At first, I repeated the truth. Eventually, I made up more and more outlandish tales about it. The one thing I never did was tell her what she and the rest of the world believed was true: it was from the person who pushed Ferris into the ravine.

The state released me on a Thursday afternoon fifteen years, four months, and twenty days after I arrived. I called Dawn to ask for a ride, and she was waiting outside the gates for me. The clothes I'd worn into the prison hung strangely on my nearly sixty-year-old body. My breasts had definitely sagged in the intervening years. When I sat down in the car next to her, Dawn said, "Should we go shopping or get you a real meal first?"

"Take me to the hospital."

"What's wrong? Someone shank you on the way out the gate?"

I gave her a dirty look.

"He's not in the hospital anymore, Diana," she said quietly.

"Where is he?"

"As soon as Shay reached majority, he had him moved to your old house."

Seamus had turned eighteen a few months earlier. Ranice sent me a photo of him -- the first new one I'd had in years. He looked just like his father. "How could he do that? Who is taking care of him?"

"As his nearest relative, Shay has medical power of attorney over Ferris now. He hired nurses to care for him, and he's living there, too."

"No...that's not right. Why is he doing that?"

"Because he believes it's his duty to take care of his father."

"Have you talked to him? Have you tried to tell him that he can't give up his life for his father?"

"Shay won't listen to anyone, least of all me. Demi and Ranice have been furious with me for years because I wrote my first book about you."

"How do you know all this, then?"

"Are you kidding?" she scoffed. "He's Seamus Bodeen! The world has been watching him his whole life. Once you and Ferris were no longer around, he became the media's favorite orphan."

"But he's not--"

"Effectively, he was. They called him 'Little Boy Lost' for years."

"Take me to my home."

"It's not yours anymore. California law states that in the event of attempted or completed spousal homicide, all property belongs to the victim or the victim's heirs."

"So where am I supposed to live?"

Dawn shrugged. "I have a spare room, if you'd like to stay with me."

The nightmare that waited for me on the outside was more horrifying than anything I encountered inside. I still had money, but not much. Most of my fortune had been set aside in a trust to care for Ferris and Shay -- another California law. I had enough to keep me afloat for a year, at best. Despite her successful writing career, Dawn lived as cheaply as she could in a small two-bedroom Hollywood Hills bungalow. Her office had an extra bed in it, but it certainly wasn't set up for a long-term roommate. I knew I would need to get out of her way as soon as I could.

I called Paul's number, but his wife answered.

"Is Paul around?"

"Who's calling?" Sheila asked, her nasal New York accent coming through loud and clear.

"Diana Mogens."

"Diana, honey! I thought you were in the big house."

"I just got out. Is Paul...?"

"Oh, sweetheart, Paul had a stroke a few years ago. He can't talk anymore. I'll let him know you're on the phone. Just a sec...I'll put you on speaker." The next time she spoke, I heard an echo. "Paul, baby, it's Diana Mogens. You remember her, right?" A brief pause followed. "He remembers you. She's out, Paul. Isn't that terrific?" Another pause. "He says that's terrific, Diana. Now, what did you want to talk about?"

I stumbled over my thoughts. There was no point in telling this feeble version of my agent that I was ready to go back to work. "I...just wanted you to know that I'm okay. I'll try to get back to New York to visit you soon."

"He's nodding and trying to smile. I think he'd really like to see you, honey."

"Okay. Give him a hug from me."

"I will. Goodbye!" She disconnected the call.

I walked out of my room in a daze.

"What's wrong?" Dawn asked as I wandered past.

"Paul. He had a stroke."

"Really? I had no idea!"

"Now what do I do?"

"You don't need Paul to find work, Diana. You were the best actress of your generation."

"Key word: 'were.'"

"You're still the best. Is that what you need to hear?"

"No. What I need to hear is 'We have a role that was written with you in mind,' preferably spoken by a fabulously successful producer. Who are the successful producers these days, anyway?"

Dawn, frowning, ticked off a few names, none of whom were familiar to me. Finally, she said, "Jager Easterbrook. Call him."

"You've got to be fucking kidding me."

"No. If you want a comeback role, he's the guy. It'll make him feel like a hero, and the guy's got the golden touch."

I didn't take Dawn's advice until I ran out of other options. I called everyone else I knew first, including other actresses against whom I had once competed for roles. Everyone made sympathetic noises, but no one seemed interested in working with me. Even the ones who had their own series couldn't see fit to throwing a guest role my way. A measly guest role! Just something to show the industry that I was still alive and hadn't lost my chops! Not even a walk-on.

Finally, I called Jager.

"I've been waiting to hear from you," he said smarmily. "You've been out a few weeks, haven't you?"

"Yes. How are you, Jager?"

"Me? Great. Life has been good to me. But what

227

about you? Did you age well? Must be hard to get the necessary beauty supplies in prison."

"Luckily enough, I have wonderful genetics on my side."

"You should let the paparazzi snap a photo. You could do with a little publicity."

I flopped down onto my bed, suddenly depressed. "I haven't seen any around."

"Really? I wonder if these whippersnappers know who you are. They might be too young to remember you. Hell, maybe they think you're dead." He chuckled evilly.

"Thanks. Listen, I hate to ask for any favors..."

"But you will, won't you?"

"I need something to get me out there. Just a little part--"

"I've been putting together a period piece. There's a role in it -- a landlady thing. It's not much...but it'll get you seen."

I swallowed hard and said, "I'll take it."

The script was set in post-WWII United States -- a world that didn't resemble our country at all anymore. Part of it -- the part I was in -- took place in Arizona. Jager and the director settled for a small town in southeastern California rather than paying for the security an Arizona shoot would require. "Besides," Jager had reasoned, "Phoenix doesn't look anything like it did a hundred years ago."

When I was nominated for a supporting-actress Oscar, I called my son. He didn't answer, so I left him a message. "Seamus, this is your mother. I've been out of prison for a while now, but I wanted to give you plenty of time to adjust to your new living situation. I understand you are caring for your father. I would like to see you both. I don't know if you saw the news, but I've been nominated for an award. I would be honored if you would escort me to the ceremony. Please call me back."

I'd lie and say I didn't get my hopes up, but I did. When he didn't call, I decided to skip the ceremony. I knew I wouldn't win anyway -- Hollywood's way of punishing me. Not for trying to kill my husband, of course, but for disappearing for nearly two decades.

The scripts started rolling in, though. Dawn, despite her busy writing career, helped me screen the first dozen. Then she suggested I get a new assistant and my own apartment...not necessarily in that order. I found a cute little condo near Beverly Hills and an adorable young man who loved to read. He and his wife became like a surrogate family to me over the years. I doted on their children even as I watched my son wither within his hermetically sealed life. The gossip websites treated him as if he were Howard Hughes -- a reclusive, eccentric millionaire with no idea how to live normally. It broke my heart.

Ferris is still alive after all these years. He's seventy-four now. He's spent more than half his life in a persistent vegetative coma -- no life at all, really. I blame myself -- there's no one else to blame. I should have allowed the state to take away his feeding tube forty years ago, but I was too selfish. I dreamt of a day when Ferris and I would be reunited and all the bad memories would be washed away. That's never going to happen, though. All I've succeeded in doing is ruining not only my life but also Shay's. He's a forty-year-old man who has tied himself to the shell of his father, as if he were serving some sort of penance on my behalf.

I can't let that happen.

Tenth

After my swim, I curled up on my bed with my towel spread over my body. I slept until four the next morning. When I woke up, I remembered that I had silenced my phone the day before. I found it in the living room and checked my messages. There was a new one from future-me -- no doubt trying to fix the mess she had made with the coordinates message. Shaking my head in disgust, I skipped over it, reading and listening to everything else first. I had a few messages of solidarity from actors and actresses with whom I had once worked. I knew the women were actually thinking how great it would be if I were taken out of circulation -- one less person to compete against. The men who had called were probably more sincere. Paul wrote a heartfelt letter expressing his deep concern for me and referring to me as the daughter he wished he'd had. He offered to fly to L.A., too -- something he almost never did. I wrote him a short note to tell him I appreciated the thought but that he should stay in New York for now.

I was shocked to find hate mail for the first time in my twenty-year career. People, most of whom identified themselves as former fans, wrote nasty diatribes about how I was evil and should be killed. They accused me of being the worst mother imaginable, since I was leaving my son without a father or a mother. Mixed in with them were letters of support from fans who refused to believe I could do anything so horrible. Normally, I would have forwarded all of them to Dawn for her to weed through. She was good at selecting one or two of the best emails to give my ego a boost. With Dawn no longer around, I weeded through them myself, deleting the nasty ones and sending short thank-you notes to my supporters.

By the time I finished with my email, the sun was coming up, spraying beams of sunshine across the floor and warming the house up just a little. I hesitated, torn between dropping the phone on the sofa and finding some breakfast or opening the email from my future. Gritting my teeth, I opened it. "For Shay's sake, take Ferris off life support."

Every ounce of my soul cried out at once, searing my flesh. Hot tears rolled down my face as I crumpled into a ball. He was never waking up.

"Do you understand what I'm saying?" Jay asked. He was leaning forward on his desk, his thick, black eyebrows drawn together.

"Yes."

"The state will charge you with murder."

"I know."

He shook his head slowly. "Either you knew what I was going to say or you aren't hearing me at all. Which is it?"

"He's never waking up. I know that. I don't want him to waste away in a hospital bed while his body continues to tick along like a clock. He's not there, and he's not coming back."

"It's never a good thing when a client gives up hope," he commented.

"There's no point in hoping for something that will never be."

He cleared his throat and shuffled some papers on his desk. "Do you want to plead guilty?"

"No," I answered quietly, my hands folded in my lap. "I didn't do it."

"If you let them kill Ferris without protesting, but don't plead guilty, the prosecutor will seek the death penalty."

"I didn't do it," I repeated.

"You and every other con on death row."

231

I wanted to sit with Ferris as he died, but the prosecutor said there was no way of knowing how long it would take Ferris to starve to death. I tried not to think about how horrible his last moments might be. I prayed to whatever might be out there that he wasn't aware enough to suffer. I consoled myself with the knowledge that he had never woken up within future-me's lifetime. If I didn't let Ferris go, this would affect Shay's future.

At the trial, Jay argued valiantly that if I had hired someone to end Ferris's life and been caught -- as I so obviously was -- I certainly wouldn't have allowed the state to remove his feeding tube without a fight. The prosecutor, on the other hand, argued that I was more interested in finishing Ferris off than in self-preservation. If I did do it, she reasoned, wouldn't the thought of him someday waking up be more of a problem than him being dead?

Jager testified about our affair, of course. And Dawn, whom the prosecution considered a hostile witness, reluctantly shared her knowledge of the anonymous email containing the coordinates. Jay, fearing I would do more harm than good by testifying, kept me off the stand. I sat and docilely watched as the prosecutor made a strong case against me. Most of the time I wasn't even paying attention. I was trying to somehow formulate an email that would fix all of this. But if Ferris were dead, what was the point in finding a way to keep living? I was too much of a coward to kill myself, but if the state wanted to do it, I'd let them.

Most of the words that flew past me over the course of the week-long trial sounded as if they were being spoken by the adults in the old Charlie Brown holiday specials: *Wah-wah-wah wahwah wah-wah wah-wah-wah.*

When the witnesses were done and the final arguments had been made, Jay took me out of the courthouse to get some lunch. His somber mood made me think of da Vinci's *The Last Supper*. I'd gotten to see it once, a long time ago. I smiled at the memory.

"What are you thinking about?"

I shook my head to clear it. "I never really appreciated my life, you know? I was always too busy looking for the chance to improve it. Nine lives, and this is where I end up. I must have lived at least one life that was close to perfect. And I still tried to fix it. How crazy is that?"

He stared at me strangely before a sly smile spread across his face. "Wow. Just wow. Paul told me you were an acting genius, but I thought that had to be an oxymoron."

"I'm not acting." I frowned, confused.

"You know that California has a law against executing the insane. You have to be perfectly sane before they'll stick that needle in your arm -- if you're found guilty, that is." He bumped his forehead with his palm. "I wish I'd thought of this sooner. We could have pleaded not guilty by reason of insanity! You'd already be safely ensconced in a sanitarium. You might not have gotten out until you were too old to do much more than go straight to a nursing home, but you would be alive! And you'd be surprised what a little money can do to make your life comfortable in a crazy house."

"I'm not crazy."

"Keep it up, baby! It's a little late, but we might be able to get a mistrial! That would just burn that bitch of a prosecutor's buns." He looked like he was two seconds from performing a field-goal dance next to the table.

I stared at him as if he were the crazy one. His phone rang and he sobered instantly. "Yes?" He listened to someone on the other end. "All right. Fifteen minutes." He closed the phone. "Too late for a mistrial. The verdict is in."

I looked at the food on the plate in front of me. I hadn't eaten more than a few bites. It didn't matter -- I wasn't hungry.

@

"Please, your Honor, I didn't realize my client was in need of psychiatric care," Jay argued.

"This should have been addressed months ago!" the prosecutor exclaimed. "If she's really sick, he should have noticed long before the verdict came in."

The judge frowned; deep lines ran from the corners of his lips down his neck. I thought he looked like a marionette. I was reminded of my trip to Austria back when I was still an ingenue. "I'd like to meet with Ms. Mogens and her attorney in my office."

"I insist on being present as well," the prosecutor said staunchly.

"Fine. My chambers. Now."

Jay came back to the table and said, "Let's go." He gave me a look that I'm sure was supposed to be conspiratorial but actually made him resemble a villain in a melodrama -- all he lacked was a mustache to twirl.

I followed behind him obediently. The judge's chambers were smaller than I imagined they would be -- not much bigger than a low-level studio executive's office. There were only three chairs, two in front of the desk and one behind it. The prosecutor claimed one. Jay gestured for me to take the other one.

"Now, Ms. Mogens, your attorney seems to think you've gone 'round the bend."

"I'm not crazy."

"That's exactly what a crazy person would say!" Jay pounded the back of my chair excitedly.

"Or an intelligent and talented actress," the prosecutor said crossly, falling back on what I thought was her most convincing argument for a guilty verdict.

"Now, now," the judge murmured before focusing again on me. "Would you agree to a psychiatric evaluation?"

"No, sir. I don't need one. I'm sane."

"We're the crazy ones, right?" Jay prodded.

"No. No one in this room is crazy," I answered quietly.

"Please, your Honor, she needs help," Jay said.

"What makes you believe this?" the judge questioned.

"At lunch, she said that she has lived nine lives."

"Mr. Janusai, there are one billion Hindus who share her belief in reincarnation. Are they all insane?"

"Not different lives...the same life, over and over."

"Again, this is not so different from Hinduism."

"Tell him," Jay prodded, pushing my shoulder from behind.

I considered my options. Every email my future-me had sent had led me to this place. Maybe this was my reward for meddling...maybe not. But there was no point in trying to escape my fate. "Jay misunderstood me. I believe in reincarnation."

"Good to know," the judge said. "Maybe you'll do better next time. Let's get back to the courtroom now, shall we?"

The death sentence was almost a relief. It meant I didn't have to sit at any more tables and listen to all the people I had ever known heap hot coals of guilt upon me. Paul hired a new attorney on my behalf to begin working through the appeals process, even though I asked him not to bother. He just put his hand against the glass window between us and shook his head.

"Really, Paul, I'm fine."

"You're not fine. You don't know how many times I have wished I'd never taken you on as a client. You were such an ambitious girl. You always seemed to know just what to do to come out on top. No matter what life threw at you, you always came out stronger. That's why I love you. You're the daughter I should have had. And I should have protected you like a father."

"Paul, what's happened, where I am...none of this is your fault."

"Did you kill him?" he whispered into the telephone-like device he held on the other side of the glass.

"No."

"Then why won't you fight for your life?"

"I'm tired, Paul. I'm just...so tired. Ferris is gone, my son is gone. My life is gone. What do I have left? Nothing. What's the point in staying alive?"

"You're depressed. It's to be expected. But that's no reason to give up. Talk to the prison psychologist. He or she will put you on something to bring your mood up."

I let out a disbelieving laugh. "Why? I have nothing to be happy about."

"We'll get this fixed, Diana. I promise."

I hung up the receiver and motioned to the guard to take me back to my cell.

I don't know who Paul talked to, but no more than three days passed before the prison psychiatrist arranged for me to see her. The guard escorted me to the door and knocked. When it opened, a tiny woman with red-rimmed glasses and thick black hair opened the door.

"Prisoner Number 93482," the guard said.

"Diana Mogens! Please, come in," she said warmly. "Officer, please remove her cuffs."

The gruff bitch looked at the doctor as if she had

just asked her to hand her weapon to me. "She's death row."

"I'm well aware of that. Please remove the cuffs."

The officer grabbed my arm roughly and turned me to face her. Quickly, she unlocked the cuffs and stepped away from me warily.

"Thank you," the doctor said. "Please wait outside."

The officer eyed her again before stepping through the doorway and closing the door behind her.

The doctor held out her hand. "I'm Dr. Chiappone. You may call me Nella, if you prefer."

I reached out and took her hand. "Diana Mogens."

Nella smiled. "Please, have a seat."

"Why am I here?"

"Apparently, you have people who care about you. Depression among inmates goes largely undiagnosed, you know. Self-reporting is almost non-existent."

"No one wants to look like the weak link. I'm fine, though."

"I'm sure you are. I just thought you could use someone to talk to." Nella flipped through a file, presumably one about me. "You were a movie star, correct?"

I smiled. "If you don't know that, then you've spent too much time studying and not enough watching television."

"Just verifying. Your friends and family have reported that you don't seem like yourself. Why do you think that is?"

I leaned into the sofa. It was the most comfortable seat I'd sat in since the judge's chambers. Suddenly, the idea of spending a few hours talking about my problems didn't seem like a bad trade-off. "I guess they've never seen me give up before."

"Is that what you have done?"

"I don't have anything left to live for. My husband -- the love of my life -- is dead. I can never get him back. On top of that, I'm sitting on death row for killing him."

"What about your son? Don't you think he needs you?"

"I've done everything I can for him," I answered, thinking of Ferris's slow starvation.

"Let's talk about your parents."

"Why?"

"Didn't your father kill your mother and eventually get sentenced to death? I find that more than a little coincidental, don't you?"

I closed my eyes, remembering those last good moments with Dad in Europe -- before we came back to the States and he found her leaving him. "I hadn't even thought of that." The urge to laugh overwhelmed me and I found myself cackling uncontrollably at the absurdity of the situation. I had emailed myself into repeating my father's cycle. How bizarre was that? Maybe I was insane.

I felt a hand, almost as cool as a wet rag, on the back of my neck. "What was your parents' relationship like?"

"Difficult."

"How so?"

"My father was a laid-back sort of a man. He ran an antique shop." I felt a smile come unbidden to my face. "Nothing made him happier than digging through other people's trash to find treasures. I think Mom felt a little like trash when she and my dad first got together."

"Please continue." She moved back to her chair and picked up a notebook.

I sank further into the sofa, wondering how many other secrets had slipped into its cracks over its years of service. "Mom's first husband was a basketball player with a lot of money and a bad temper. He threw her out when she was four months pregnant with my sister."

"Half-sister," Nella corrected.

"We never made that distinction."

"You may not have, but your sister is of mixed race, correct?"

I nodded.

"You both must have felt the stigma of that."

"We ignored it."

"I'm sure you tried to. Unfortunately, you probably had more than your fair share of disapproving stares."

"What does this have to do with me being crazy?" I asked.

"I never said you were crazy. Do you think you are?"

"No." I shifted, suddenly uncomfortable.

"We'll come back to your childhood later. Let's talk about your relationship with your parents as an adult."

"My mother and I were never close. After I left for college, we rarely spoke. On the other hand, I talked to my dad at least once a week."

"How did you do that? Weren't your parents living in the same home?"

"I called Dad at his shop."

"Were your parents happy at this time?"

"Happier than when we -- my sister and I -- were still at home. Their lives smoothed out. At least, I thought they did."

"How did that make you feel?"

I stared at Nella blankly, unsure of how to answer.

"Take your time."

My eyes fell on her shelves. I remembered, back when I was young, how shelves like those used to be filled with books, CDs, and sometimes DVDs. My father had been a bibliophile. He never sold books in his shop, but he always found one or two books a week to add to his personal collection. Some of Mom and Dad's loudest fights had been about the multiplying books. I had nightmares as a kid about the house filling with books until there was no more room left for Demi or me. "Unnecessary," I finally said.

"Interesting word choice."

"Was it wrong?"

"There are no wrong answers here, Diana. However, many people would say that children are unnecessary -- at least, within their own lives."

"But my parents chose to have Demi and me."

"That doesn't mean that either of them would have deemed you necessary, in the strictest sense of the word."

"I guess I felt...less than important to them."

"Yet you maintained a strong bond with your father."

"He always supported my dreams. He knew I would be successful."

"What do you think he would say if he saw you now?"

Her shelves were filled with knickknacks -- not a book or CD to be seen. None of the items had sharp edges, but, if someone were so inclined, a few of them could be broken into sharp weapons. The orange ceramic vase, for instance, had potential. She must not have been afraid of her patients -- or maybe she simply sought to project confidence and security.

"Diana?"

"I think he would be heartbroken."

I saw Nella twice a week for years. She said we had a "till-death-do-us-part" commitment. I once asked her what kind of sense it made for the state to spend money on a shrink for a convicted murderer. She said the state wanted to be sure I was mentally healthy when I died. I laughed. "Do you think that will happen?"

"I'm an optimist," she answered. "Tell me about the emails."

"What?"

"I got a copy of your trial transcript. Your assistant said you got an email the day Ferris disappeared. It gave you the coordinates that turned out to be the location of Ferris's body."

"He was still alive," I answered stiffly.

"I'm sorry." She reddened and cleared her throat. "Of course he was. But that's not what I want to focus on today. She said you claimed to have sent the email to yourself."

"I don't want to talk about this."

"Why not? Are you afraid you'll sound insane?" Nella had a sneaky grin that only crossed her face when she thought she may have found a weak spot in my mental armor. Once I recognized the grin, I would usually change the subject -- at least for the time being. Eventually, she would worm her way in and find the secret I was keeping -- but not right away. Today, though, I decided to give her something for her trouble.

"Have I ever told you about my college boyfriend?"

She frowned and sighed. "The one who wanted you to move to California and live with him?"

"Right. Joe Stones."

She blinked. "Joe Stones, the technology wizard?"

I shrugged. "I don't know. There must be a hundred Joe Stones in the world."

"Okay. So why are we talking about him?"

"He had a theory about this glitch that started appearing in his emails back when we were in college together. He thought there might be a way to use the glitch to...communicate with yourself."

She smiled disbelievingly. "Sounds like he watched too much science fiction."

"Probably," I acknowledged, "but I started getting emails from the future a few days after he told me his theory."

"How do you know they were from the future?"

"They were all sent on December thirty-first of twenty-sixty-nine."

"How many have you received?"

"Nine."

"What did they tell you to do?"

I closed my eyes and tried to remember each one. "The most recent one told me to let Ferris die because that was the only way to save our son. The one before that was the coordinates -- the one Dawn saw. There was one that told me to take my dad to Europe for a long vacation. I got that one right before he killed Mom. And then there was one that told me to make up with Demi and let my dad pay the price for his crime."

"How do you know that they are from you?"

"Who else would have access to my private email address and know exactly what was happening in my life at any given moment?"

"What if it's just been Joe Stones all along? What if he has been manipulating your life for his own pleasure?"

"How could he know exactly when to send an email? How would he have known where Ferris fell off the trail? No. There are too many details that only I knew for this to be anyone other than me."

"So you believe that Ferris fell and died in other lifetimes?"

I nodded.

"Then why wouldn't your future self try to prevent the series of incidents that led up to his death?"

"I must have thought I could fix it. Maybe I thought I could save Ferris if I found him soon enough."

"Have you ever ignored any of the messages? You know, just to see what would happen?"

I closed my eyes again. "Once."

"And what happened?"

"Ferris died."

Dawn came to see me. Somehow, she finagled the system so that she was allowed to visit me in a private room. I thought my lawyer was the only one who could do that, so I was surprised to find her in the room instead of the suit.

Nearly a decade had passed since we had seen each other. She was one of those lucky women who wore her age well. Not that she'd ever been ugly, but age had brought confidence and a sense of power to her bearing. A scattering of gray hairs mixed in with her natural blonde strands. "How are you, Diana?" she asked with a sympathetic smile.

"Not too bad. And yourself?"

"Good, actually."

"How did you work this out?" I asked, gesturing at the room.

She shrugged. "You're a celebrity and, despite the max-security prison, you aren't considered a threat. In fact, the warden tells me you are the most docile and polite death-row inmate here."

"Good to know. Of course, it's not like I get a lot of visitors." I hadn't seen Demi or Ranice in years now.

"I'm sorry."

"About the visitors or the testimony?"

"Both. If I could have fixed it, I would have."

I sat down across from her at the table. "Why are you here?"

"I'm writing the screenplay for your biopic."

"Seriously?" I laughed.

"Yes. I was hoping to get a little help from you on your early years."

"Why would I do that?"

"Because, like a lot of people, I don't believe you are guilty. And I want to get it right."

"What about the email?"

"I won't claim to understand where it came from.

But you let Ferris die, which led directly to you sitting on death row. I've interviewed doctors and specialists who tell me that he could have lived on indefinitely -- he was unconscious, but he had enough brain function to keep his organs going. You were sitting on a fortune; paying for his care would have barely made a dent in it. I think your lawyer gave you bad advice, and that's why you are here."

I stifled a chuckle because she looked so serious. "It's not Jay's fault that I'm here. I made the decision to let Ferris go by myself. Jay gave me the pros and cons of both options."

"Did you talk to the doctors?"

"I knew they were only giving Ferris a five-percent chance of waking up." I almost mentioned the last email I received from my future-self, but I decided against it. "Have you spoken with Jay?"

"Of course. He's a real bastard. He says you're crazy, but that you refused to use your condition in your own defense."

"Jay's okay. He did everything within his power to help me."

She looked as if she wanted to say something else, but instead she pulled out a notebook. "I've talked to Demi about your childhood. What I really need are the details about your college years."

"I think Demi and I have different views on our childhood."

"She says you and your mom were never close. You preferred your dad."

"Did she tell you why?"

"Not really. She just said you and she were constantly at odds."

"I looked just like her -- before her first husband shattered one of her cheekbones, anyway. She never showed me any real affection."

"I talked to Louella, too."

My eyes widened. "How is she?"

244

"She's well. Sad about what happened to you, but...you know."

"Who else have you talked to?"

"Co-stars, directors, Paul of course. Everyone who would give me time."

"Jager?"

She snorted. "Why bother? Everyone knows his take on you."

"Why are you doing this? Really."

"I owe it to you. You and Ferris were like surrogate parents to me. And no matter what I think about the emails you claim are from the future, I don't believe you would have hurt Ferris."

"Emails?"

"Louella told me you got one years ago...right after your dad killed your mom." She paused and looked down at her notebook. "Look," she finally said, "you don't have to tell me anything. Just give me a few names to start with -- people who actually knew you before you were famous. Everyone from your class claims to have been your friend back then. Just tell me who is telling the truth."

"Talk to Joe Stones. Let him know that I still remember him fondly."

"Joe Stones? He wasn't in your class."

"No. But he was in my bed," I said, smiling.

"That seems like a good place to start." She jotted down the name and put the notebook away. "Is there anything I can do for you?"

"No."

"You know you're just about out of appeals, right?"

"If I'd had my way, I would have waived all of them. I'd already be dead."

"Do you believe in heaven?"

"We're not supposed to, are we?"

"Not officially," she said, reaching across the table to caress my hands. "But Ferris did."

"Ferris had faith. More than once, I envied him for that."

"It's not too late, Diana. I could get you a Bible...if you want one."

"'Faith is the final source of comfort for those who should not be comforted,'" I said, quoting a once-powerful politician. His name was on the tip of my tongue -- he had done what the Civil War had failed to do. He split the country with his rhetoric. Douglass -- that was the guy's name. Atheistic son of a bitch believed that faith led inexorably to terrorism.

Dawn was staring at me.

"What?"

She didn't change her focus. "I'll bring you a Bible," she said.

You couldn't buy a Bible, a Koran, a Torah, or any religious text in digital form. To buy it in digital form implied that you intended to read it, and reading religious texts was explicitly outlawed in the United States. However, all religious texts were still sold in traditional book form -- primarily for use in ceremonies and courts. The last time I had seen a Bible had been at my trial, when every witness had been asked to swear to tell the truth, the whole truth, and nothing but the truth. I heard rumors that there was a Bible present at every execution, too; unfortunately, the only way to confirm that was to actually be executed.

Dawn was true to her word, though. The next time I went to see Nella, she had a package waiting for me.

"What's this?" I asked as soon as the guard left the room.

"A friend of yours sent this to me," she answered.

"You didn't open it?"

"No. I trust your friend. She wouldn't send anything illegal. Besides, it passed through the metal detector with no problems."

"Do you mind if I open it?"

She hesitated. "I'd prefer that you didn't. When you leave, just stash it in your waistband and take it back to your cell."

I sat down. "Do you have faith in something outside of yourself?"

"Are you asking if I believe in God?"

"God...a higher power...something that isn't you."

She smiled and laid her notebook on her lap, crossing her hands over it. "I was raised Catholic."

"So was Ferris."

"What about you? Did you ever attend church?"

"At Christmas sometimes."

"With your family."

I shook my head. "Louella would take me. Louella believed in God."

"What about your Mom and Dad?"

"I guess it never came up."

"Do you believe in a higher power?"

"I always considered myself agnostic."

"That's the coward's way out of religious discussion, isn't it?"

I chuckled and said, "Yeah, I suppose you're right. This will sound ridiculous, but I don't want to end like this. I've tried to set myself on the right course nine times."

"If we accept that the emails are from you," she inserted.

"Right. And now, on my tenth try, I won't even be alive when the loophole opens."

"It does seem unlikely that you will reach eighty-one."

"To say the least."

"But at this point, what would you do to fix your

life?"

"I haven't the foggiest notion," I sighed. "I think I've painted myself into a corner this time."

"Why not just start over -- go back to the beginning?"

"Because who's to say that I wouldn't just repeat the same choices I made in the past? No...starting over means I'll just repeat the same mistakes. I feel a bit like Doctor Faustus."

"What do you mean?"

"I must have made a deal with the Devil. Those never end well. We humans are too myopic and greedy to believe that we have lived a good-enough life -- to be satisfied with wherever we end up. No matter how happy I was, wouldn't I always be tempted to send another email?"

My appeals ran out last month. Fifteen years after Ferris fell, I will finally join him -- whether in oblivion or Heaven. I don't know, but unlike Saint Thomas, I will not allow my doubt to overcome my faith. The Bible Dawn and Nella smuggled to me has not gone to waste. I have read it from front to back; I have accepted God's gift of salvation. If nothing else has come of ten lives, at least I have found Jesus.

Dawn came to share my last meal with me. I requested a hamburger, french fries, and a chocolate milkshake, which may seem odd to most people. I spent years avoiding this meal, though -- two-thousand essentially empty calories. The last time I indulged was during my pregnancy. Now, my son is grown up. He turned eighteen a few days ago, and, though I haven't spoken to him myself, Demi and Ranice tell me that he is a strong, smart, and well-adjusted young man. He starts college in the fall. Dawn sat across from me as I enjoyed my french fries, dipping each one in my milkshake before popping them into my mouth. "Don't look so sad," I said between bites.

"How should I look?"

"Happy. This is a going-away party."

The guard opened the door to the private room and Nella appeared. "I missed dinner, huh?" she said, walking to the table.

Dawn pushed her sandwich and fries toward the doctor. "You can have mine. I don't have much of an appetite."

Nella smiled sadly and picked up a fry.

"You two have met before, right?" I asked.

"Yes," Nella answered. "Dawn and I have been friends for a while now."

I let out a surprised snort. "I should have known!"

"I didn't want you to think I was sharing your secrets with anyone, not even a friend."

"That's all right. You two should feel free to share any and all of my secrets once I'm gone. Maybe you'll write a new script, Dawn -- one that's more accurate." I winked at her as I raised my napkin to my lips.

She straightened and I realized I had offended her. "I told the truth in that movie. You don't deserve to die."

I shrugged and smiled in an attempt to defuse the situation. "Maybe, maybe not. It's a moot point now, don't you think?" I glanced up at the clock: nine-forty-seven. In two hours and fourteen minutes, I'd know what was on the other side of this life.

Dawn started crying quietly, as if the water within her had simply reach the tipping point and had no choice but to spill out. Nella dug in her bag and found a fresh handkerchief for her.

"Please don't," I begged quietly. "I don't want to be sad. I've reached the end...at last. No more starting over for me."

"Isn't there anything we can do?" Dawn asked, her voice thick.

I shook my head. "Tell me something good. What did Joe say about me?"

She smiled and brushed the tears away. "He said he never stopped loving you."

I closed my eyes and conjured up Joe's sweet, handsome, young face. It seemed like all of my lifetimes had passed since the last time I'd set my eyes on him. "He was a good guy. Did he marry?"

"Yes. Tessa is his wife. She said you were roommates in college."

I couldn't even remember what she looked like. I frowned. "How odd."

"She told me she had been in love with Joe since the first time you introduced them. She asked me to thank you for passing him over."

I shrugged my eyebrows. "The first email I received told me to go to New York instead of California. If I had ignored it, maybe my life would have turned out more like Tessa's -- normal and happy."

"I wouldn't call them happy. Tessa loves him, but, like I said, he still carries a torch for you. That can't be the basis of a great marriage."

"If you don't know that you can change it, maybe good enough is wonderful."

We finished our meals in silence. When the food was gone, I hugged them both and told them I loved them. I was glad that Demi and Ranice had opted not to drive upstate for this; there was no reason for them to witness my death. The guard -- the same one who years ago had warned Nella against being alone with me uncuffed -- hugged me as she opened the cell door. "I'm sorry it's come to this," she said.

"It's okay. Thank you."

"For what?"

"I don't know...everything, I guess."

Unlike the movies from the last century, no priest or preacher was sent to me. Apparently, they stopped doing that when organized religion was outlawed. I knelt next to my bed and opened my Bible to Psalm 23. I allowed my eyes to scan the poetic words before bowing my head in prayer. "Lord," I said in a whisper, "into your hands I commend my tortured soul. Do with it what you will." A single tear rolled down my cheek, landing on the words of David: *I will dwell in the house of the LORD forever.*

The End

Author's Note

This book actually grew out of a glitch – a flaw in Apple's iPhone programming that causes me to occasionally receive emails with no sender dated 12/31/69. Because I don't have a brain that easily dismisses such trivialities, I began to wonder: what if someone from the future is trying to reach me? In fact, what if I am trying to reach me? Hence, Diana and her many lives came to be.

Thank you to Dan Bennett, Chris Wells, Jerry Wells, Nikki McBroom, and Grace Guerra for reading this manuscript and providing feedback before I sent it on to Inknbeans Press. Thank you to Jo and Alan for giving my work their undivided attention so that it could be polished to a high shine.

And, Dear Reader, thank you for spending a few of your precious hours reading this book. In this digital age, I know you have access to an enormous selection of books, both fiction and non-fiction. The fact that you chose to read mine means more than you will ever know. I hope that you will spend more hours with me in the future.

Happy Reading!

Susan Wells Bennett

If you've enjoyed Just One Note, we encourage you to send Ms. Wells Bennett an email from any point in history to :
SWB@inknbeans.com

Be sure to look for her other titles wherever fine books
are sold:
Circle City Blues
Thief of Todays and Tomorrows
The Prophet's Wives
An Unassigned Life
Forsaking the Garden
And The Brass Monkey Series:
Wild Life
Charmed Life
Night Life
New Life

Look for these other fine authors from Inknbeans Press:

Enjae Edwards, *You'll Wake Up One Morning*
Annarita Guarnieri, *The Importance of Being Shine*
Jim Burkett, *The Nick West Series*
Rusty Coats, *Out of Touch*
Kitty Sutton, *Mysteries From the Trail of Tears*
Dea Lenihan, *Out of This World Series*
Dawn Hood, *God's Pinky Promises*
David Rowinski, *The Open Pillow*
Dorothy Legge, *Poems of Faith and Love*
Ey Wade, *In My Sister's World*
Perle Butcher Lyon, *The Dutch Doctor*
Eric Pullin, *Digweed the Cat*
Hugh Ashton, *The Deed Box of John H Watson, MD*
Nickie Storey, *The Grimsley Hollow Series*
Jt Sather, *How to Survive When the Bottom Drops Out*
Virginia Czaja, *Get Real*
Jackie Williams, *the Tori-Jean, No! series*
Liam McCaughey, *Collected Werks*

Fresh Books Brewed Daily

www.ingramcontent.com/pod-product-compliance
Lightning Source LLC
Chambersburg PA
CBHW071139170626

46809CB00002B/689

* 9 7 8 0 6 1 5 7 6 4 4 2 9 *